Snowed In
-for-
Christmas

Snowed In
-for-
Christmas

JAQUELINE SNOWE

FOREVER

New York   Boston

Copyright © 2023 by Jaqueline Snowe

Cover and illustration by Sarah Congdon
Cover copyright © 2023 by Hachette Book Group, Inc.

Forever
Hachette Book Group
1290 Avenue of the Americas, New York, NY 10104
read-forever.com
twitter.com/readforeverpub

First Edition: October 2023

Forever is an imprint of Grand Central Publishing. The Forever name and logo are trademarks of Hachette Book Group, Inc.

The publisher is not responsible for websites (or their content) that are not owned by the publisher.

Forever books may be purchased in bulk for business, educational, or promotional use. For information, please contact your local bookseller or the Hachette Book Group Special Markets Department at special.markets@hbgusa.com.

Print interior design by Taylor Navis

Library of Congress Cataloging-in-Publication Data

Names: Snowe, Jaqueline, author.
Title: Snowed in for Christmas / Jaqueline Snowe.
Description: First edition. | New York : Forever, 2023.
Identifiers: LCCN 2023020947 | ISBN 9781538739815 (trade paperback) | ISBN 9781538739822 (ebook)
Subjects: LCGFT: Christmas fiction. | Romance fiction. | Novels.
Classification: LCC PS3619.N693 S66 2023 | DDC 813/.6—dc23/eng
/20230508
LC record available at https://lccn.loc.gov/2023020947

ISBN: 9781538739815 (trade paperback), 9781538739822 (ebook)

Printed in the United States of America

LSC

Printing 1, 2023

To the blizzard of 2013 that was the inspiration behind this story. Being snowed in with my husband for an entire week ended up shaping my life in so many ways. It caused us to move to the Southwest to escape the cold, but also, it's when I really discovered I wanted to be a writer. Publishing this story is a dream come true.

Snowed In
-for-
Christmas

CHAPTER ONE

BECCA

HGTV had to be created with magic—it sucked me in within the first second, and I hadn't moved in three hours. *Love It or List It* was my catnip. Three entire hours of sprawling out on the massive leather couch when I had shit to do. Lots of shit. As the house mom for Betas, I had to make sure the chef was paid, and since the cleaning service had two weeks off for the holidays, that had become my responsibility, too. And considering the fun fact that there was a blizzard coming, I had to make sure I had enough food to shelter in place for a week. If I wanted to get into specifics, I needed to make sure I had enough sugar, chocolate, and wine to survive the holidays alone. *Again.*

"Becs? My mom wants to know when the doors are officially locked for winter break." Marissa Kelly patted my shoulder as she came to a stop behind the couch. I would never rank students in the Beta house in order of favorites, but if I was forced at gunpoint, Marissa would be in the top three.

"Friday, girlfriend."

I looked away from the TV and cringed at my outfit: hot pink pajamas covered with little suns wearing sunglasses tucked into purple-and-green fuzzy socks, with a stain on my chest from either chocolate or coffee and a clear view of my stomach because I forgot a button. *It's no wonder I'm single.*

"Is it sad I wish I didn't have to leave for two weeks?" Marissa joined me on the couch and sighed with as much angst as a nineteen-year-old could.

"You have a home here waiting for you when you get back. Trust me, enjoy the time you have with your family while you can, because adulthood comes fast and hard." I adjusted my position, moving so we sat shoulder-to-shoulder, and snuck a look at her. Her typical smile disappeared. A deep frown that made her look years older replaced it. I nudged her shoulder with my own. "Hey, talk to me. I haven't seen you this sad since the infamous breakup freshman year."

She shrugged. "My parents are going through a rough time, and it's hard seeing them fight. It never used to be like that."

Poor Marissa. My soul hurt for her. "I'm sorry. I really am. I wish I had some profound advice for you to help or make it better, but that is out of my realm. Just...maybe try to find things to do with your parents separately. Offer to help with dinner or cleaning. You can always text me if you want."

"You're the best, Becs." She leaned her head against me.

A rush of *this-is-why-I-love-my-job* bloomed over me in a

full-body hum of happiness, and I couldn't stop my smile. "I *am* your house mom, and yeah, I can be the best."

She laughed, and I put my arm around her shoulders for a half-hug. She leaned into it, and a lightness filled my chest.

No one in my education-focused family understood why I did what I did. They always asked how it was going and what I actually did, but it was so foreign to them that their eyes would gloss over and they'd nod a lot. They appreciated the fact that I helped college students, sure, but it wasn't the same as teaching in their eyes. Yeah, I loved my parents, and I knew they loved me, but they didn't understand me. None of my endless stream of first dates ever understood me. Very few people did. *Except these girls.*

"I guess I better start packing since it'll take me forever to clean my room."

"Yeah, honestly, you're a great human but a slob, Issa." I earned another smile from her.

I was about to offer to help when Amanda Lee rushed down the spiral staircase to my right, face flushed and eyes the size of saucers. "Becs."

"Yes?" I sat up straighter, already imagining the crisis I would have to deal with. Was it her creepy boyfriend? Her slipping grades? Her secret stash of vodka I knew she kept behind her desk but we never talked about?

"I tried opening the window and it wouldn't work, so I forced it, you know, to get fresh air into the room. I do live on the highest floor so it gets stuffy, yeah? So I shoved it and the window shattered and I tried cleaning it up but then the wind picked up, and anyway...my clothes are on the roof, and you know how my mom feels about me losing *any-thing*," she rambled, slurring words and syllables in an almost incomprehensible way. But I knew her well and pieced it together.

"Your clothes are on the roof?"

"And all over the yard." Her bottom lip trembled. "My mom will kill me if I lose those blouses. My grandma made them for me."

Save the clothes and then look at the glass. "Okay girls, get your coats. We're going on a recovery mission."

I marched from our huge living room to the closet, shoving my feet into my favorite pair of sequined Uggs, bundling up with a head-to-toe hot pink parka and ridiculous yellow hat I'd knitted myself two years ago. Not my best-stitched work, but it was warm and that was all that mattered in winter. Marissa, Amanda, and another pair of girls joined us and bundled up, and we set out the back door. Sure enough, colored shirts decorated the dull landscape. It had been a brutal December in the Midwest. Poor central Illinois was already prepared for a blizzard before Christmas, and the wind burned the exposed parts of my face. I didn't complain though—we had a mission to complete.

We each took off in different directions, grabbing shirts before they blew away, and a bright red something caught my eye next door. Damn it, Amanda. It landed in *his* front yard. Of course, I'd be wearing something totally uncool as I trekked around Harrison's property in search of a runaway shirt. He probably wasn't home anyway. He had family in state—a niece and nephews, if I remembered correctly—and it was Thursday before break. Yeah, he wouldn't be home, and I'd be fine. *No need to panic.*

With a quick glance at Harrison's front window, I blew out a relieved breath at the dark stillness within. Yes! He's not even home!

I sprinted toward the yard and snatched the shirt. Unfortunately, whoever was in charge of my life thought it'd be hilarious to increase the wind and send the shirt flying onto his front porch.

Rats.

Okay, I can do this. He wasn't home, and even if he was, I had nothing to be embarrassed about—even if he did ghost me on the after-date call he'd promised.

Ten steps. That's all it'd take. I scanned the house once more, and then I moved stealthily in case I was wrong. The last thing I needed was to come face-to-face with that man.

Each crunch of the ground beneath my boots echoed, and my heart raced. Tiptoeing on the bottom step, I winced as it creaked. My eyes shot to the window, hoping his handsome face and infamous frown wouldn't appear.

A long moment passed before I moved again. Then, blowing out a breath, I snatched the shirt off the railing. Thinking I was home free, I almost did a victory dance. But before I could stop myself, my right foot slid out from beneath me on a patch of wet leaves, and I crashed onto my butt on his porch. Hard. With enough noise to wake the dead. Fate was seriously messing with my life.

"Shit, shit, shit!" I yelled, my lower back hurting more than I'd like to admit. I lay there for several seconds before heaving myself upright, and as I stood, the front door flew open. I tried to never let the girls hear me curse. But the pain caused it to slip out.

It was like a movie, a slow-motion action scene where my heart crept up my throat and my palms sweated despite the freezing temperature. I took one deep breath and met the intimidating and perfect green eyes of Harrison. "Hello, Harrison."

"Becca," he grumbled. His rough, deep voice was way too sexy and commanding for his own good. And oh, baby, I hated how he affected me.

"Great porch you have here. Just wanted to say have a nice holiday." I marched down the stairs with more trepidation than before. I winced, but my back was to him so he wouldn't see. *Just let me escape, please.*

"Why are you on my porch?"

"You wouldn't believe me if I told you," I said into the wind, still not turning back.

"Try me."

I snuck a glance at him again, hating how his gray Henley showcased his sculpted arms and strong chest—broad shoulders were my weakness—and the shirt paired well with his black jeans hugging his massive thighs. It wasn't fair he looked like that when my pink, girly pajamas peeked out from under my coat. Channeling my tiny inner badass, I gave him my best smile.

"Okay." I held up the red shirt and motioned to the sorority house with my chin. "One of the girls broke a window on the top floor, and her clothes escaped her room. She blamed the wind, but now that I think about it, it's a bit suspicious. Was she waving clothes out to signal someone? Smoking a doobie? Airing out a fart? I just don't know." I frowned for a beat before chewing on my chapped bottom lip in the awkward silence. "Anyway. So yeah. We're on a dangerous recovery mission before the elements destroy her clothes."

His expression never changed beyond a slight lift on the side of his mouth. "Recovery mission?"

"Yes. For the clothes." I held the shirt up like I was wearing it, pretending to be a model. "See?"

"Yeah, I see. You expect me to believe it just *landed* on my porch?" He arched one disbelieving brow.

"Yes." I gave him a firm nod.

"What was the crash I heard?"

"Oh, that." I tried thinking of something that would explain the sound of my tush hitting his stairs, but the longer the silence grew between us, the more I felt the need to ramble. "A raccoon. I saw a raccoon, and we fought over the shirt."

His nostrils flared for a second before he tilted his head to the side. "You fell."

"Okay, fine. Yeah. I fell. Happy?"

"Not particularly. Are you okay?"

Did his face look like he was actually concerned? My heart skipped a beat at the thought, but it settled down just as quickly. No, he must be cold.

"The diagnosis is that I will survive. It'll take a couple of hot baths, but nothing more than my ego and butt is bruised."

"Glad you're alright."

Those simple words should not have caused me to blush like a teenager around her crush, but they did. I had to get out of there, like five seconds ago. "See you around, Harrison."

I took a couple steps back toward the sorority house when he spoke again. This was the most words we'd exchanged in over two years...since that night. Since that *kiss*. Weird didn't cover how I felt about it.

"Are you staying in the house alone over break?"

"Yes." I didn't stop walking.

"That's a huge house for one person."

I spun around and narrowed my eyes, giving him my *no bullshit* look I always gave the girls. My mom referred to me as a tough marshmallow when I tried to be mean, but it was all I had. "I'm a big girl, and I've done it before. I'll be fine. It's my job."

"Make sure you fix the broken window. You shouldn't wait too long to repair it with the blizzard coming."

I squeezed my eyes shut. He was right. *Ugh.* I had to call someone to come out today or tomorrow or I'd have an open portal into the frigid negative temperatures that would last for an entire week. My heart rate sped up like I was running.

"I gotta go." I waved over my shoulder, still too humiliated to face him again.

"Have a nice holiday, Becca."

I didn't respond to him. The window was my priority. I had never had to get one repaired before. Did I just call a window guy and beg? Were there window guys? Oh my gosh, how could I be a house mom and not know how to fix a broken window?

I rushed by the girls carrying various shirts and waved at the few sitting in the front parlor with their suitcases. Parents started picking up their girls today after finals, and I doubled back to say goodbye. They couldn't see me with anything but a smile. No one ever saw my panic. *Remain calm, stay positive, and always have a plan.* That was my motto for life.

"Ladies, have a wonderful time at home. I'll miss you."

"We'll miss you, too, Becs." Ashley, Beatrice, and Maria all hugged me, and I squeezed them back. "We left you presents under the tree. You can't open them until Christmas, though."

"You did?" I almost cried at their genuine expressions. "I said no gifts!"

"We know, but you're unlike other sorority moms. You invest yourself in us, and believe in us, and well, you deserve a nice holiday."

My eyes watered. "I told myself no tears when you all left but look at me, already weepy."

"You cry at animal rescue commercials, every rerun of *Friends*, and when we get good grades. Never change, Becca Fairfield."

"Don't forget every single Hallmark movie," Beatrice added.

"Okay, leave already." I gently pushed her away, causing the three of them to giggle.

I peeled off my coat, refilled my cup of coffee with the newest hazelnut roast and coconut creamer, and sat. I had a crisis to deal with, and I had no idea how. But the first step: clean up the mess.

That I could do. I grabbed the broom, a trash bin, and heavy-duty gloves I still had from an intense scarecrow costume for Halloween and marched up to the third floor still wearing my puffy coat. Amanda's room faced north—the exact direction of Harrison's house—and sure enough, the wind whipped around her room. Pieces of glass decorated the floor, the windowsill, and the window ledge that spilled onto the roof.

I am their house mom. It is my job to take care of them when they are away from home. I can do this. I will do this.

"Becs, do you need help?" Kristin Garrison, the president of the Betas with enough potential to run the world—despite her terrible taste in men—entered the room.

A rush of happiness flooded through me at her offer. "I'd rather you don't cut yourself. But could you find me a tarp and lots of duct tape? We should have some in storage outside."

"You got it. Be careful."

"You too. That shed is a piece of work out there."

Kristin left, her face set in determined lines, and I scanned the damage. It took ten minutes to sweep up the floor, the desk area, and the windowsill. So far, no cuts.

Outside the window, there were huge pieces. I stepped onto the small porch on the roof—just one foot—and balanced, picking up the broken glass and tossing it into the bin. The wind blasted and I stumbled, slamming my shoulder into the window frame—right where a minor shard stuck out.

"Balderdash!" The cut hurt. The sharp sting stole my breath for a second, and I maneuvered myself back into the room. I unbuttoned my top and surveyed the damage. Yup. A small shard impaled my arm, leaving a trail of blood dripping down my pale skin.

My head spun...oh no. I hated blood. I did. It was the worst.

I needed to sit. Yeah, just for a second. I found my way to Amanda's twin bed and put my head between my knees. Everything turned fuzzy, and I focused on my tasks.

Clean up damage.
Repair area with tarp.
Make insurance claim.
Call repairman.

I repeated it three more times as everything went black.

CHAPTER TWO

HARRISON

Only during a cold day in hell would I voluntarily watch my younger brother be interviewed about his team playing in a bowl championship on TV. There wasn't enough beer in the world to numb the rampant feelings of jealousy, anger, and injured pride coursing through me. The jealousy wasn't about his coaching ability—I'm good at what I do—it was the envy of having professional athletes who took their careers seriously.

Winter workouts were not going well, and there wasn't a single thing I could do about it. College players were getting drunk and high, and throwing away their future for a good time. Team and responsibility meant nothing to them. *All a coach can do in the off-season is pray.*

My strength-and-conditioning staff gave me weekly reports on the guys, and they weren't incredible. They also weren't garbage. Our team defined the word average. I pinched the bridge of my nose and cracked open my second beer. Yeah, it was only midday, but since we didn't make it to any championships, it was my first holiday break in three years.

Probably my last break, since I'll get fired next year if we don't start winning.

The amber liquid loosened the tightness in the back of my throat. Thinking about getting fired had the potential to ruin any day at any given time. It didn't help that my folks constantly pointed out the differences between my younger brother and me, like they had to convince me he was talented.

Oh, Hank is just made to coach. He's a natural.

Hank will have offers with the NFL, I know it.

Hank played football one year of his life and had a string of luck to get him where he was. I could only blame myself, since I got him his first coaching job. Funny how life works.

My phone went off, the dull buzz drawing my glance to a text from my mom.

> **Mom:** Since Hank is in the Bowl, we are flying out to see him play in California for the holidays! This is huge! Aren't you so proud of him? You're more than welcome to come, as we'll do Christmas there this year to support him.

Of course, they would fly out there even though the game wasn't until a week after the holiday. I didn't get a chance to respond before my sister—my favorite family member—texted me.

Blair: We're not flying out to see His Holiness.
Come stay with us. The kids miss you. I miss you.
Ben will have beer.

Harrison: Thank God we're the normal ones. I'll
be there.

Blair: He is the classic youngest child, isn't he?
Always the favorite, never to blame. We'll always
have each other, Harrison. Don't let them get in
your head.

I didn't respond and hated how some family members could make me feel insignificant even as a thirty-four-year-old man. My career was filled with accomplishments and awards. I was proud of myself. I didn't lack confidence or patience or even self-awareness about my strengths and weaknesses. It was the constant embellishing of Hank's average, yet lucky, career that drove me mad.

Hank could be average at anything and get praised for it, while I had to work three times as hard to get any acknowledgment. I'd coached in two bowl championships, and no one except Blair and her family came to watch. My parents canceled last minute both times. Hank had to *focus on his own career* and couldn't take off work to watch. Yet our mom wanted us to fly out there? I groaned and ran a hand over my face.

When I first started, Blair told me that I needed to stop caring what they think. That was easier said than done.

Damn, why am I thinking about my parent issues when I could be three beers in?

I finished my second brew and shuffled into the kitchen for another. Downtime for me consisted of napping, watching football, drinking beer, or heading to the gym. I had already completed an aggressive workout that morning, so I could do whatever the hell I wanted the rest of the day. And what I wanted? Napping and beer.

The fridge sat next to a window, and I glanced out into my yard, hating how dark and drab the landscape was. I needed to make my property a priority in the spring, because if I had another losing season, I'd get fired and be forced to sell it. Then what would I do?

Stop. I couldn't worry about that now. Not without the facts. My ex-wife always told me my outlook was too negative, and look at me now, refusing to think about getting fired until it happened. I was growing as a person after all. I snorted and cracked open a third beer just as the wind howled and the screen rattled against the glass. I paused at the sound.

Becca.

She'd mentioned a broken window at the house. My lips twisted. The bright pink pajamas, the wild honey-colored hair, the wide eyes and full lips. That woman was too fucking happy and full of energy and trouble. I knew how those lips felt against mine, and if I thought about it too long, I'd forget why it would be a terrible idea to kiss her again. Even though her face and body were gorgeous.

Becca could talk for minutes without stopping, created

ridiculous stories when she was nervous, and always had a smile on her cute face. Hell, the woman played the ukulele and sang during our one dinner together. If anyone could be described as my complete opposite, it was her. She was petite and fragile, she loved everyone, and everyone loved her.

And she shouldn't be trying to repair a window on the third floor of an old house.

"Son of a bitch." I wiped my hand over my jaw. My chest tightened, and I swallowed. Becca needed help, and I couldn't sit here when she might hurt herself. I threw on a down coat I used when I camped, found my warmest boots, grabbed my toolbox, and headed next door to the large house.

I had no idea how Becca could live with fifty college girls. The thought made my body cringe with horror, but she clearly liked it. She'd been there as long as I had: four years.

Neighbors for four years, one date, one insane kiss, and maybe ten conversations since that kiss. Great track record on my part. I marched through the backyard and frowned when I spotted a tiny woman struggling to open the shed. "Need help?"

"Hi Coach Cooper. Yeah, Becs needs a tarp out of here." She blew out a breath and put her hands on her hips. "This is stuck."

"Let me." I set my stuff on the ground and yanked at the door. It was jammed hard and took three tries before it opened. The tarp lay folded in the corner—because how else would Becca store it? The woman sorted her food and ate all her potatoes before moving on to something else. *Why do I remember this date from two years ago so well?*

I shook the thoughts from my mind and cleared my throat. "Here." I handed her the tarp and shut the difficult doors. "Care to show me the room with the damage?"

"Please. I love Becs but it looked bad, and I don't want her hurting herself. She's helpful, really, but pretty clumsy."

"That's putting it nicely." The woman fell on my porch not twenty minutes ago.

The girl laughed. I followed her into the brick house, through a living room three times the size of mine, and up a spiral staircase that reminded me of the movies. Pictures with girls all wearing light blue shirts covered the walls. It looked like different graduating classes, but I just saw hundreds of girls in the same pose. If the lighting was dark, it would've been a little creepy. The stairs creaked with my weight, and I studied the railing and photos to make sure they were secure. With a quick check, they proved sturdy, and it pleased me.

The house was well taken care of, but that wasn't a surprise. Becca cared deeply about her job. Our passion for our work was about the only thing we had in common, justifying why that one date did not lead to two.

"It's on the third floor."

I nodded and continued following the young woman. The cold air blasted my face the second we stepped onto the top floor, and I sucked in a breath. It was a small, narrow hallway with three rooms on each side.

The girl pointed to the first door and opened her mouth to say something when she paled. "Becca! Oh my God!" She darted into the room with me right behind her. The young woman bent over the bed, her voice squealing. "She got hurt!"

"Let me see," I commanded, assessing the scene and taking note of what could've happened. The young woman didn't wait a second before jumping out of the way and providing me with a view of my neighbor. My heart leaped into my throat. She lay there, eyes closed and her creamy skin pale and covered in blood. Her jacket and shirt hung halfway off, giving me a view of her silky bra. *Shit!* She'd passed out.

"Do you have a first aid kit? Something to clean the blood?" I asked as I sat on the edge of the bed, noticing for the first time the glass shard in her arm. *What did you do, Becca?* "Tweezers, too?"

"Uh, yeah. I think. Um…what?" the young woman stuttered, her concern for Becca almost tangible. A part of me wondered how my players would feel if I ever got hurt. Would they care? Help? Notice?

Not the time.

"Tweezers, first aid kit. Hurry." I jutted my chin toward the door.

The young woman rushed out of the room, and I removed my gloves and coat. I touched the side of Becca's neck. Her pulse beat strong, thank God, but her soft skin was freezing cold.

I set my jacket over her torso, carefully avoiding the spot

in her upper arm. With a soft shake of her uninjured arm, I asked, "Becs, can you hear me?"

Nothing.

Not great.

The shard was a few inches long, and the sight of it impaling her skin made my stomach churn. She should be obnoxiously happy, spouting off about all the good things in the world...not pale as hell and covered in blood.

Her silence was jarring. While her incessant gabbing could go from charming to annoying in a second, I much preferred hearing her voice than not. I carefully cupped the back of her head with my hands and traced her jawline with my fingers, trying to be gentle. The last thing I wanted was to scare her.

"Becca."

Her eyelids fluttered, a soft groan escaping. If it were any other time, in any other situation, that sound would've driven me wild. But this was now, and she was hurt. "Becca, you passed out. Can you hear me?"

"S-what?" she mumbled, lightly moving in my hands, her teeth chattering and her lips pressing together. "It's c-cold."

"I put my coat over you, but I need you to stay put until we remove the glass from your arm."

"Window. Four steps. I...I...clean, repair, insurance, phone."

Damn. She was cute. I smiled, the foreign gesture almost hurting my face. I moved my fingers over her neck, hoping to...what? Warm her? Help her? The need to keep touching her grew stronger.

"I'll help you with the window. Can you open your eyes for me?"

"Maybe?" Her lids fluttered open but then closed again.

"I think you can." I pressed my lips together, preventing a laugh from escaping.

"Are you the window man?"

I snorted. "No. It's Harrison."

"My sexy neighbor?"

Sexy neighbor? My grin spread, and my heartbeat kicked up. Nothing could make me leave her in this moment. "Yes. I came to help with the window and found you like this."

"Sexy window man."

"Not the best nickname, or the worst, but I'll take it." I chuckled.

Even in her distress, she smiled and turned her face so her cheek pressed against my palm. Her skin felt like ice. We needed to remove the glass and get her dressed in fifteen more layers. Where was that damn woman with the first aid?

"Your hand is warm. It's probably weird you're touching my face. But I like it. It's big. Do big hands help with window repair?" she asked, still not coherent enough to realize who she was talking to.

My chest tightened at how goddamn cute and vulnerable she looked. I swallowed hard, unsure what to say.

"Coach, I couldn't find the first aid kit, but I found some cleaning wipes, tweezers, and a handful of bandages and wraps. Hopefully they'll work."

I blew out a long sigh of relief. *About damn time.*

"That will do. Does Becca have a sweatshirt or something we can change her into since she's covered in blood?"

"Yes, I'll run into her room. Should I bring a hot chocolate? It's her favorite pick-me-up."

Of course it was. "Yeah, that's a great idea."

The young woman stepped out just as Becca opened her eyes. Her light brown irises had specks of blue in them. It bothered me that I'd never noticed before. Those almost-too-large eyes narrowed at me, and the brief warmth in them disappeared. She wrinkled her brow and blinked several times, her frown deepening.

"Wh-what are you doing here?" Her voice came out weak.

I scooted closer to her on the bed. "Helping you."

"I didn't ask you for help, did I?" She bit her lip as a light blush crept up her neck and cheeks. "I can't remember if I did. I wouldn't want to bother you, so I'm confused why you're here."

"No, you didn't ask. One of your girls flagged me down when I was on my way to offer help." I caressed her skin with my calloused fingers, convincing myself I did this to give her warmth and distract her from pain. That was it. She leaned into me just a bit, but I didn't think she realized it.

"Flagged you down?"

"She was worried. You must've bumped into the window and got yourself pretty good." I moved my hand from her jawline and placed it on her arm, inches away from the small shard. "I'm going to remove the small piece of glass from your arm, okay?"

"Glass?" Her voice rose an octave, and she blinked faster. "I *hate* blood."

"Ah, that's why you passed out then."

"Rats." Glancing down where my hand rested, she winced. "It's probably best to rip it out just like taking off a Band-Aid, right?"

"Yes. Look toward the window. Trust me, you don't want to watch this." I gently tilted her head away from her shoulder and ran my hand down her neck, over her shoulder, and stopped when I got to the glass. The wound wasn't that big, thankfully, and it looked worse than it was. In a world of cleat injuries, this was a pretty shallow wound. "It might hurt."

"I can handle it." She whispered affirmations to herself, somehow making her sunshine personality even cuter. "Just get it over with so I can figure out how to fix the window."

I picked up the tweezers, cleaned them with an alcohol swab, and placed them around the thickest part of the minor shard. "On three. One, two—" I pulled.

She released a little *oomph*. "I did *not* like that. Nope. Not even a little."

"You're a real champion." I fought another grin.

"I don't like skin pain. I know that's a weird thing to say, but when I tried getting a matching tattoo with my mom, I couldn't handle the pain. So now I have half of a four-leaf clover because the pain was too much. It looks like weird butt cheeks, which is not a cool thing to show off. Everyone has cute or meaningful or beautiful tats, and I have butt cheeks."

Skin pain? Butt cheeks? Good lord. I snorted. I should *not* be smiling at her. "Where is this tattoo?"

"On my hip. If you give me two drinks, I'll probably show you." As soon as she said the words, her eyes went wide, and her muscles tensed beneath me. "I didn't mean that. Ignore it. It's the blood loss. It's loosened my inhibitions and common sense."

She grunted a few times and tried to pull out of my arms without success.

"No, stay put. I need to clean your cut."

"Surely one of the other girls can do that?"

"I'm sure I have more experience with this sort of thing, and I don't mind." I found a cotton ball and covered it with the saline. "One of the young women is making you hot chocolate and bringing you a shirt since this one is covered in blood."

"My shirt?"

"Yeah."

She looked down, and her eyes widened even more. "Am I naked?"

I fought a laugh. "No. You kept half your shirt on, half your coat hanging off your other arm, and you're wearing a bra."

"I don't remember if it was a cute-bra day or an old-bra day."

"Cute. Trust me."

That must have satisfied her because she sighed. "Is it clean yet?"

"Almost." I'd already used five cotton balls cleaning up

the now-dried blood from her arm. I tossed the used materials into the nearest trash can. "Let me put a bandage on it, and you'll be good to go."

"Thank you." Her voice was quieter than usual.

I finished with the bandage just as the woman brought a sweatshirt and a large white mug with a Beta sign that said *happy happy happy* in red. "Done."

"Here, Becs." The woman placed the mug on the night table and stared at Becca with worry lines around her eyes. "Are you okay? We're sick downstairs just thinking you're hurt. The girls wanted to come up, but I made them wait."

"I'll survive this time, Kristin." She sat up and smiled— not at me but at Kristin. "Will you go reassure everyone I'll make it? I don't want anyone up here since there's still glass on the floor."

"Are you sure?"

"I'll help her clean up," I interrupted. "Thank you for getting the supplies."

She nodded and left us alone in the room. We hadn't moved from our positions so our thighs pressed together. My entire body tightened with need, with awareness of how warm and soft she was. It unsettled me. Becca took a sip from the mug and met my gaze over the rim, her brow furrowing for a second before her forehead smoothed out.

"Feeling better?" I asked.

She ignored my question and let out a long, deep sigh that I swore I felt in my gut. "I'm sorry you're the one who had to help me."

"Why?" Her words shouldn't have hurt me, but they did. Was I that bad of a guy?

"I hate when people feel guilted into helping me. It was nice of you to check on me, though, so I appreciate it. Thank you." Her stiff tone had me sitting straighter.

"I wasn't guilted, and you're welcome." I rose from the bed and began the pickup. My coat still covered her, and I tossed her the sweatshirt. "Do you need help putting that on?"

"I think not, sir." Pink tinged her cheeks.

I turned away to hide my amusement. Finding a broom, I swept the broken glass into the pan. She'd done a good job repairing the window before her injury, and I could put the tarp on soon. I stuck my head out the window, frowned at the large fragments there, and was picking them up when she let out a loud, frustrated sigh. I stilled, afraid to turn around. "You good?"

"Um, well, see the thing is . . . I need help with this shirt. My arm hurts, and I'm stuck."

"To clarify, I *can* turn around?"

"Yes, Harrison."

I did. Becca's sweatshirt covered her face and only half of her body, leaving a sizable part of her chest exposed to me. The lacy blue bra teased me. Her nipples strained against the fabric, like the bra was a bit too small. My mouth watered. Yeah, my attraction to her was never a problem. Not even a little bit.

"Sure, I can help." Shit, my voice sounded gruff.

I stepped toward her and maneuvered her arm into the sleeve and then studied the front of the sweatshirt: *Friends, Coffee, Betas, I'm a simple woman.* I couldn't stop the smirk overtaking my face. "Cute shirt."

"Shut up." She pushed up from the bed and grabbed the edge of the desk.

Reaching out, I put my arm around her waist before she could fall. She leaned against me, her vanilla scent making me inexplicably hungry for something sweet.

"I got up too fast." She closed her eyes.

"I noticed. I don't mind helping you. Seriously. Just drink your hot chocolate and relax. My only plan today was to drink beer and nap. This is better."

She chewed on her full bottom lip and narrowed her large brown eyes. "It feels weird to just watch you work."

"It's not weird. You deserve a break. Rest a bit, okay?" I lowered my voice and gave her my coaching stare—a scowl, my eyes going into slits—the one where players backed out of an argument and submitted to me. She did no such thing. She wasn't intimidated, and I liked that. *Huh.*

She nodded but still remained standing. "I need my phone to see what's next on the list. I think I need to file a claim? Put up a tarp?"

"How to fix a window list?"

"Exactly." She jutted her chin out just as she shivered head to toe. "Now, should we put up the tarp to stop this cold air?"

I rubbed the back of my neck, hoping to calm my annoyance at her use of the word *we.* "Becca, you just passed out. I will put up the tarp."

"I can—"

"Yeah, yeah, yeah. You're badass, independent, and can do it. I understand. But I'm capable, not minutes from regaining consciousness, and don't want you to hurt yourself. Sit your cute ass on the bed and watch or get out of the room."

She blinked three times before plopping down on the bed and crossing her legs in a very sassy move. "Are you always this bossy?"

"When I'm pissed, yes." I pointed at her. "Don't get up."

I got to work, nailing the tarp into the walls on the top and repeating the motion on the bottom, then lining it with duct tape around the edges. The wind still breezed through and, with the blizzard coming in less than forty hours, I double lined it. "There, this should hold until someone can come out and fix it."

"Thank you."

"Was that hard to say?" I joked.

She rolled her eyes, and one of her famous crooked smiles greeted me. She used to smile at me like that every time we crossed paths on campus before I promised to call and never did. Definitely my fault that she stopped flashing me those smiles.

"Yes, but it was necessary," she admitted. "I wouldn't have done as good a job as you."

"I'm happy to help."

She took another sip from the mug and tilted her head to one side, almost like she was studying me. "I'll get you some cocoa to go. To-go-coa!" She laughed at her joke and bounced out of the room without any modifications to her movements even though she had just passed out.

I chuckled. This woman...I'd avoided conversations with her the past two years for a reason. She got underneath my skin and had me wanting more.

And that was something I just couldn't do. *Again.*

CHAPTER THREE

BECCA

Chef Ramirez and Claudia's House Cleaning got their final checks before the holidays, enough food was stocked so I could survive an entire zombie apocalypse if needed, and all the girls were scheduled to be picked up early to avoid the blizzard. The only blip, if I'd even call it that, was the broken window that couldn't be repaired until after the snowstorm. After hours on YouTube, I barricaded the window three more times and secured the bedroom so most of the wind and cold would remain tucked inside. After confronting Amanda and interrogating her roommate, they insisted the window broke by accident, but it still concerned me. I prided myself in my house-mothering skills, knowing things the girls thought were secrets.

The sneaking in past curfew.

When the hallway smelled a little too much like recreational activities.

I trusted them to make a few mistakes, but an entire window breaking sent my instincts on alert.

Perhaps it was the wicked winter wind.

I sighed and finished folding some blankets and stacked them on the back of our couch.

Two more hours until I had the house to myself for two weeks. My only vacation until the summer months. I wasn't crying at the thought of not seeing the girls for that long. Nope. It was winter allergies...or something. They were totally a thing.

"It's just Kristin and me left, Becs. Your favorites," Marissa said as we huddled on the couch watching reruns of *Survivor*. We started it as a joke during spirit week back in October because the theme was *Survivor*, but we couldn't stop watching. We were already on season eight.

"I don't have favorites, Issa."

"Uh-huh. *Sure* you don't." She grinned. "You're going to miss us."

I winked at them and focused on the TV instead of the fact that I'd be alone for fourteen days. "I'm not going to shower the entire time and just eat all the food. It's going to be great."

"You know, you could ask our hunky neighbor Hot Henley Harrison to visit. Hm?"

"Who?" I ignored her comment about *him*. "Mr. Bixby, the eighty-year-old? Or Mr. Huntley who just had a hip replacement?"

"Avoidance is a huge red flag, Becca. You damn well know I'm talking about Coach Cooper."

"Oh, him." I pursed my lips, hating the way my body heated up thinking about him. Yeah, he'd had his hands on me, saw me in my bra, and set my skin on fire with his heated gaze. He also promised to call and didn't. "Hot Henley Harrison isn't exactly my type."

"False. He's every heterosexual woman's type."

"Uh, I'm bi and wouldn't mind giving him my body for an entire night," Issa said.

"Ladies, he is too old for you!"

"But not too old for you." Kristin wiggled her eyebrows. "I saw how he treated you. He was worried."

Harrison worrying about me? No. He felt guilt or a duty or something. I shook my head and waved a hand in the air, dismissing the thought entirely. "I was covered in blood. Anyone would be worried. Mr. Bixby would've been worried."

"Listen Becs, you take good care of us, but you can take care of yourself, too. When was the last time you went on a date?" Issa patted my arm.

"Did my mom put you up to this?" I joked, hating how I felt the need to defend myself. "She did, didn't she? That woman is obsessed with helping me find *the one*."

"What? No. Would she do something like that?" Issa asked.

"Many times. My dear mother meddles in my dating life more than I meddle in yours. Trust me."

"So when was the last time?"

"Uh, let's see…my mom set me up with an uptight doctor who told me I was the strangest woman he'd ever met. That was a month ago. Before that, there was a dude named Rickon who was an engineer with as much personality as this couch. And before that, a man named Todd told me women were only good for birthing and cleaning." I scrunched my nose and omitted mentioning the date from two years ago that I thought was one of the best ones yet. Stupid feelings.

Kristin shook her head. "They sound like they sucked."

"They did." I laughed, despite the pang of unease at the reality. My mom insisted on setting me up with guys who weren't my type. But I never enjoyed focusing on the negative and forced a smile. "I'm so busy with you gals, I don't mind my lack of love life too much."

"When we get back, prepare yourself for a love-tervention. We'll get you signed up on dating apps, style some new outfits, and it'll be awesome! And we'll get guys that don't suck. Trust me." Issa nodded with a lot of aggression.

"It can be our New Year's resolution! Becca gets boned!" Kristin threw her hands up in the air.

"Okay, that's enough," I said between bouts of giggles. "I appreciate your misplaced concern but shh...they are voting someone off the island, and I want to watch."

The girls shared a look, and I pretended I didn't see it. It was hard continuing to put myself out there. All those first dates...never any second ones...the continual phrases of *no chemistry, not a good fit, too strange* ringing in my ears.

I didn't lack confidence. I loved myself, but it grated on me when people consistently told me I was *too much* or *too odd.* I spoke too loudly, or too often. My clothes weren't sleek or cool. My favorite though: no explanation at all. The promise of a call or another date that never came.

Maybe it was time to take action.

Especially if my mom tries setting me up for the holidays again.

"Okay girls, you're right. After break, we're doing this."

"Yay!" They cheered in unison and left me alone for the rest of the show.

Soon they were all on their way home for the holidays, leaving me alone for the first time since summer. And while I never looked forward to having the girls gone, the peace and quiet was nice. I picked up the remaining cups and the debris from outside and made myself a cup of tea before settling into my room on the west side of the house. It was modest, but I had my own bathroom and suite separate from the girls. Tomorrow, I'd read one of the books I'd checked out from the library and hunker down for the blizzard that had scared central Illinois into buying bread by the tons and emptying store shelves of all the flashlights and batteries.

Something wasn't right. I woke up chilled to my core. Condensation from my warm breath swirled in the air, and my skin felt like ice. *Am I in a nightmare?*

I wiggled around in my bed and eyed my watch—*7:00 a.m.* The extreme weather alert at the top of my phone filled in the

missing pieces. God, the blizzard must've hit hard. I shivered
as I pushed off the covers. This wasn't right. The house should
never be this cold. *Amanda's room!* I needed to make sure the
tarp held.

I crept toward the third floor. My teeth chattered, and my
entire body trembled. I wrapped my fuzzy pink bathrobe
tighter around my body and switched on the hallway light.

Nothing.

I tried it again. No light. I ran into the first room. Again,
no light. *Oh my goodness, the power is out.*

I jogged to the closest thermostat and gasped at the number. Thirty-four degrees in the house. Holy moly. I needed
more layers and a plan.

I speed-walked back to my room and fumbled with the
bedside drawer, retrieving the device I stored there for
moments like this. I flipped on my emergency flashlight and
then searched my closet for three pairs of sweatpants, three
pairs of socks, and an old fleece bathrobe. I shuffled downstairs toward the fireplace, panicking at the five remaining
logs of wood. We didn't have a generator in the house since
the last one blew a couple months ago. Why hadn't I prepared better and stocked more wood?

Thank goodness the girls aren't here.

But what the heck am I going to do?

I found lighter fluid and set up the first couple of logs. The
cold would last a week, but the snow should stop after a few
days. Then I could drive to my parents' house and stay warm.
That left me with forty-eight hours of warmth to create.

There used to be a stockpile of logs in the backyard, and if they weren't there, the kitchen chairs it was. Okay, start a fire.

I could do this. Totally do this.

Twenty matches in, there was still no fire burning, and my hands were so dang cold. I blew my hot breath into my gloves. *This is not good.*

Before a wave of panic came over me, someone banged on my front door. Three loud knocks echoed in the foyer. *Who would be here at 7:00 a.m.?*

"Becca, let me in. It's fucking cold."

Harrison.

I got up in a rush, unbolted the door, and ushered him inside. "The power is out! I'm trying to make a fire but it's harder than I thought and I'm having no luck."

"I know. Heard on the radio everything west of Lincoln Street is out." Still standing at the front door, Harrison squinted toward the living room where I'd made a temporary setup while trying to start the fire. "How much wood do you have?"

"Uh, a couple of logs, but I think there's more in the backyard."

Focus on surviving, not his face. Most definitely not his lips.

He shook his head, shut the door with a loud boom, and entered the hallway. It was just the two of us in the dark, narrow foyer. "There's no stockpile in your yard. I checked on my way over here."

"Okay." I hoped my voice didn't give away my worry. My

stomach rivaled a pinball machine of anxiety at the severity of the situation. *Think. What's the plan?* "Uh, I have kitchen chairs and tables." I ran my hand over my face and took a few steps toward the kitchen. "I could break the legs off, yes. That shouldn't be too hard."

He scoffed, and cupping his hands around his mouth, he blew into them with his hot breath before rubbing them together. "Becca. Pack a bag and stay with me, at least until the power comes back on."

Stay with Harrison. At his house. Alone. *With the guy who ghosted me?* With the guy who made me question if I was too much? No. No way. Was this a prank? Another act of misplaced guilt? My gut churned, wondering at his motivation behind the invitation, and I dug my hands farther into my pockets. I wasn't pathetic, and I was sick of men being guilted into spending time with me. They felt bad, or my mom begged them, or they owed a favor to a mutual friend, and *that's* why they were on a date. The list was endless, and I gritted my teeth.

"I'm not helpless, you know. Just because I had the glass incident doesn't mean you need to take care of me." Despite the cold, heat crept up my face.

He rolled his green eyes, framed perfectly with long, snow-covered lashes. "I checked on our neighbors, too, okay? Not just you. They have generators or are out of town. Now come on. I can help you grab some stuff to bring over."

He barged past me, heading up the stairs with his own flashlight. He didn't know where my room was located, but he sure walked with a confidence I could appreciate.

I followed him, needing to stop the insane idea of *rooming* together for a few days. "Harrison, stop. I'll figure something out. I always do."

"Again, I admire you." He stopped walking and got nose-to-nose with me until his breath hit my face. His minty, warm breath. His eyes were hard, so beautiful, and filled with annoyance.

Awesome.

He tightened his jaw and stared at me like he wished I was anyone else. "Becca, people *die* during power outages like this during a blizzard. The power companies can't risk going out with negative-forty temps, so it could be days before the electricity is back on. I have enough firewood to last a month, food, and a gas water heater."

Unease and foolishness hollowed out my stomach, and I took a step back, hating how nervous he made me. I shook my head, wanting him to get out. I'd call someone or bury myself in a closet. "No, I—"

His facial expression softened, and he spoke over me. "It's better to have a buddy, right? You teach the girls that."

I rolled my eyes. "Yeah, for going out at night, not blizzards!"

"Same thing, Becca. If I freeze to death, I don't want to die alone."

"We won't die," I said, even though my heart raced as the severe realization came over me. I could remain stubborn, but doing so would be dumb. I'd rather not die.

I couldn't get a fire started on my own, and I didn't have any wood.

Harrison narrowed his eyes in a silent warning.

"Okay fine. *Fine.* I'll get my stuff."

"Good girl. Hurry. I want to get my fire going."

He followed me up to my room, and I ignored how close he walked behind me. He must've thought I'd fall down the stairs—which had happened before—but I wasn't going to complain because his natural body heat warmed me. I could surely survive a few days with him. God knows what we'd talk about or do, because we weren't friends. Hell, we were barely neighbors. But an uncomfortable few days beat dying, so my reality was what it was.

"Could you point your flashlight around my room?" I asked, hoping it would speed up the packing process.

He didn't respond but did as I asked.

Finding an old duffel bag, I shoved leggings, socks, underwear—the semi-sexy kind—sweatshirts, and every long-sleeved shirt I owned inside. I threw in two lip balms, my phone, and toothbrush. It wasn't like I was moving in with him...just for like two days to escape death. That's all.

"Do you need help?"

"No, I'm done." I hoisted the bag on my bad shoulder, winced, and switched to the other.

Noticing, he yanked the bag off my arm. "Here. I've got it."

"Hey!"

He shook his head. "I need you to grab all the ingredients for your hot to-go-coa."

My mouth fell open at his playful expression. Near-death

temperatures raged outside, and he chose that moment to make fun of me. "Did you...did you just use *my* joke?"

"Yes."

I burst out laughing at his proud expression and left him in my room. Smug looked really good on him. *Gorgeous grump.* "I'll grab the goods. Do you have enough food? We can take some over."

"We can come back if we run out. It's only next door. We could get cabin fever after a couple days."

Couple of days? Two days with Harrison? I gulped. Could I survive more than a day with my sexy, grumpy next-door neighbor? Sleeping under the same roof together?

Guess I'd find out.

I cleared my throat as my entire body flushed with how inappropriate my thoughts *almost* got. He'd ghosted me. Thinking about how he slept or what he did—or didn't—wear to bed was none of my business. "Come on, friendly neighbor."

He took his time leaving my room despite his insistence on rushing. "I can't figure out what that heap of stuff is on your chair."

"Yarn. I got into knitting a couple years ago and love to make hats and scarves. Oh! I want to bring that." I brushed past him again and shoved the materials into my arms.

His lips twitched as though he was trying not to laugh at me.

Feeling silly, I blushed. "I don't care that you might not think it's cool. I like it and it relaxes me, so don't judge me.

Sports aren't my thing. I trip over my own feet all the time, if you hadn't noticed."

He didn't say anything else as I rambled, but I decided I didn't care. We were doing this for survival. Nothing more. Partners out of necessity. Buddies to escape death.

We walked in silence down the stairs with our flashlights illuminating the dark passage. There were no windows on this side of the house. Even with the wicked snowstorm out-side, a tiny stream of sunlight hit the kitchen and provided enough light to grab some food. Harrison waited while I found the necessary ingredients in the kitchen and then grabbed my tea and kettle.

"My books!" I turned toward the living room.

"Your books?" He furrowed those dark and strong brows.

"I checked out ten books to read over break. I think I left them in the living room. Can you wait a second more?"

Again, he didn't respond but followed me into the room and watched me grab various novels I'd stored in random places. Four should be good enough.

"There. I'm ready." I stood to my full five-foot-three height and gave him my best smile. Yarn and books spilled out of my arms.

"Why were your books all over the place?" His lips were curved up in a slight smile showcasing his delicious dimples.

"Well, I like to place them where I can easily grab them when the fancy strikes. It's a system I've used my whole life. Books on hand at all my favorite hangout spots."

"Okay then." He reached out and adjusted one of the

books in my hand, his gloved fingers accidentally brushing against the outside of my coat. "Ready?"

Feeling like a teenage girl around her biggest and most embarrassing crush, I looked away. "Yes, sir."

We approached the door, and as I placed my hand on the knob, he stopped me. "It's bitter out. Can you put on a hat and scarf? A coat? Maybe gloves?"

Oh my goodness. I'm still in my bathrobe.

"Uh, yeah. Give me a sec."

Setting my stuff down on the front table, I tossed my bathrobe in the closet and searched for the right winter gear. It wasn't like I wanted to be sexy for him, but that bathrobe was ratty.

We'd already taken up a good twenty minutes in the cold, and his impatience grew with each second. I rummaged in the closet and found a green-and-red scarf I'd knitted. It was way too long, so I wrapped it around my neck three times. The hat was large and a dark red color. The gloves didn't match but they had snowmen on them, and I loved them.

"Ready," I said, closing the closet door.

He shook his head at me, his green gaze roaming all over me. My face, shoulders, torso, and legs.

Fine. Let him mock me, I didn't care. I held my head high. "Lead the way."

He clenched his jaw for a second before adjusting my scarf so it covered my cheeks. "Look down and walk fast. It's the worst weather I've ever experienced."

Shaken by that oddly sweet gesture performed by the

handsome giant, I locked the door even though the neighborhood was deserted, and we trekked the short distance toward his house. Wind whipped from every direction, stinging my cheeks like little daggers. My eyes watered, and each breath hurt my lungs. Despite the short walk, my entire body hurt with the cold, and I shivered so hard my jaw ached. "W-whoa, it's f-freezing."

He ushered me into his house first then shoved my bags inside. "There's a blanket on the couch. Use that until I get the fire going."

I dove onto his leather couch and bundled into the blanket without taking off a single piece of my winter wear. His house was warmer than the sorority, and my gratitude for him overwhelmed me. How dumb was I, thinking I could've done this alone... by burning kitchen chairs? I snorted into my fist while looking over his living room.

Yikes. His pile of wood, no pun intended, was eight times the size of mine, and it didn't take him more than a couple of minutes to get the fire going.

"How you doing over there, Becca?"

Not staring at your butt. Not at all. "Better. This b-blanket is amazing."

"I'm glad." He faced me and smiled.

I stared at his expression. "What?"

"You have a great smile."

"Uh, thanks."

He cleared his throat and rubbed his hands together in front of the small flames. "Your arm okay?"

"Hurts a little if I put pressure on it. I'm a side sleeper so I had to switch from my right to left. Took me a while to get comfortable, but other than that, I haven't noticed. I'm what one would call a *yearning dreamer* when I sleep. It means I'm open and inviting, hesitate to let people in, but very determined once I make up my mind." God, his stare made the little control I had on my filter disappear.

His dimples returned. "Well, I can agree you're stubborn."

"What kind of sleeper are you?"

Oh my goodness, I just asked him the world's stupidest question. I could've asked about his taxes, or football stuff, or why his pants were so tight, but no. I asked about *his sleeping position.*

If the blanket could swallow me up whole, I'd be grateful.

His lips twitched, and he plopped down onto the floor with his back to the fire. He crossed his legs and rested his beefy forearms over his knees. "Stomach."

My pulse increased with a sick combination of excitement and warmth. "Like a baby or a skydiver?"

"Uh, what?"

"A baby? Hello?" I rolled onto my side and brought my knees to my chest. My hands were almost in a prayer position on top of the pillow. "Or more like this?" I moved both hands under the pillow and turned slightly onto my left side, with both knees lined together with my legs slightly bent.

"That." He pointed, his brows wrinkling. "The one with the leg kicked out."

Nodding, I felt all kinds of silly that we were talking about sleeping positions.

You're too different.

You're too much.

You're too weird.

The words of my first dates came back. A sharp reminder that Harrison had ghosted me...no, just refused to acknowledge me or the incredible date I'd *thought* happened. If he'd see me coming, he'd cross the street, avoiding me at all costs. His actions set me back in the confidence department.

My face burned red, and I snuggled back into the couch, promising myself I'd bring up normal topics like weather or dogs or the best Christmas movies. I knew better than to reveal too much of myself. I'd end up hurt or feeling dumb, or worse—getting my hopes up for something that wouldn't happen.

The silence went on for too long, and the need to fill it overwhelmed me. "The snow is really coming down out there."

Jeez Louise, I was *that* person. My self-loathing knew no bounds.

Harrison cleared his throat and shifted positions. "Wait, aren't you going to tell me what the skydiver or whatnot means?"

I sneaked a glance at him over the blanket, prepared for a frown or raised brows. Instead his expression was open and curious. *Interesting.* It couldn't hurt to tell him since he'd demanded I come over here anyway. Plus, this wasn't a date.

"Well," I cleared my throat, "skydivers are usually direct

with what they want. They tend to be brash, fun, and risk-takers."

"Hm." He nodded a few times. "Not far off."

"I like showing the girls the descriptions. They read into it like horoscopes, and it's so fun seeing them accept how great they are. The article I share doesn't have negative traits, not really. Yeah, you being brash is true, but it's not necessarily negative, you know? It's powerful, command-ing. It gives the girls confidence, and I love it."

"You care about them a lot."

"I do," I said as warmth burst through my chest. "It might not make sense to you, but I love it. I don't get paid well, but I have free room and board, free meals, no bills, and I get to know these amazing, incredible, inspiring young women."

A line appeared between his eyebrows, and he did his head-tilt thing again. "Why wouldn't that make sense to me?"

"Uh, well, every time you see me doing something with the girls, you always give me this look like you can't believe what I'm doing."

He crossed his arms over his knees and leaned a little closer toward me. "What do you mean?"

"Just...never mind, okay? I didn't sleep well last night because of the cold. I'm going to try and nap if that's okay." *Yes, avoid him. Avoid his cute facial expressions and the charming way he tilts his head when he's confused. And above all, avoid all feelings.*

"Sure, get comfortable."

I turned my back to him and snuggled closer into the

back of the couch. As my mind raced, his footsteps grew closer. I stilled, holding my breath, as he grabbed the blanket and tugged it up to my face.

Harrison tucked me in. "Rest, Becca. Then we can talk about that comment."

CHAPTER FOUR

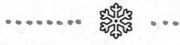

HARRISON

I could add being a creeper to my list of less-than-redeeming qualities. Watching Becca sleep was the last thing I should be doing. But here I was, staying warm in front of the flames and admiring the innocent expression she wore as she slept on my couch, wrapped in my blanket, her golden hair cascading in every direction.

Becca Fairfield slept on my couch.

I'm an idiot.

An idiot who was now stuck with her until the blizzard passed. Why did I do this? Ask her to stay here?

Right. Her safety. That huge house without power. The damn woman suggested burning kitchen chairs for warmth. She would have frozen to death or burned the entire house down. Either was plausible for her. Here she was at least safe. Sure, having a woman in my house freaked me out. I never dated. Since getting divorced three years ago, no woman besides my sister visited. Marrying Vivian ended up being the worst mistake of my life, and I had no plans of repeating that mistake again.

And yet, my beautiful but slightly annoying neighbor lay three feet away from me, her mouth parted as she snored softly. Her full, soft lips caught my attention. Even when she rambled on about nonsensical things like sleeping positions, they drove me crazy.

Her previous description of how I slept caught my attention, though. Was I a risk taker? Open? Maybe I was before the divorce and the losing team. When had I stopped being adventurous and going after what I wanted? When did I become so damn unhappy?

Becca shifted in her sleep. My lower gut tightened, and a wave of lust hit me, warming my skin despite the freezing temperature. *Stop thinking about her mouth.*

Great, I now had conversations with myself inside my head. Must be the cold getting to me.

I warmed my hands over the fire, rubbing them together. With one more glance at her sleeping figure, I walked into the kitchen. Enough natural light shone through the various windows, making it easy to cook some eggs and bacon on the stove. Thankfully, I had a gas stove. I turned it on and grabbed a lighter, carefully lighting a burner. It had been a while since I cooked for two.

The thought of eating canned beans and bread for the week made me cringe. I spent hours in the gym staying fit and planned my meals down to my snacks. I required a certain number of calories per day or I'd get really hungry— and that tended to make me hangry and more unpleasant than normal. Or so I'd been told. My ex-wife's complaints skewed my perception of myself, and I never cared enough to learn the truth.

I switched on my battery-powered radio to a low volume and set it on the counter next to the stove. I hoped there'd be an update on the power situation or something else of value to help us out. Last I checked, the front stretched from Illinois to New Mexico—so it could last days.

The familiar static and muffled voices brought me back to a million summers spent in the basement, waiting out tornado warnings. The memories made me smile. Times were simpler then, back when my siblings and I built forts and never fought. Now was so different. Blair and I were close still, but the divide with Hank grew each year. I was an easy scapegoat for him, and I wasn't sure if it was out of jealousy or anger. He was smart as hell and learned early on that blaming me, with or without truth, meant my parents would side with him. Even as an adult, he fell into the same trap. We were at the point that it wasn't worth trying to fix, and it hurt. I didn't enjoy not liking my brother.

> *It's Aaron Hodge with the National Weather Service, and thousands are without power, but until the gusts of forty-mile-per-hour winds stop, power companies are not cleared to work on the electrical lines. We advise not going outdoors for any reason. Stay warm and inside. Reserve power on your phone for real emergencies. We'll be back with reports on the latest soon.*

"Shit." I rubbed my hands over my eyes. Not good. If the gusts were that strong, the house could be damaged. Hell, windows could shatter. I squinted through the window facing the sorority house and could barely see the north side through the flurries.

What if Becca was still there, alone? I shivered at the thought and cleared my throat. We were safe, for now.

While the eggs sizzled, I chopped peppers and mushrooms. My open floor plan allowed me a view into the living room, but I focused on the food. Becca rolled over, making a cute groaning noise as she sat up on the couch. Hair escaped from her ridiculous holiday hat and indentations from the pillow were on her cheek—she shouldn't look that good, but damn, I liked her just-woke-up face.

She sniffed the air before her gaze landed on me. "Mm, you're cooking."

"Yes. I made some eggs for you, too. Do you like peppers or mushrooms?"

She yawned loudly and nodded. "I eat everything besides zucchini, eggplant, Brussels sprouts, and salmon." She counted off each item on her fingers.

She sounded so confident about her food list that my mouth twitched. "Okay then. That's a very specific list."

"I know what I want to eat and what I don't. Those are a definite no." She stood and wrapped the blanket over her shoulders, making her look like an oddly shaped burrito. Then she dragged her feet toward me and sat at the kitchen table. My breathing accelerated at the sight of her in my place, sitting at my kitchen table, and waiting for me to deliver her breakfast. It weirded me out how easily she fit into my space, even though this wasn't a morning after a hookup or anything down that road. I needed to get a grip on myself.

She chewed the side of her lip, and her cheeks tinged pink. "Thank you for making some food. I didn't realize how hungry I was until I smelled it. I can totally cook the next one." Her chipper voice contained a slight waver as she traced small circles on the table with her pointer finger.

Is she nervous? Uncomfortable?

I hated thinking I made her nervous. Was it because of that damn date two years ago? Or the silence? I didn't have a lot to say, so being quiet felt more natural, but her nervous ticks made my chest tighten. I wanted her feeling safe. My muscles strained with unease, and I thought about sneaking downstairs to get another workout in. My home gym had everything I needed, and I'd risk the cold at this point just to do something to ease the awkwardness. Having this energy in my house was new to me.

Hoping to reduce her awkwardness, I said, "We'll figure it out. I don't mind cooking."

I found two paper plates on a shelf and served the eggs, topping them with vegetables. The fact that I still had paper plates from an old football party worked out perfectly because I sure as hell didn't want to do dishes in freezing cold water. And not cleaning wasn't an option. Hanging out with smelly players in locker rooms for most of my days made me obsessive about the cleanliness of my own house.

I handed her a fork, and she dove in.

Becca shoveled eggs into her mouth like it had been years instead of hours since she'd last eaten. She released the smallest moans with every bite. It distracted the hell out of me. Her throaty sighs and happy expressions reminded me of our one date. She'd savored every bite that night and insisted on having me try her food. It was so different having someone offer me a bit of food from their own fork that I froze, probably hurting her feelings.

I had never met anyone who enjoyed food the way she did, or who ate like it was a special event. I liked knowing my cooking made her happy. It was an odd feeling.

I hadn't touched my plate yet, content with watching her. She stopped with the fork midway to her mouth.

"Why aren't you eating?" She jutted her chin to my plate.

I stabbed the plate with my fork a little too hard, shaking the tabletop, before shoveling some eggs into my mouth. "Mm."

Mm? I said *Mm*? What the hell was wrong with me?

She brought another bite to her mouth and ate with more grace this time. No groans. No frenzy like the food would evaporate into thin air. Damn. I missed her enthusiastic way of eating, but my staring had probably freaked her out.

"This is good, Harrison. Thank you."

"Welcome."

"Honestly, I never would've pegged you for a guy who could whip up a good breakfast. That's for sure. Very pleasant surprise." She smiled, her lips stretching across her entire face.

"Why not?"

"Why not...oh, why is it a surprise?" Her brows came together, and her pretty lips parted into an O shape.

"Yes." I set my fork down so it balanced on my plate and I gave her my full attention.

Her comment bothered me. Did she think of me as a total asshole who wouldn't cook for her while she stayed? Or was it something else? Like maybe I was so unskilled that I ordered takeout every night? My muscles tensed.

Her hesitant gaze met mine, and her face softened. "Well, you coach football and are single." She dropped her fork with a loud clink and squeezed her eyes shut. "Oh, yikes, I can't *assume* that. I don't know you. Or your dating life. You could be very *not* single. You could have a serious girlfriend. Or be engaged!"

I covered my mouth with my hand, hiding my smile at the embarrassment on her face. I considered letting her stew a few seconds longer, just to see how red her face could get or how much her hands could flail in the air, but I was a decent guy. "Becca, it's fine. I'm not seeing anyone. I'm single."

She released a long breath, picked up the fork like a wand, and met my gaze. "I stereotyped you, and for that, I'm sorry."

This time, I didn't hide my smile. "I'll let it slide this once."

Missing my joke, vivid red splotches lit high on her cheeks. She gave me a firm nod. "I know better than to make assumptions. You being a football coach has nothing to do with your abilities in the kitchen. Or anywhere, really. You could be a great knitter or juggler or dancer. I don't know, and it's not my business to assume a dang thing."

Wow. The knot in my chest loosened. "I'm not a great knitter or juggler or dancer."

"You could be."

"True. I guess you could also be all those things. I would never assume." I teased her again. It was too easy, and damn, there was something about her that made me comfortable.

She missed my joke again, and a line formed between her brows, her expression serious. "I'm an average cook, an average knitter, I can juggle for about ten seconds before I get distracted, and dancing is all your own interpretation."

My mouth twitched again, a bubble of laughter forming in my chest. She had a unique charm about her, and I wanted to see more of it. She was so unpredictable while my life was built around discipline. I had no idea what would come out of her mouth, and I liked it.

Even though Becca and I were not in a relationship—not at all—her presence threw me off-balance. I cleared my throat, hoping to pause and straighten my thoughts. Distracting myself from Becca was harder than I'd expected.

Her jacket swished, her teeth hit the fork, she let out a little groan, and she sighed—all within a matter of seconds. I didn't dislike the sounds filling my home. They were better than the wind whipping around outside, threatening to destroy the house.

She took another couple of bites before her large eyes focused on me. "Tell me...how did you learn to cook such a good breakfast?"

I smiled. "My grandma. I spent a lot of time with my grandparents in the summers growing up, and she always made me and my siblings cook as payment for staying with her."

She grinned. "That's lovely. Were you close with her?"

"Yeah, I was."

Wow, when was the last time I talked about her? Years? The nostalgia hit me hard and fast. Those visits with my brother and sister were awesome and some of the best memories I had growing up. The three of us would play board games with her for hours. I missed my grandma. Her death six years ago was rough, but it was right around a championship game so I never got to grieve. Life went on, and I kept pushing, and guilt ate me up from the inside.

My grandma would be so disappointed in me. Divorced, obsessed with a job that wasn't forever, and barely spending time with my family. To her, family was everything. My chest tightened.

Becca's singsong voice penetrated the self-pity taking over my brain. I focused on her.

"I never met my grandparents on either side, which stunk. My dad's parents didn't like the fact my mom was divorced before marrying him, so they stopped talking to us. I know it upset my parents, but they got over it. My parents never let the drama stop them from being happy. I love that about them. My mom lost her parents when she was young and grew up with an aunt. I always envisioned her parents as warm, huggy people who smelled like coffee and old pages from books. I'd create these elaborate stories about fake trips we went on whenever my mom got sad. We'd go to the library and take piano lessons and play card games." She turned, her attention drawn to the window. Then, like a switch, she stiffened and stopped talking. "You never asked me about mine. Uh, sorry I started talking." She pushed back in her chair, preparing to stand.

"Don't apologize," I pleaded, hoping she'd continue sitting with me. I paid attention to everything she said, but responding was difficult.

She frowned, staring at me like I'd said giraffes had ten feet and played strip poker.

"I liked hearing about your family. It was a nice distraction. Mine did smell like coffee and moth balls, but I try not to remember that part. And we played *a lot* of rummy." I smiled, hoping the effect was reassuring. "I'm sorry you never got to meet yours. I can't imagine my childhood without them."

Becca nodded. How did I make this okay? I didn't want her uncomfortable again because of my dumb ass.

"Where's your trash?" Standing now, she grabbed her paper plate.

"Under the sink," I said.

Disappointment weighed me down. I replayed the conversation in my head, wondering where I'd messed it up. This was exactly why I didn't date. It was too exhausting; worrying about saying or doing the right thing took up way too much energy. I wasn't a talkative person and that rubbed most women the wrong way. Hell, it even pissed my other coaches off, too. Sometimes there just wasn't a response formed in my head, and people interpreted the silence as an insult.

"Ah, found it." She disposed of the plate and fork then returned to the couch without sparing me another glance.

Yeah, I'd definitely upset her. I sighed, running a hand over my face. I glanced at my watch. 11:00 a.m. Seven more hours of usable daylight, less than forty hours until the power would, hopefully, turn on. If we were lucky.

What were we supposed to do? Small talk was clearly not an option. I'd just piss her off more or make myself look like a bigger ass. We were trapped under the same roof, limited to the kitchen or living room because of the heat source. I was in new territory.

My cute neighbor, who talked about everything with everyone, was silent, and I only had myself to blame.

CHAPTER FIVE

BECCA

I thought that the last date I went on was decent, but it ended with the guy telling me I talked too much. The random dude my mom set me up with said he'd lost interest because my rambling was boring. The insult hurt—a lot. Even though the girls at the house reassured me that my *ramblings* were a part of my charm, self-doubt and worry remained. Even now, two years after the date where Harrison promised to call and didn't, I got nervous and told him *all* about my family.

He never even asked about them!

My face burned brighter than the sun, and it took all my energy not to fling myself into the fireplace. It'd at least be warm in there, and he wouldn't look at me with those intense green eyes. His entire body had tensed, and this vacant, almost dazed, look had crossed his face. There was no other explanation than me being me. The weirdo. The over-talker. The oddball.

My love-tervention plan needed a lot of work if I wanted it to be successful. Which, I did. For sure. But that meant putting myself out there, knowing I could get hurt or insulted. Again.

I adjusted my position on the couch, the movement shifting the blanket and sending a whiff of laundry soap and wood smoke into the air. It smelled like him. Clean, woodsy, and masculine, with a hint of warmth. Ugh. I rolled my eyes at myself, the situation, the whole dang thing. Sure, it was bizarre. A guy who kissed me like he was into me, ghosted me, and then spent the better part of two years making sure he crossed to the other side of the street when he saw me.

The guy wasn't interested in talking to me. He didn't have to, normally, but his house felt smaller than my car. Every time he breathed, I heard it.

Distraction. I needed one or I'd go insane, analyzing every single moment. I could read or knit. Yes. Those would work. I clicked my tongue, proud of myself for taking action on something I could control because that was a hard lesson I was still learning.

I couldn't control what others did or said or thought. Sure, I'd like to know why Harrison hadn't called two years ago or why all my dates thought ghosting was the nicer option when a simple *I'm not into you* would suffice. That was an answer I'd respect. But I didn't want to bring it up. The diss stung, all these months later. Ugh, this was going to be the longest few days of my entire life.

I leaned over and grabbed one of the books—an adventure romance during a natural disaster—but changed my mind and put it back. I had no desire to read about a tornado where two people caught feelings, not while I was in the same room as Harrison. Instead, I found a crime novel and nuzzled into the blanket, finding the perfect position.

"Hey, Becca," Harrison said.

Way to ruin my momentary bliss.

I hadn't even read page one. I shut the book, my eyes turning to my rescuer. Despite all the turmoil and doubt, he offered for me to stay here so I could be safe. That meant something.

"Hm?" I glanced up at him.

"I found a deck of cards." He held up a red pack, his shoulders bunched by his ears. "I thought, maybe, we could play?"

"Right now?"

He tilted his head at me, uncertainty swirling in those green orbs, before he took a step back. "Never mind. Yeah. Stupid idea."

It was *almost* adorable, the way he looked so unsure. Almost, though he still spaced out when I talked too much, and he hadn't bothered letting me down like a decent human might after our date. Still…was this an olive branch? *Wait, were we fighting?*

"Wait!" I shook my head, clearing the unnecessary thoughts. "What game?"

His shoulders dropped, and the tight lines around his lips faded. Instead, his dimples teased me with his amusement. "Whatever game you want."

"Huh." I pushed my legs off the couch, my blood

pumping faster. Sports were so not my thing. If I had to choose between sports or beekeeping, I'd chose beekeeping every time. It was less sweaty and took less coordination. But card games, those were my jam. My bread and butter. My way of mopping the floor with Harrison Cooper as I screamed victory. Excitement thrummed under my skin, and I wiggled my toes deeper into my fuzzy socks.

Okay, too far. Bring it back.

I cleared my throat. "What would you like to play?"

"You're my guest." He picked up a side table and set it between the couch and the recliner.

The movement allowed me a great view of his jeans as they pulled tight across his ass, but I promised myself I'd only look for a second. Okay, two. The view was spectacular, after all. Harrison unzipped his jacket, giving me a view of his Henley.

Oh, baby. *Focus. It's game time.*

"You should pick, Becca." His tone dropped.

Was that excitement? Flirting? He wouldn't be flirting with me, would he?

I puffed out my chest, and all the previous worries disappeared. I loved competition outside the sports world. Spirit weeks, costume contests, face painting, cards. I owned that world.

I bit the inside of my cheek, holding back a victorious smile. "Ah, but dear neighbor, while you can throw a ball around, I can play cards. I'm good. It's only fair that you pick."

His eyes lit up, and he chuckled. "You seem confident."

"I am. You should be worried. *Really* worried." I winked.
"Card games are my Super Bowl, pal."

He flashed a grin. "We can start with Speed."

"Ah, a man who likes adrenaline, hm?" I said, unable to filter myself. "You like it fast?"

Oh my goodness.

"The cards," I corrected, my face burning hotter than the crackling fire. "You like playing fast card games."

The smug jerk pressed his lips together before clearing his throat. "Sure. That's what you meant."

Okay girl. Settle down. This is NOT the time to flirt.

"Well, buckle up cowboy, you're about to be ridden."

Seriously. What was wrong with me? I squeezed my eyes shut for a full ten seconds before sneaking a glance at Harrison, but he didn't give any clues that he thought I was bonkers. I was unique, but my words and brain and hormones—let's be honest—were not on the same page. They weren't even in the same book at this point.

The uneasy knot in my chest loosened as Harrison sorted out the cards into four piles, one on each side and two in the center. The object of the game was to match numbers or put the one right before or above it, all while doing it fast. We had to discard the cards in our hands before drawing another one, and if we both were stuck, we would flip one card from the farthest deck.

My fingers twitched, and my heart raced as he divided the cards evenly between us.

"Ready?" he asked, his voice a deep timbre.

A shiver shot through my limbs.

"You're on, Harrison."

The game started. The snow fell hard outside, the fire crackled, and I played to win. *Five on five. Four on five, then three, then two, then ace. Boom!*

I placed ten more cards down before I was stuck and found my neighbor had barely played three cards. "Ah ha, I'm I too quick for ya? Thought you could move faster, football boy."

"Wow." He ran his tongue on the inside of his cheek and studied me with intense eyes. "I wouldn't have pegged you for a trash talker."

"You don't know me. You don't know what I'm about." I stared him down.

He closed his mouth and then opened it again, his face twisting into a grimace before his eyes lost a little of their playfulness. "You're right. I don't."

The mood shifted. Did he think I was trying to make him feel bad? Was I? *No.* I wasn't that petty. I had my moments but, really, why would the dude have any clue that card games turned me into a borderline Monica? That I'd sacrifice a friend to win a game? That I ended up grounded from games as a child because I was too intense?

I chewed my lip as the silence grew. The familiar wave of self-doubt washed over me. Why did I have to say anything at all? I made it worse. Ugh.

"Should we flip?" He sat up straighter and pointed to the deck on the sides. He was all business now.

It didn't take away my urge to win. Not even a little bit. *Maybe there is something wrong with me.* "Yup. Flip it, good sir."

The game continued. *Ten on Jack on Queen on King on Queen on Jack on ten on nine on eight on eight.* My little fingers flew circles around his large ones and *Bam! Boo yah!*

"Yes!" I jumped from the couch, victory coursing through my blood. "Suck it, Cooper!" I fisted my hand in the air and twirled around. "This is my victory dance if that's not clear." I clapped twice and kicked one leg, then the other. "It doesn't matter if it's a card game, a bet, Monday night bingo, or a silly race across the street, I always do my victory dance. The girls love it so much, I swear they let me win to see it come out." I wiggled left and then right. "I'm making my future husband do this with me because he'll definitely be a winner if he married me," I said, the high of the win making words spew out even more.

Man, it felt good. My smile almost hurt my face. Until my attention turned back to Harrison, and I found him staring at me like I'd grown eighteen Christmas trees from my head. My smile fell.

Hard eyes. Lines between his strong eyebrows.

He must think I'm insane.

"Uh," I started, unsure what direction to go.

Did I apologize for winning, or no? Was he used to women petting his ego with football talk? Was the dance too much? My stomach fluttered, and I sat back on the couch, willing my heart rate to return to normal.

"Best two out of three?" I offered, needing something to ease the tension.

Harrison might think me a dork, but I refused to pretend

I was anything other than myself, especially if we were rooming together for a few days. A lightness rushed through me at the knowledge that I could be my unapologetic self without regret. I didn't need to impress him at all. He had his chance with me that night when he kissed the heck out of me but then deemed me unworthy of even a dang text message.

With new resolve, I picked up the cards and shuffled. "Your lack of response is feeding my ego, bud. You're either too afraid to play me because you know I'll kick your butt, or I beat you so badly you're embarrassed and need some time to recover. Which is it?"

He ran a hand over his jaw, letting out a deep, grunt-like snort. "You definitely kicked my ass. You and your girls must win all those silly competitions Greek life does, huh? Your competitiveness is next level. I'm equally horrified and impressed."

I balled my hands into fists. "*Silly* competitions?"

He flinched and opened his mouth to speak, but I cut him off. "You might think they're silly because they aren't a sport, but they are important. It promotes collaboration, fun, a way to show off pride for your house. It helps create a healthy culture for the girls. Most of them raise money for charities, Harrison. We raise thousands each year and collect canned goods and items for a women's shelter. If you actually asked me about them, I could've told you."

I was sick of men belittling what I did and what the girls stood for. *Silly competitions.* Throwing a ball to score points was silly! The level of my voice gave away my anger, but I didn't care.

He shook his head, his mouth gaping before he said my name, loud. "Becca, stop."

"What?" I arched both brows and thought about tossing him into the fire. He outweighed me by three times with all those muscles, but I'd figure it out. I was the house mom, and he insulted my house children.

"I'm sorry. I really am. I misspoke." He rubbed his palms over his eyes and exhaled.

His warm breath hit my face, and I crossed my arms tight over my chest. He did look sorry, and seeing his turmoil helped ease the irritation brewing in my gut. But what he'd said was uncalled for in the first place. I wanted more—no, I deserved more—of an apology.

"Was that your entire explanation?" I arched a brow in challenge.

"No. I'm trying to figure out how to explain it in a way that doesn't make me an asshole. This is...hard for me."

"Having a conversation?"

He barked out a laugh, but it wasn't filled with humor or warmth. More like sarcasm. "Honestly? Yes. I'm a bit of a recluse off the field, and I haven't had women—anyone, really—at my house since my divorce. I say the wrong thing all the time, if I even speak at all. Trust me. It wasn't my intention to insult you."

"Then what was your point?"

"To compliment you." The worry left his eyes, and a real smile transformed his already too-handsome face. "Your energy is contagious, and I'd bet my entire stash of firewood that you and your girls always kick ass."

"Hm. Keep going." I stuck my nose in the air.

I waited for him to grovel a bit more. He was getting the full Becca Fairfield without reservations.

"I have a bit of animosity toward those spirit weeks and competitions," he explained. "The guys on the team refuse to do any of the bonding stuff, and I've tried to get them involved but they don't care. I tried to sign us up for a race, to mow lawns on campus, or even to run a gym for younger kids. They just...I took out my issues with my team on you with that crass comment. I really am sorry. If I don't understand an event, I'll ask you about it first."

I rubbed my lips together. Should I forgive him? He had no idea how many times people said something similar to me and didn't apologize. He had done it, twice. But he apologized. Plus, his comment about the team piqued my curiosity. He had a great reputation, from the little I knew about him. He hid his struggle well.

"What's going on with your team? I didn't realize you were having issues with them."

Instead of answering, his jaw tightened, and he shook his head, his narrowed eyes ending the conversation.

Okay then. No questions about the football team.

My chest tightened like I'd somehow wronged him. The constant unknown exhausted me.

"Should we play another round or something?" I asked, hoping to stop the growing frown on his face. "I'll even give you a five-second head start since I'm feeling nice."

"Later. We'll do a rematch later." He pushed up from the recliner and set the side table back in place. He didn't glance my way once as he placed another log on the fire and walked toward the kitchen. *Great. Cool.*

My blizzard buddy wanted to avoid me, and I had no idea why.

CHAPTER SIX

HARRISON

You have no consideration for anyone who doesn't play for you! My ex-wife's words bounced around my head as I gripped the edge of the counter. I'd disregarded most of her criticisms, but now, with Becca in my house, her lips turned down on the sides, maybe my ex had been right. Hadn't I thought the same thing about Hank, that he didn't care about anyone but himself?

I turned up the volume on the radio, filling the silence I'd caused with holiday music. Becca wanted to play another round of Speed, but I needed a breather. My brain short-circuited around her and brought out all the things I sucked at.

Communication. Being fun and carefree. And currently, the lack of leadership for a group of guys unwilling to commit to each other. Hell, they wouldn't even commit to a season. I pinched the bridge of my nose.

Becca shifted in the same position on the couch. I glanced

over at her, preparing myself for some hurt behind her soft brown eyes, but she didn't look in my direction. Instead, she held a book with the word *murder* in the title and angled it toward the small window next to the couch. She grunted and shifted her weight again and then repeated the process a third time. I watched her for a full minute before she tossed her book onto the floor.

"Do you care if I move a kitchen chair or something closer to the back window for more light?" Glancing my way, she scrunched her nose. Lines etched her brow, and even her tone lacked her typical joy.

I narrowed my eyes at the curtains. "The cold will be pretty strong if we open the curtains much more. I can feel the wind if I hover near the glass."

"Right. Of course." She adjusted herself on the couch for the *fourth time* and blew a raspberry with her lips. Seeing her upset bothered me. If anything, I should try to ease whatever worry she had. I just had no idea how.

She scanned the room with a frown. "Do you have a candle?"

Did I? My ex had bought them, but she took all her stuff when she left. I checked under the kitchen sink and came up blank. There was literally no other location I would house one. "Nope, I don't."

She let out a humph and nodded. It was the oddest thing, watching her make a decision without voicing it. I couldn't stop watching her. She got up, found the crazy pile of yarn on the chair, and returned to her position before winding the red and green string around her knitting needles. The metal utensils clinked each time they touched but, other than that slight disturbance, silence and the distant sound of the howling wind outside filled my home. I rarely felt the urge to fill the quiet, often causing the lack of conversation. With her, though, it was different.

I gripped the back of my neck, shrugging. "I'd offer a flashlight, but we should save those for the night."

"I understand."

"Can you knit without good light?"

She nodded. Her smile lit up her entire face "Yes. I'd prefer to read but this is relaxing. I refuse to let a pesky little storm deter my plans to read, so I'll find a way somehow once I make progress on this scarf."

She fascinated me, and I wanted to know more. "Earlier, you mentioned reading ten books this semester. Why?"

"I made a reading goal for myself, and I hate losing. Thus, I will finish it." She pointed to the crime book.

My always-happy neighbor read about murder. Another surprise. Maybe she wasn't anything like I'd assumed two years ago. A warm sensation spread in my chest, watching her smile. *What the hell?*

She never once stopped moving the sticks in her hands, and a scarf-like strip of finished knitting had taken shape.

"Do you have a candle or something at the house?" I didn't want my lack of candles to be a reason she didn't meet her goal.

She gave me a sly grin, like we shared a secret. "They're

not allowed. You kidding me? Fifty girls and flames? No freaking way." She lowered her voice in an unassumingly sexy way. "I *do* have some in my room, but I'll never tell the girls. They smell so good, you know? Scents matter to me so much. I swear, most people I know have their own scent, but not in a creepy way. Like Marissa, one of the girls, wears this vanilla-orangey lotion that I can smell miles away. I know when the girl is in the house or not." She paused, a red tinge creeping up her cheeks, and cleared her throat. "Could we make a run over there?"

Her voice was lined with so much hope that I couldn't resist. "You won't. You stay safe here. I can, though. Where are they? I'll go now."

Quirky, overtalkative Becca broke her own rule for candles, rambling on about scents until my attraction to her seemed to grow. I was sure she hated me, and I didn't do relationships. Maybe the cold would whip some damn sense into me.

She set her yarn down, stood to her fullest height, and placed her hands on her hips. "Harrison, I can go over there and get them *with* you."

"Becca," I used her same tone, "it's dangerous outside. I'll go. It won't take long."

She huffed. "But what if something happens and you don't come back? There are huge icicles and frozen trees that could fall. I should be there to help you dodge them or help if you get hit."

Frozen trees?

"I'll be fine," I assured her. "Just tell me where they are."

"Buddy system. We're blizzard buddies! You said so. What you do, I do."

Something in her voice gave me pause, stopping me from ranting about all the reasons she would make the trip more unsafe. *Fear? Nerves?* She was worried about something, and if tagging along helped her out, then I could adjust.

I shrugged. "Okay. You want to head there now?"

She nodded a bit too hard, and some of her hair fell in front of her petite features. She pushed a strand back and reached for her ridiculous hat before layering on her winter wear. Not one item matched with another. My entire life was about uniforms and wearing orange and black. Her lack of care—wearing six colors in various patterns—confused me as much as it intrigued me. Who just let go enough to wear a rainbow?

Catching me staring at her, she flinched. "It's my hat, isn't it? I know it's ugly, but I made it myself and I'm immensely proud of it. My mom scolded me for wearing it to one of the awful dates she always sets up for me, but it's my way of rebelling."

"I wasn't staring at your hat."

"Oh." She glanced down at her mismatched array of winter clothes and shrugged. "Then what is it?"

"I'm used to wearing only orange and black." There, I went with the truth. I wasn't sure how she'd react since my track record sucked.

Her eyes warmed as she continued buttoning her coat all the way up to her throat. Shoving mittens on each hand, she laughed and held them up to me. "I could never be restricted to two colors of clothes. Just these babies alone have ten colors. I guess it's a good thing I'm not a football coach."

I smiled at the image of her on the field, wearing a headset and an orange polo, shouting orders behind a clipboard. But getting a glimpse of what would be under her polo made the picture more entertaining, so I kept my mouth shut. It took me ten seconds to bundle up before I assessed her, making sure she was covered everywhere. "You're absolutely sure about coming with me?"

"Mm-hmm."

"You lead the way. I don't want to walk too fast and lose you."

She saluted and waltzed toward the front door, pausing for a deep breath before opening it.

The frigid air stung every exposed part of my skin, and I winced. *We shouldn't be doing this.*

Becca didn't stop. She marched down the stairs and headed next door toward the sorority house. The wind whipped snow almost at a horizontal angle, and ironically, I was glad her coat stood out against the white. *I'll see easily if she falls.*

We walked for a full minute before a bitch of a wind gust hit and I had to rebalance my weight into a crouching position. I covered my eyes with my arm, and by the time

I looked back up, Becca was half-buried in the snow. My heart leaped into my throat. *Shit.*

"Becca!" I bent to my knees and slid one arm under her legs and the other around her rib cage, lifting her slightly.

She scrunched her nose and pressed her lips together so tightly that they looked white.

"Do we need to head back?" I asked.

She shook her head and pointed to her ear.

I moved closer, almost pressing my nose into her face. Despite the blizzard blowing around us, she smelled like vanilla, and a surge of lust went through me. "You sure you can go on?"

She mirrored the gesture, bringing her mouth so close to my ear her lips almost grazed the outside. "Yes. The wind knocked me down, and I bruised my butt." She reached around and rubbed the back of her thigh.

"You're a petite thing. I imagine it wasn't hard."

The expression in her eyes changed, and she gave me a warm, inviting look. But I didn't get time to react to it. Another gust blew at us, and I pulled her closer to my chest, hoping to block her from the worst of it. Her grip was almost painful, but I didn't dare adjust my hold on her until it passed. Ten, twenty, thirty seconds went by.

The wind finally relented, and I didn't ask before quickly placing her on her feet. "Walk fast, Becca."

I kept my hands on her shoulders the rest of the way and breathed a huge sigh of relief when we reached the front door. Brushing past her, I pulled it open against the wind

and gently shoved her inside before following behind.
"Damn."

"It's b-bad out there." Her words trembled out of her
almost-blue lips.

My first thought was to kiss them. For warmth.

Get it together.

"The candles are up in my room," she said.

"Let's hustle then and get our asses back to the fire."

Her jaw shook—from what I assumed was cold because
mine was also shaking. She bolted up the stairs in all her
colors.

"Becca, slow down. You've gotten stabbed by an aggressive window and taken a fall. I can't have you tumbling
down the stairs, too. I'm a horrible nurse."

She slowed her pace. "You do have a terrible bedside
manner."

I caught up to her and matched her stride to the third
floor. She led me toward her room, keeping her hand on
the side of the wall. We entered the small room, and while
I wanted to study her setup and learn more about her, it was
cold and not the time. Reaching her bed, she bent down
and rifled through the drawers of a wooden nightstand.

"Bingo!" Standing upright again, she held up four large
candles.

"Four contraband candles. I would never have pegged
you for breaking the rules, Becca."

Damn, is my voice just dripping with innuendos?

"Life is way too short for all rules and regulations," she
said, completely missing my double meaning. "There are

nonnegotiable rules in life, and the rules you can flirt with. Sneaking candles into a sorority house is negotiable. The speed limit is another one. Same as having dessert before dinner."

"I agree with your logic."

She flashed me a proud smile. "Let me get my matches."

"They aren't in the same drawer?"

She huffed. "No. I always store them separately just in case matches catch fire on their own. They need to be in a place most likely for them to fizzle out, so I keep them in the bathroom."

Matches catching fire on their own? "They can't burst into flames."

"You can't prove it, and if it makes me feel better about sneaking *contraband* items in here, then so be it." She held her head high and disappeared into the small room off to the right before returning. "Got them."

"Anything else you want to grab? I'd prefer to not head outside again."

She sucked her plump bottom lip into her mouth and scanned her bedroom. I followed suit, admiring the pictures covering one of her walls, each depicting the graduations of her sorority girls with only a couple images of herself scattered in. I studied the photos a moment, my eyes zoning in on one of Becca with her parents. A grin formed on my face because it was so...Becca. Wearing a huge smile and a purple and blue tie-dyed dress, her hair was shoulder-length with curls. Beside her, her parents wore tight-lipped expressions matching their simple black-and-white outfits. *Becca and her rainbow of colors.*

"Do you have enough blankets for us to get through the night?" she asked.

I mentally counted all the down blankets and quilts I had. "I should, yeah."

"Toilet paper?"

"Went to Costco last week, actually." I puffed out my chest. My ex insisted I would never do it, and look at me: adulting and living my best life.

"Then I guess we shouldn't delay the inevitable. Let's head back." She winced and reached behind her back. "I might've landed on something when I fell. My upper thigh really hurts."

Damn it.

"Becca, this was why I didn't want you to go," I barked, hating that she was hurt again. "Show me where it hurts."

"No, no, it's fine." She waved a hand, but her eyes remained narrowed.

She blinked a few times, and I put a hand on her waist, pulling her closer to me.

"Harrison," she said, her voice a whisper.

My body hummed with how good she felt against me, even with all her winter layers. "I don't want you hurt."

"I'll look when we get back to your house." Her chest heaved.

I wondered what she would do if I pressed my lips against hers. I knew how soft they were and how she kissed with so much passion.

My body heated, and I stepped back. "You better. I need you to be okay. Now, let's get back."

I almost said *home*. It unsettled me. Her being with me, in my home, and somehow fitting in there threw me off. She was a talkative woman with a fierce competitive streak who snuck candles into her room. There was no reason to want anything more. Right?

CHAPTER SEVEN

BECCA

The wind rattled the house, refusing to relent. Snow fell, but it was hard to decipher how much with the constant gusts. My skin still prickled from the frigid temperatures, and I shivered. Gratitude washed over me that I was in Harrison's house and not the sorority house without any warmth.

My lilac blossom candle provided the perfect amount of light in the bathroom for me to use the facilities with ease but not enough to admire the black-and-blue bruise covering the back of my right thigh. I winced as I traced my finger over the skin, fighting the sting behind my eyes.

Don't cry. It's fine.

It hurt, and I had no idea what I had fallen on. Pain radiated from the bruised area and pounded with each heartbeat.

"Are you okay in there?" Harrison's deep voice cut through the door, and every muscle tensed, preparing for a fight.

How embarrassing. He thinks I'm using the bathroom this long.

"Uh, yeah," I answered. "I'm trying to see how bad my fall was. This bruise is pretty bad."

"Do you need me to look at it?"

I gulped. It was near my butt, and I had already suffered enough humiliation for twenty-four hours. Heck, more like my entire life.

I shook my head but then remembered he couldn't see me. "Uh, no?"

"Not making a pass, Becca. If it's hit hard enough, you could get nerve damage. You might need to ice it or at least put muscle rub on it. You were limping. Let me take a look, please."

The sincerity in his voice confused me, and my stomach did a weird swoopy thing that I did *not* like. I tried shifting my weight to get a better look but it was no use with most of my winter gear still on. The bruise sat in a tricky position so that I couldn't see it, no matter which way I bent.

With a disgruntled sigh, I pulled up my sweatpants, mentally prepared myself for Harrison, and opened the door. He leaned against the wall, arms crossed, with a casual air about him. The expression on his face was intense, like he always was, but his brows were drawn together in concern. It was dangerous to enjoy being the momentary recipient of his care, so I tried not to. Every time he did something nice, I remembered all the ways he'd made me feel silly. It was the safest way.

"So…" I blew out a frustrated breath. "I can't see the bruise no matter how I bend."

His lips quirked up a bit on the side, and he motioned with his chin to the living room. "The light is best in there by the window. I'm sure it's fine but I'll feel better knowing it isn't serious, Becca."

Did he have to say my name like that? All warm and nice and sexy? I swallowed hard and did my walk of shame to the couch as my entire body heated with humiliation. Did I just lay down, drop my pants, and say *take a look*? I sweated just thinking about it.

"Don't be so nervous. I'll be gentle and quick, okay?" His footsteps faded, and his voice came from somewhere else in the house. "Get on your stomach and adjust your waistband so I can see the bruised area. I'm getting some supplies."

Adjust your waistband. That was the most professional and least sexy way any man has ever told me to take off my pants. I giggled and kept my face turned toward the couch.

His heavy footsteps creaked on the wooden floor with his return. "You might not like it, but you'll probably have to put ice on it."

"Ice?" I almost screeched and spun to face him. "Are you sure?"

"Just a guess, but yeah." He winced and moved to sit on the edge of the couch, his thighs pressed against my side.

We were so close. Way too close. My breathing hitched at his warmth and size.

Oh my, when is the last time I had sex? Months? More?

Stop thinking about sex in Harrison's house.

"Let's see it."

He's about to see my butt. Be cool.

I wiggled my hips and pulled down my sweats enough for him to see my bruise. Goose bumps erupted on my skin—this time from his nearness more than the cold. Every part of my body tensed, waiting for his response.

Oh, such a weird butt you have.

No, he wouldn't say anything like that. If he did, I'd take my chances in the blizzard. Instead, he said nothing. Not a word. He sucked in a breath and shifted his position on the couch, making me lean farther into him.

"This is a bitch of a bruise," he said, after what felt like six hours of silence.

"It's not pleasant," I mumbled into the pillows, thankful he pulled me from my weird trance.

"I'm going to check to make sure nothing is raised, okay? That means I will touch *just* the bruised area."

I groaned.

The pads of his calloused and warm fingers skimmed lightly over the area, leaving my skin prickled with heat and awareness. He didn't press down enough to hurt but used enough pressure that wave after wave of shivers washed over me.

Oh, wow. Hot Henley Harrison is touching my butt.

"It seems surface level so I'm going to have you put this on it for twenty minutes." He shuffled items around, and a blast of ice cold touched my skin. I bucked, almost smacking my head into his, but he gently held me down with his massive hands. "Shit, I should've counted down or something."

"Yeah!" I grabbed the blankets and wrapped myself tight.

Finding another heavy comforter, he positioned it over

me with an odd expression on his face. It was almost like he was fighting off a smile. He was enjoying this.

"Is my misery amusing to you?" I snapped.

The cheerful expression evaporated, and he sat on the other love seat about ten feet away. He narrowed his eyes, and his wicked mouth flattened. "Absolutely not."

"Then why the smirk, huh?"

He gave me another long look, first studying my hairline and then moving down and stopping on my mouth. He grinned again, and the startling difference between smiling Harrison and grumpy Harrison was too much for me to take. Why did he have to be so good-looking? It wasn't fair to my brain. Or my hormones. My pulse raced, and my face heated. I'd about had it with my next-door neighbor.

I shot him my best angry scowl. "Stop laughing at me."

"I'm not, I swear. I'm thinking about your tattoo."

He knows about my . . . oh, snap.

"It's on the other hip." I lifted a defiant chin. "You didn't see it."

"I know. I was disappointed."

Finding a coaster on the side table, I tossed it at his face and then huffed out a frustrated breath when it landed three feet to the right of him. "I told you that under stressful circumstances, buddy, so it's off-limits to bring up. You don't get to mention it ever."

"Don't think it works like that, Becca."

He continued smiling, and I was struck by how much I liked it on his face. The way his lips curved up slightly on each side, the distinctive laugh lines around his mouth showcasing his lips, and even the way his eyes lit up and made him seem happier. Harrison didn't smile often, but when he did, it was a sight.

"Why are you looking at me like that?" he asked.

Shoot. He caught me staring at him like a lunatic.

"You have a great smile. I was thinking about how nice it looks on you. It isn't something I've seen a lot. But to be fair, I don't really see you so you could smile all the time, and I'd have no idea. I'm not the smile police."

Stop talking. Just shut your mouth.

My filter was officially broken. The longer he stared at me, his smile growing more by the second, the more words escaped without my permission. "You're a handsome man, you know this, but the smile makes you even more handsome."

Oh my goodness, shut up. Stop talking. Stop opening your mouth.

His grin deepened for a second before he went back to his normal, unfazed expression, leaving me feeling like the most awkward person in school. It was like that time when I was a freshman and confessed my crush to the popular guy and the entire school heard it. They called me Ten C for at least a year.

The *Ten Chaser*. The girl flirting way out of her league.

Why did Harrison usually look so bored and annoyed? The expression wasn't *Resting Bitch Face* like the girls talked about. Instead, it was *Resting Unamused Face*. RUF. He definitely had a RUF whenever I talked, and even though it bothered me, I admired my own cleverness. I snorted at the thought, and avoiding further embarrassment, I buried myself into the blanket and covered my face. I could live here forever now. Piece of cake.

"Is there a reason you shoved your head into the blanket?" His tone held a hint of amusement.

"Not one I'd like to share with you." White-hot flames of embarrassment crept up my body.

I needed to shift the direction of our conversation, move it away from how I said he was handsome with a smile. *Yikes, was I like those creepy men who always told women to smile more?* No. I couldn't be. But I did tell him he had a nice smile. No, that was different. Phew.

Content with the fact I wasn't creepy, I changed the subject to a safer area. "Thanks for helping me with...the injury. Injuries, actually. Dang, two times within twenty-four hours."

With his gaze on me, he let out a deep chuckle. "You're welcome. Both times."

His gaze held mine, and a million thoughts swam in my head. The wind howled outside, causing the window near me to shake a little, but instead of the bone-chilling cold, I was hot all over.

I cleared my throat. "I guess I should read since we went to all the trouble of getting the candles, huh?"

He didn't respond. Instead, he offered a slight nod and pushed himself up from the chair before disappearing into a different room.

I blew out a long breath. Harrison Cooper was the most handsome man I had ever seen, and while it wasn't easy to forget about our date from two years ago, it was even harder now when I couldn't escape the sight of his full lips. There were very few times a kiss was *that* memorable. My first one in seventh grade by the water fountain with Matt Hack. Despite his braces, he'd slid his tongue into my mouth and seared the memory into my mind forever. I had felt so scandalous...until a teacher caught us.

Then there was the night I'd had a one-night stand with a guy in college. I'd wanted to experience a night of passion without names, and I did. But while it was fun, the process taught me that I wasn't a one-night girl. It was the first time I'd done anything remotely on my own terms so, for that reason alone, it was memorable.

And then two years ago: Harrison's kiss. Strong, aggressive, *hungry*. He kissed like he coached on the field: full of determination, passion, and talent. I was the sole focus of his attention for a full minute. That one kiss left my knees buckling and my stomach fluttering with excitement. Unfortunately, the temporary bliss evaporated when he turned out like everyone else in my life. Ghosting me without a reason and making me doubt myself.

So screw that, Harrison. Take your kissing elsewhere.

Grunting from the bruise on my butt, I picked up my crime novel and settled into the perfect reading position with pillows propped behind my back, my legs covered with a down blanket, and a water bottle nearby. The ice rested against the bruise for another ten minutes. I would've preferred my hot chocolate, but I couldn't have it all.

I read a chapter before Harrison's heavy footsteps stomped

toward me from the hallway, followed by the sound of something dragging. Something heavy. Cursing myself for forgetting a bookmark, I searched his coffee table drawer for something to use. Remotes, coasters, pens, a deck of cards, and a gum wrapper. Perfect.

"Uh, did you just pull a wrapper out of my drawer?" he asked, hands on his hips and his mouth quirking up on one side.

"Yes." I took a deep breath, pushing down the desire to kiss him, and closed the book before setting it on the side table. "I refuse to bend the pages of books, and I forgot my bookmarks in the mad dash to the house."

"One could argue that's very peculiar. Books are meant to be read."

He still hadn't changed his stance, and it was distracting how well his layered shirts fit against his chest. I was a sucker for muscles, so I trained my eyes on his face. It was safer. Him touching my skin to assess my bruise had really messed with my strict *blizzard-buddies* relationship. Here I was thinking about kissing and sex after he'd touched my butt for two seconds.

"I understand books are meant to be read, but I like it when the pages aren't creased. They look nice and perfect." I pursed my lips, refusing to hear his side of the argument. He was wrong. Plain and simple.

"Couldn't you argue the more a book is read, the better? The creases or stains are visible evidence of how much people loved and used it. My favorite books as a kid had writing on them, food spots, dirt. You name it, and I got it on the pages."

I cringed, the thought of destroying a book sending a shudder through me. "No. No, thank you. You're wrong in your assessment."

"Beg to differ. There's something gritty about seeing a used book and knowing that all the people who read it made a mark. My sister for instance." He laughed, and the lines of his face softened. "She would reread the same books over and over. Nancy Drew, I think, and she would write the date in the corner on the same page each time she reread it. God, it's been years since I thought of that. But one page had probably twenty dates on it, showcasing her youth. I like the thought of that."

His half-smile transformed into a full one again, and my next words in defense of my proper care of books disappeared. Disarming. That's how his smile was, and I needed to get a grip if I planned to stay here for another two days.

I cleared my throat, but it didn't do any good.

His gaze dropped to my crime book, and he shook his head, a slight red coming to his cheeks. "You're an odd one, Becca."

His tone was warm, and while I had been called odd before, this one didn't hold the same sting. He said it like a compliment rather than an observation, and I liked it.

"I like what I like." I shrugged. "Erik Larson does a phenomenal job of writing the truth about crimes, events, what have you, in a narrative form. This one combines the events of the World's Fair and a serial killer in Chicago. Also, how wild is this? My mom said her grandma lived on the street this serial killer did, at the same time! That just boggles my mind. Like, they could've crossed paths."

I shrugged, my face heating from *oversharing yet again*. I waited for a condescending remark like most of the dudes my mom set me up with because they'd tuned me out. *Oh, that's interesting you read crime.* Or *Wow, cool.* The best, though, was when they didn't respond and instead talked about themselves, unprompted. Men were the worst sometimes.

Harrison did none of those things.

"Life's too damn short to settle. It takes a certain level of confidence to own what you like, and I commend you for it. Also, that's crazy about living on the same street as a murderer," he said.

"If you want, I can leave this book with you so you can borrow it?" I offered.

He nodded. "I'll give it a try."

"Great."

We waited a beat, staring at each other as the room grew warmer and smaller. I cleared my throat as he disappeared in the hall for a second, returning with an entire mattress. Not a small one, either. He pushed the biggest mattress I had ever seen into the living room and tilted it against the chair he'd recently vacated.

My eyes bulged. "What the—?"

"I'm gonna have to move the furniture to fit this guy in here."

"You brought your entire bed?"

"Yeah. The air mattress won't fill up without power, and I'm too old to sleep on the floor." He pushed the chairs from the main area toward a den-like room.

"Here, I can help." Moving to stand, I moaned in pain.

He spun toward me, pointed his finger at me, and shook his head. "No. Sit."

For one second, I imagined what he was like as a coach and how intimidating he could be. Would he tell me to do push-ups? Jumping jacks? Punch the air? Wow, I knew nothing about sports. But I was a grown woman, not a college football player, and I could argue with his bossy gestures.

I huffed out a breath. "What? I think I can move some pillows at least. I'm weak, but not that small."

"Hmm. Fine." He frowned and continued arranging the mattress until it sat two feet away from the fireplace.

He'd restocked the woodpile earlier, and thirty logs sat in the corner of the room. Seeing how prepared he was sent another wave of gratitude through me. There was no way I would've stayed warm enough in the huge house without firewood, and if I didn't stop my thoughts, I would derail into a handful of what-if scenarios that all ended with me freezing to death.

I shivered while helping him move a lamp and a couple of pillows. Finished, I stared at the new living room. The couch I'd vacated, the firewood, and the bed took up the whole room. "You have a huge bed."

"I'm a large guy."

I'll say. My gaze darted to his frame, taking in his massive hands and long legs.

He slid me a coy smile.

"Did I say that out loud?" I gasped.

"No, but the look on your face is amusing, and I wish you did share your thoughts." He moved to a small closet door and returned with more blankets for the bed. "We'll sleep on this tonight. I think I have enough to keep us warm when the temperature drops at night."

"We?" I squeaked.

"Yes, Becca." He gave me the same intimidating look that had weakened my knees. "As you said, this bed is big enough for the two of us, and I want both of us close to the fire. I have no plans to lose any fingers or toes."

He was serious. Another wave of fear went through me. "Thank you, Harrison."

"What for?"

"For letting me stay here." A shiver of *what if I didn't come here* went through me, making my teeth chatter together.

He stepped toward me and rubbed his hands up and down my arms and shoulders. "Are you cold now? Come on. I'll put more wood on the fire." He moved his large hands over my arms six or seven more times, his touch relaxing me, before gently nudging me to sit on the edge of the bed nearest the fire. He threw a deep blue blanket over my shoulders and added three more logs to the fire. "Feel any better?"

"Y-yes." I pulled the material tighter against me. "I'm glad I'm here with you."

He stilled, the hardness of his stance obvious, but it didn't last long. Relaxing, he said in a soft tone, "Yeah, I'm glad you are as well. It's safer for both of us."

Picking up the poker, he arranged the logs into a position I assumed was meant for more flames. The quiet gave me time to think about what would happen when the dark took over. We had a couple flashlights and my candles, but would those last more than a day or two? Would the cold get so bad we'd die in our sleep? Would we have to spoon for warmth, just for survival?

Or just for fun?

I shook my head.

"I can practically hear your thoughts from two feet away," Harrison said. "You fidget. What's on your mind?"

"Uh, well." I stammered and avoided his attentive stare. If he could hear my thoughts, it wouldn't be good for me. I pressed my nails into my palm to gain my bearings. "I think the thought of it going dark and getting colder is freaking me out a bit. This morning, waking up to the cold, was terrifying. I've never felt anything like that before, and my mind has the ability to snowball one bad idea into an even worse one."

He sighed and sat next to me on the mattress, leaving a couple of inches between us. Even still, his strong body radiated heat, and I fought the urge to scoot closer to him. He was just so big.

"I'm not looking forward to it, either," he admitted. "We can't waste batteries in the flashlights unless we need to. We'll have the fire going, which will provide some light and hopefully a lot of heat."

"Were you a Boy Scout? Do you know tricks to survive in the wilderness?"

He laughed. "No. My brother was, but I refused to participate in anything unless it had a football."

"Damn it, I was hoping you knew all sorts of survival skills. Did your brother teach you anything? Is he in the area? Can he help us? Maybe a phone call for tips? I always wondered what it would be like to have siblings. That has to be awesome."

The laugh lines around his eyes disappeared, and his shoulders tensed. He replied with a curt tone. "No. He's not in the area. He's in California right now."

Then he got up, leaving me in the living room alone.

Did I upset him? Frowning, I replayed the entire conversation in my head but couldn't figure out how I'd made him mad enough to walk out. *Story of my life: the inability to understand anything about the opposite sex.*

Becca's Blunders: The Netflix Series.

I sighed and fell back onto the bed, ignoring how good the sheets smelled, and lay there for a good five minutes before my phone rang.

Mom.

I scrambled to answer it, feeling terrible for not calling them earlier and knowing they were probably worried.

"Are you okay?" I asked instead of a hello.

"Of course, sweetie. Your father has three generators just in case the end of the human race starts. You know him. But how are you? I keep thinking about that big drafty house and those old windowpanes. I'm upset that you weren't able to leave yesterday and come stay with us. Those girls are capable of locking up on their own, aren't they?"

"I'm glad Dad's extra preparedness is helping this time. And don't worry about the house. I'm staying with a neighbor until the power returns."

"A neighbor? Just any of them? Who? Are you safe? Becca, I know you're trusting, but did you think this through?" she asked, her voice laced with concern and judgment. Per usual.

I glanced over my shoulder, but there was no sign of Harrison. "Mom, it's the football coach. He's trustworthy."

"Is this the one who never called after the date you swore was wonderful?"

"Yes, Mother." I rolled my eyes. "Why can you remember every detail of my dating life but forget when you borrow my jewelry?"

"Priorities, dear. Now, you're staying with the hottie who hurt you? Is that the best idea? I just don't see how that will be good for your self-esteem. You need a dependable man."

Hottie who hurt me?

"Ha, surprisingly, yes, it is the best idea. A window broke in the house, and I had zero firewood. It's better I'm here." It hurt to admit but it was true. Harrison got major points for it.

"Well, to help you get through these troubling times, get excited for a dinner date on New Year's Eve! He is just the cutest. He's a doctor, Becca—a pediatrician—and he's so handsome. It's Lisa's grandson. I work with her at the shop, and oh, he is just a doll."

"Mom...no more dates, please, I beg you." I smacked my forehead in dismay.

"Becca, trust your mother, okay? I want my baby girl to find love and have a family because it'll be the best thing in your life. That's all I want. Can you blame me?"

I groaned louder and stomped my foot against the floor. "We are in a blizzard with subzero temperatures, and you're still focused on finding me a boyfriend? Put Dad on the phone."

"He's busy, and there's always time to talk about your love life."

"No. My love life is off-limits. Now, I need to go."

"To make the hottie regretful that he never called? Did you bring sexy pajamas?"

"No! I did not bring sexy pajamas to make Harrison regret ghosting me. I brought warm ones. Gah! I'm hanging up. I love you, Mom, but you're insane."

"Love you more!"

I tossed my phone on the couch but missed. Getting up, I grabbed it from the floor and, noticing Harrison standing in the kitchen—looking right at me with a huge grin—all the blood left my face. Shit. *Shit.*

"No sexy pajamas? Damn. It was the one thing I was really looking forward to seeing."

CHAPTER EIGHT

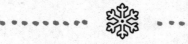

HARRISON

I was a bastard. I knew it, accepted it, and made no attempt to ease Becca's discomfort. Her blush was cute, and her already large eyes widened as she bit down on her full bottom lip. While I meant to flirt and fluster her, the image of her in black lace was a practical way to warm up.

Her long hair spread out over the sheets, her ample breasts bare for me . . . Shit. I coughed into my fist and tilted my head, still not saying a word. It took her a full minute to speak, and it was worth it.

"I only wear my sexy stuff on date three," she deadpanned.

"Why not the first date?" I prompted, my mind going to the images I'd created in my head that had no business being there.

She blinked a couple of times and ran a hand over her throat. "Because most of my dates never get to a second or third, and at some point, I stopped trying."

I fall into that category.

"Ah."

Becca snorted at my one syllable response and glanced outside, a line appearing between her eyebrows. I waited for her to mention our date or the fact I'd never called even though I'd said I would. I tensed, searching for the right words that would make it better, but she didn't mention it. I was really in the doghouse with her.

Sighing, she tilted her head to the side, shaking it a little. "My mom is one of the most loving people in the world, but she's a little wacko about me finding a man. She means well, but because she loves me so much, she thinks that having a kid is the only way to have happiness. I disagree with her."

"I see." *I didn't.* "So that's why you were talking about sexy pajamas?"

She shot me a goofy smile and nodded. "Exactly. No time like subzero temperatures to seduce my neighbor." She snorted again. "Obviously, I'm kidding. But I swear, she sets me up on these dates with weenies."

"How would you define a *weenie*, exactly?" I sat on the edge of the couch to be closer to her. It was uncharacteristic of me to ask all these questions, but something about her intrigued me. Maybe it was the way her lips moved when she spoke or how she couldn't keep her hands still and gestured for everything. Or maybe it was her ridiculous use of the word *weenie*.

She raised both hands and made circular motions. "You know, like... 'Why's a girl like you single?' Or, 'Should we really get dessert here rather than at my place?' Or, maybe my favorite: when they ask a question only to answer it themselves. I once went on this date with this schmuck who asked about my favorite vacation. I told him a trip to Florida, and before I could even finish two sentences, he decided to tell me in minute detail about his trip abroad in Paris."

"So, assholes?"

"Hmm, some were, some weren't. An asshole isn't always the worst because I at least know what I'm getting into. The passive aggressive, quiet jerks are worse. The ones who think they're different than the other jerks when really, they're disguising their jerk-ery." She sighed and shrugged. "The ones who make empty promises are their own type of monster."

She eyed me, and we both knew she was thinking about me and our date. I opened my mouth, hoping inspiration would hit me when I tried talking, but she bounced up off the bed and headed to the kitchen. "What's our food situation? I'm hungry."

While I could be a dick, I wasn't an idiot. She'd clearly avoided bringing up our date directly, and I would follow her lead. My muscles relaxed at her change of direction because I wasn't sure what to say. Words and communication were already hard for me, and owning up to a decision I made two years ago was difficult. There wasn't a good reason I could give her that would ease her mind, and she deserved more. Saying nothing was better.

I glanced at my watch. It was only 5:00 p.m. but it would be best if we ate earlier rather than later. Once it got dark, I wanted to bunker down. "We can make some grilled cheese."

"Oh, that sounds good." She shuffled through the fridge and pulled out the ingredients. She held them up, showing me, and did a little wiggle with her body. "And you have ham! Hot damn!"

Goofy. She was so goofy. "Glad you're happy about it."

"Did you know a grilled cheese with ham is called a bikini? I'll show you once it's cooked, but you have to cut them into triangles. They look like the little part of the swimsuit, you know, that covers the lady parts." She smiled to herself and stopped, glancing at me with those damn wide eyes again. "I don't know why I told you that."

"I'm not upset about it." I chuckled and took the food from her. "I'll make them but only if you tell me why the hell you know that."

"Are you sure? I can cook a mean grilled cheese. It's actually one of my best talents. It's all about the butter; plus, you *did* make breakfast for us."

"I like cooking, and it's nice not having to do it for one."

The second the words left my mouth, the weight of how true they were hit me. I was always alone if I wasn't at the stadium or in the gym. I preferred it that way, but this was a nice change.

"Now, the bikini story, please." I pointed the cooking utensil at her, and she plopped down at the table. I'd like to think she'd be this interesting even if we weren't stuck together in a house with terrifying weather conditions.

"I really wanted to study abroad in Barcelona when I was in high school. Like, I would buy all these maps of Spain to start learning all the different parts of it. Barcelona is actually in Catalonia, and I read everything I could get my hands on to prepare for the possibility of moving there. I didn't want to be some idiot American without a clue. I'm already blond, and don't know a lick of Spanish, so it wouldn't have been a good look. So I discovered little things, like the bikini fact or that they still have siestas every day! Could you imagine having a set nap time in our society?"

I buttered the bread and warmed the stove, enjoying the rise and fall of her voice when she was excited. "No. But it would be nice to have a midday nap."

"I know." She sighed and leaned back onto the kitchen chair. "I read that everything shuts down except cafés. Schools, businesses, stores, banks...it's forcing everyone to calm down and take a minute to breathe. I would've loved it there, I know it."

"Why didn't you go?"

She deflated. "My mom got sick. They found a lump about three months before I was supposed to leave, and the results weren't good. She went through chemo for a while, and it went into remission, but that year was tough. I couldn't imagine myself galivanting through Spain while my mom was fighting for her life."

Dang, to want something that bad and be so close. Missing it must've been devastating. "I'm sure she would've understood if you went."

"Oh, she was furious at me for backing out, but I don't regret not going then. The timing was off." She traced a line down my table with her index finger.

An unknown feeling took hold of me. I wanted to

comfort her, tell her what she did was admirable and amazing, but the words got stuck in my mind and stayed there. Despite the way they acted lately, I'd do the same thing for my parents. How could I not? I was grateful for the life they provided us. But would my parents ever sacrifice anything like that for me?

Probably.

I don't know.

My mood soured, and I focused on cooking. Being jealous of Becca because her mom was so involved in her life was ridiculous. *I'm a grown-ass man.* I exhaled, hoping all the negative energy inside me would escape, and flipped the sandwiches. Becca hummed from the table, and I snuck a glance at her. She had a half-smile on her face, and her hands were flat on the table.

"You know an *embarrassing* amount about me now, from my tattoo to my obsession with Spain. It's only fair you share some of your stories. Does your mother set you up on dates and obsess over you finding a partner? What was your favorite trip of all time? Do you know any random facts about countries that will make me feel like less of a dork?"

"That's a lot of questions at once, Becca."

"Well, take your time. We literally have all night."

Her response had me smiling again, and I answered her first question. "My mom doesn't try to set me up with anyone. Honestly, my parents couldn't care less about what I do or don't do. They never quite got over my divorce. They firmly believe that a marriage should be suffered through because of vows, even though it wasn't a healthy relationship. We both wanted out, and it was amicable. My sister, however, would plan my entire life down to the minute if she could."

"Yeah? Older or younger?" she asked with her usual warm tone.

"Older. Definitely older. She calls or texts every day and has tried setting me up with most of her friends. She blames me every time it doesn't work out but—what word did you use? Weenies? They were weenies."

"You cannot steal my word to describe women. Women are not weenies, Harrison," she scoffed. "I think I like your sister."

I barked out a laugh. "I imagine she'd like you."

"Weenies," she mumbled under her breath. "Find your own word."

I fought a smile as I finished up the sandwiches and then set them on paper plates and grabbed two bottles of water. She thanked me, and we ate in silence. My own word. I thought of a couple I wanted to say but saying them would seem rude.

I settled on one and clapped my hands. "Okay, I got my word."

"And?"

"Ungenuine. A lot of those dates, the women didn't seem genuine. They were too worried about saying the wrong thing, it seemed like an act." *They aren't like Becca who is 100 percent herself all the time.* "I grant you *weenie* back."

She snorted into her fist, and I fought my own laughter. "I aim to amuse here."

"I'll say. *Grant you weenie back.*" She shook her head and moaned as she took her next bite. "This is the best grilled cheese I've had in months. Probably because I didn't make it. There's something about someone else cooking for you."

"Bikini, you mean?"

She met my eyes, and a warm sensation started in my stomach at our shared joke. It was stupid, something she'd rambled minutes ago, but the way she looked at me had me looking down at my plate.

"You'll never forget that fact, I bet you. Now, I'm not forgetting about my other questions, but you need to share a weird food fact so we're even. It can be about anything. The weirdest food you tried or know how to cook, or a food horror story like you thought you were eating bacon but it ended up being rattlesnake. Happened to my dad once, I swear."

My face would hurt from all these damn smiles by the time this storm was over. How she moved from one topic to the next without taking a break was a talent I would never have.

I racked my brain for something, anything, like she'd mentioned and could only think of one thing somewhat related to food. The day I thought my sister would actually kill me dead.

"Okay, got one," I said. "The same sister—she has monster children, and I babysit for her once in a while. This one night, I brought over a bunch of fruit because she feeds them all artificial crap, which is awful. Don't get me started on correct protein; that's a rant you don't want to hear. But anyway, the cranberries were ripe, and we discovered they bounced.

"Really now?" Becca's mouth hung open in awe.

"Like a bouncy ball. The kids thought it was hilarious, and George, the oldest of the bunch, started throwing them at the wall." I paused, took a swig from my water bottle, and snuck a glance at my temporary guest. A slight blush graced her cheeks so I kept going. "I thought she would actually murder me when she and her husband got home and saw the damage."

"Did it look like a murder scene?"

"Exactly."

Becca burst into laughter and slapped her hand on the table. "Holy moly. That's hilarious. How many kids does she have?"

"Three. Two boys, one girl." I smiled. "George, Brodie, and Gabby. I hadn't thought about that memory in years."

"That's a great one. Are you close with your siblings? You mentioned a brother, too, right?"

The momentary bliss disappeared at the mention of my brother.

I'd been in a funk since our season was in the gutter, my ex was getting remarried, and our brother's ego was the size of Texas since his team qualified for a championship game. My sister's text from earlier in the day weighed heavy on my conscience. **The kids miss you.** I couldn't believe my parents wouldn't try to spend the holiday with their grandchildren. At least they sent presents, though.

My throat tightened, and I gripped the water bottle hard.

"Just the two siblings. My sister and I are close. My brother and I grew apart as we got older."

She opened her mouth as though to ask more and then stopped herself and finished eating. Swallowing her last bite, she waved her hands as she spoke again. "I would've made a deal with a wizard to have siblings. It was just me and my parents. I love them, but all my adventures were solo or with them. I bet you have hours of wonderful and exciting stories from growing up with them."

I guess I do. It was difficult to remember all the good times growing up with Hank and Blair because most of them were tainted by Hank getting away with something and me getting blamed. I loved him and protected him at every turn. We were best friends until high school, where everything became a fierce competition. The nice memories dulled with all the bad ones. Like the time he snuck out of the house and broke a window—I had a game the following day, and I would never have risked not playing my best, but my parents believed Hank when he said I did it.

Or the time they found weed in the house, and Hank pointed at me. He said they'd go easier on me, which was bullshit. They believed him, and I was grounded for a month.

Or the time Blair insisted Hank instigated the fight, but Hank played the victim and got me in trouble and then winked at me behind my mom's shoulder, mouthing *they like me more.*

He once insisted our parents' expectations were different

for us, that my life was easier than his. It sounded like an excuse, so I didn't care enough to figure out why. That was fifteen years ago.

The list of his dumb behavior kept growing, and it wasn't a shock I disliked him. He lived in his own world and didn't understand how his behavior affected me. Every time I tried talking to him, my thoughts jumbled, and no words would come out. Regular communication was hard enough for me when it didn't pertain to football, but throw in the complexity of family? I was the worst at it.

I gritted my teeth for a beat and focused on Becca. With her always-present smile and zero judgment in her eyes, she looked so hopeful. I made myself nod. "We did have some good times."

She made a humming sound and stood, picking up my empty plate as the radio made the familiar, gut-wrenching sound of three deep bell sounds. We froze, and her soft brown eyes met mine, hers laced with fear.

My stomach hollowed at the update. Maybe it was good news rather than terrifying. A guy could hope.

Aaron Hodges here from the National Weather Service. Meteorologists are predicting windchills up to sixty degrees below zero tonight. We advise not leaving shelter for any reason or wasting heat. Leave water on a trickle so your pipes don't burst. Multiple shelters have opened with heat and sleeping bags. If you are stranded, please call 911, and services should be out moving as soon as they can. The wind is expected to increase as night falls, and the snow is not letting up until midday tomorrow. Stay safe everyone, and we'll be back with more information soon.

Becca looked out the window, her brows drawn together. Glancing back at me, she asked the question already forming in my mind, "Are we going to be okay?"

"Yes," I said, wishing I was as confident as I sounded. "I'm going to turn on all the faucets before we get ready for bed."

She frowned, and my shoulders felt heavy with worry. Would we be okay on our own?

CHAPTER NINE

BECCA

The temperatures that night dropped to negative sixty outside with the windchill. The blizzard continued its warpath, not caring that people wanted to travel for Christmas. Neither reading nor knitting helped distract me from the building anxiety of nighttime. We each wore numerous layers but the cold in my bones ached inside out. Negative sixty? I'd lived in the Midwest my entire life and never experienced those extreme temps. I had no idea what we'd do if the pipes burst or if the fire went out or if the wind shattered the window exposing us to the elements. I snuggled deeper into my spot on the couch and shivered.

"What's on your mind?" Harrison asked from the cozy chair across the room.

Like me, he fidgeted every couple of minutes. It was possible he was as worried as I was. Getting a read on him was more difficult than getting fifty college girls to agree on a Monday-night TV show. Seriously.

I blew out a breath. "The weather. All the what-ifs running through my mind. My brain can spiral pretty quickly, going to the worst-case scenario within seconds."

"You'll go crazy if you do that. Try to relax if you can."

Relax? With the weather? With him? With my butt still throbbing and me needing to pee every ten minutes because of said nerves? Sure. I was as cool as a cucumber. "What if the window breaks or we run out of wood, or freeze to death?"

He exhaled an impatient breath. "We won't run out of wood, I promise. Not for at least a week." He ran a gloved hand over his jawline and studied the wall behind me, staring at it so hard that I turned around to see what in the world had caught his attention.

Just a window.

"If a window breaks, we'll try to barricade it." He narrowed his eyes as though he was thinking out loud. "If that doesn't work, we can either take wood to the sorority house or load everything in my truck and head to my sister's. I'd prefer not to drive anywhere if we can help it. Honestly, Becca, try not to worry. I paid extra for sturdy windows."

"Okay."

Those solutions all made sense, and I placed my yarn on the table beside me. It had grown dark outside, and the room was too dim with only the flames from the fireplace and a lone candle. Plus the adrenaline from the day had worn off hours ago. It could've been the confidence in Harrison's voice that soothed my anxiety, but an overwhelming sense of exhaustion hit me. My eyelids drew heavy, and my muscles ached. "Maybe I'll try to sleep."

"Good idea. I might lie down, too. There isn't much else to do without light, and we should preserve batteries. I don't have a large supply of those."

Does he mean with me? In the bed? Together? Next to me? On top of me? Right now?

I blushed at the million questions—and images of us—in my mind and moved from my position on the couch away from the large mattress. "I'm going to use the restroom really quick."

He didn't look up from staring at his lap. "If you want to use the restroom in my bedroom, you can. It's right in the back."

"Sure, thanks, yeah."

His bedroom. *Jeez. Is this his attempt at privacy?* I'd used the hall bathroom all afternoon, so why offer the nicer one? Maybe he had to fart or something and needed me out of the room. I snorted, content with why he may have offered the one in his room, and turned on the flashlight.

The beam barely made a path in his room, and the stark difference without the fire left my teeth chattering. It was freezing. Cold and shivering head to toe, I quickly used the toilet and brushed my teeth. Frost lined the lone window in his bedroom, and I fast-walked back to the living room with the fire.

Diving headfirst onto the mattress, I faced the fire. "D-damn it's c-cold outside of t-this room."

"Give it a minute, you'll warm up." He moved away from the warm room.

I tried giving it a minute, but it did no good. I was so cold that my toes, fingers, and jaw hurt. A small whine left my throat, and I bundled up even more. *Think warm thoughts. The beach. Summer. Harrison's body* . . .

"Becca." His voice came closer than a minute ago.

A part of me wondered if I'd accidentally said his name aloud. "Yes?"

"Are you warming up at all?"

"N-no." I tried sounding normal, but I couldn't. "C-could we add more w-wood?"

"Yes, I'll do that." He shuffled around and, kneeling less than a foot from me, added logs to the fire. After positioning them with the poker, he moved from the floor and sat on the edge of the bed. His back touched my legs, and he looked down at me, his brows furrowed and his lips drawn in a firm line. "You have me worried."

"I'm f-fine, just c-cold."

He ran a hand over his face and nodded a couple of times. "I'm joining you."

"Hmm?"

He crawled over me and slid under the covers, moving closer and closer until one arm slid under my head and the other came over my middle. He pulled me against his chest in one smooth motion, leaving my brain without time to digest his actions.

"Slurred speech, shivering, and drowsiness are all signs of hypothermia." His warm breath fanned over my ear.

"You'll warm up faster with my body heat. I'm not chancing it."

I didn't speak, afraid I would say something stupid. I attempted to settle my overactive senses. *Hypothermia? Me?* That only happened to people in movies or TV shows. My breathing picked up, and I had difficulty settling.

Harrison moved his hand, rubbing it up and down my arm. "Focus on the movement, Becca. Try and match your breathing to my pace."

Up and down, over and over. He continued the pattern for a couple of minutes until my lungs filled with air. Relief spread through my body, relaxing me, and I snuggled deeper into his embrace. He was so damn warm and comforting, and he didn't seem to mind when I wiggled against him. If anything, he tightened his grip.

Now that the fear of freezing to death had subsided, my brain caught up to the position we were in. He smelled like firewood and linen, and he'd placed his face against my neck. His breath tickled my exposed skin, and tiny goose bumps broke out over my body. Not from the cold.

Despite all the clothes we wore, awareness of how hard and strong his body was against mine washed over me. His lips were so close, almost touching the spot just below my ear. His quickened breathing. The way his hand now rested against my stomach. The crackling sounds of the fire and the wind howling outside painted the perfect romantic picture. Sadly, nothing about this was romantic. He was only helping me warm up. And it worked—now I had to be responsible and tell him.

"I think I'm warm enough now." I said, moving to put some distance between us.

"Couple more minutes." He pulled me even closer, his deep voice vibrating against my back. "Are you feeling okay? Comfortable?"

"Mm-hmm," I hummed, enjoying his body pressed against mine a little too much. "Very comfortable."

Big guys weren't really my type, but I liked how large he was. It made me feel petite and safe. Nothing would happen to me if we stayed like this for the entire week. I was sure of it.

"Good." He hugged me closer and rested his chin on my shoulder.

His chin was in the perfect position to kiss my neck if he wanted. *But he won't kiss me, right?* I froze as he adjusted his position, momentarily pressing his very cold nose against my skin before relaxing against me.

"Sorry. My leg fell asleep. I needed to change position," he whispered.

I cleared my throat, hoping my voice sounded normal when I spoke. "If you're uncomfortable, I'm fine, really."

It was too much: the cold, Harrison, the ping-pong of my brain wanting his kisses but also not wanting to deal with it. Okay, who was I kidding, I wanted him to kiss me, but it would be inappropriate. We were blizzard buddies. He thought I was super weird and unworthy of a second date. *Remember that, Becca. Don't let the temp mess with your mind.*

Kissing my neighbor was not on my to-do list.

He tightened his hold, and a tiny, almost inaudible sigh left his chest. I wanted to bottle up that sound and listen to it on lonely nights. It was adorable. Cute, little, content Harrison in his hot Henley shirt. I could write a poem about his sound.

Uh-oh! My mind is officially discombobulated.

"No need to guilt-cuddle me. I can move all my toes and fingers." I wiggled my fingers against his hand resting at my waist. "Even my broken pinky toe."

"You broke your pinky toe?" he asked, still not letting go of me.

"Dance-off with the girls. I got second place." I thought about how confident I'd been doing the worm. It had worked until I kicked the TV stand and pain exploded in my foot. *Becca Fairfield—second-place dancing queen.*

"Of course, it was dancing." His voice was thick with amusement.

I needed to stop *Operation Cuddle My Blizzard Buddy* before I turned around and kissed the hell out of him. Just to shut him up. Not at all because I liked him.

"Well, I'm toasty now." I cleared my throat, my stomach swooping every time his lips grazed my neck. Each goose bump reminded me how long it had been since I'd hooked up with someone. *Too long.*

"Maybe I'm enjoying this, Becca, and that's why I'm not getting up yet."

Wait! What?

Enjoying this? What did that even mean? My entire body tensed with indecision. Did I respond? Wait for more? Wiggle my ass against him for encouragement?

"I was cold, too. This helps," he said after a moment of silence.

Oh, right. Duh.

Nervous laughter bubbled up and escaped before I could stop it. "I thought you were flirting with me for a second. How reassuring that you weren't."

"Who says I wasn't?"

Oh, snap.

We were at an impasse, neither responding nor moving, and the silence drove me crazy. Thank God I faced the fire and not him—even though his face was right against my neck. He admitted to flirting. Kind of. A thrill rushed through me because I hadn't imagined it, but why would he flirt? He didn't like me...did he?

The more the silence dragged on, the more my thoughts rambled, and word vomit was a real possibility. *Do I mention the date from two years ago? Do I admit I want to kiss him? Do I pretend I'm asleep and start snoring?*

Was there any harm in wanting to kiss him? Did it make me a bad person that, even though he'd ghosted me, I wanted to kiss him again?

Before I could embarrass myself, Harrison patted my side and rolled the opposite direction. "I'll be right back, don't worry. Stay bundled up, and we can sleep close. Do you need anything?"

His voice was both soft and kind, gentle and sweet like

one a lover used. Shivers escaped my body at the combination of his tone and the loss of his body heat.

"No, thank you," I mumbled into my pillow.

He'd said we could sleep close. What did he mean, exactly? Confused as hell, my stomach swooped like a teenager's—like the time my freshman crush winked at me in class. Turned out I'd misread him, and he was winking at the girl behind me, but in those glorious few minutes, my stomach was a hot-mess express.

Sleeping next to the handsome Harrison Cooper, though...what an interesting turn of events. The girls at the house would freak out if they knew. Hell, two years ago I would've jumped up and down with glee at the thought of his hard, toned body curled up around mine. It had been years since I'd legit slept with someone. Sleeping—not the sex—was such a vulnerable thing, and I preferred having a relationship with someone before sharing a bed for an entire night. So much happened during the night. Sleep talking, snoring, drooling, or even sleep stripping—something I had done since I was a child. Knowing he might witness all of that was nerve-racking.

I paused my thoughts. Why did I care what he thought? I didn't. That's right.

Ugh. I buried my face into the blanket and let out a frustrated groan. The kiss was the problem. I had kissed a lot of frogs in my lifetime, and Harrison might've had frog behavior two years ago, but the way he'd used his mouth sure as hell hadn't been frog-like.

And a frog wouldn't save me and help me get warm.

"Should I be worried about the sound you just made?" he asked.

I tensed, not realizing he'd returned to the room. "You're a big guy. Why don't you make any noise when you walk?" I rolled over, facing him as he stood at the edge of the kitchen. "You should have loud footsteps."

"I'm light on my feet." He shrugged and blew out a candle on the end table. "How's your phone battery doing? I found one of those portable charges with a little juice left but mine is still at eighty percent."

I felt around the floor, and finding my device, I shrugged. "I'm good still. I changed it to battery save mode when the power first went out."

"Efficient." He blew out another candle, leaving the fireplace as the only light in the room. "We need to stay hydrated, so I brought a couple bottles of water. Try and have one before we fall asleep."

"You're right. Thanks." I moved onto my butt to sit criss-cross and then took the bottle from him and opened the top. He joined me on the mattress and leaned against the edge of the couch. Here we were, staring at each other in silence, drinking water like we were pals.

He gave me a long look, his gaze dropping from my face and down to my body all bundled up in the blankets. "You're different than how I would've imagined you."

"Uh, okay?" *Here we go again. You're too different, Becca.* I tried thinking of a good comeback but came up empty. Instead, my tone defensive, I replied. "You're different, too."

He smiled, the white of his teeth visible in the dim lighting. "I think you misunderstood my intention there. It was a compliment."

"A weird compliment, then." I faced away from him, hiding my reaction. It shouldn't have surprised me he'd go down this route, *again*. Same words, same letdown. *Story of my freaking life.*

"Look." He moved closer to me on the mattress. Reaching out, he placed a massive hand on my shoulder and squeezed gently. "We haven't talked about it, but I think we should."

"Talked about what?" My heart raced at the direction of this conversation.

Does he mean the date? The time he never called like he'd promised? The way I'd overanalyzed the date, wondering what I'd done wrong?

"Two years ago," he clarified.

And there it was.

Play it cool.

"Remind me, what about two years ago? *So much* has happened since then." I hated how my voice sounded as I masked my embarrassment. This was really happening, and all the responses I'd planned those first few weeks after our date disappeared. All the rants I'd practiced in my head, imagining how coy and fierce I'd be if I saw him. All of it was gone.

"Becca." His tone lacked amusement. "We went on a date."

"Did we? Hmm, easy to forget. I go on dates all the time, like so many. Where did we go? Was I nice to you?" I rambled, my face turning hotter by the second.

"Yes, you were nice to me. We both had a great time." He scooted closer to me. "I was an asshole, okay? I know that."

I blinked, hoping he couldn't hear how fast my heart beat against my ribs. It was like mini bolts of thunder. "Be more specific, please."

He took my hand and placed it between both of his. I tried pulling out of his grip but he wouldn't let me. "Hold on. This is important."

I stopped fidgeting.

"I didn't call you, and I should've. I said I would, but I chose not to. You deserved an explanation."

"It's fine." *Downplay the hurt. It's better this way.* "It's not uncommon, honestly. Just filed it away like all the other dates."

He blew out a breath, his brows furrowing together. "I won't sit here and say our situation right now is ideal, or that we would've had this conversation if not for the weather, but I want to apologize for my behavior."

"Thank you? Feels like it's two years too late, but sure." *Sure, it affected my self-esteem for a hot minute because I'd never read a date so poorly before and thought I did something wrong. But yeah. Fine.*

"I'm not done, Becca." His tone softened, his mouth twisting into a grimace and his green eyes filling with regret. "Look, I didn't call because I *can* be an asshole. You were...*are*...young. I'm older than you and figured you'd be high-maintenance. You wear a lot of bright colors and fancy clothes, have a lot of friends, chat with everyone. You always look incredible, which probably takes a lot of time, and well...Nothing wrong with being high-maintenance at all, but I wasn't at a point in my life to dedicate time or energy into dating. I assumed you'd want or need someone who could give you the attention you deserve. It was easier to not call than to explain myself to you. It was a bad move."

My throat felt full of cotton and swallowing hurt. *High-maintenance?* That was a new one for the list. He cleared his throat, probably expecting an answer, but I wasn't sure what to say. *Fancy clothes? Friends?* Sure, I talked a lot, that wasn't new information, but I hated how my traits were seen in a bad light by him. It was two years ago, yet the sting was no less dull. I took a drink of the water and offered a shaky smile. The confidence he'd carried the last fifteen hours was gone.

"At least I have an explanation now." My stomach tightened at how awkward this was. He wasn't the same guy, and I appreciated him owning up to it. But...two years later?

The lines around his mouth tightened, and he said again, "I'm sorry."

Maybe it was the regret in his voice or the flirting with hypothermia I was experiencing, but annoyance at all my past dates, him included, flared up.

"Harrison, it would've been nice to hear the truth *then*. A simple text. A thirty-second conversation. Anything. Being ghosted is horrible and makes you second guess yourself and analyze what went wrong. It's maddening when a date doesn't have the guts to be honest." My chest heaved. I pulled a blanket over my head, and I snuggled under the covers. "I'm going to sleep. Good night."

CHAPTER TEN

HARRISON

You're such an asshole. That's what the fierce winds seemed to say as they tried knocking down the walls of my house.

My list of transgressions against my sweet neighbor was ten miles long, and my stomach burned in the same way it did when I made a wrong call on the field. Regret. While I didn't regret *not* dating Becca then, because my head wasn't in the right place, I could've handled it better. We could've been friends.

Bullshit.

With the way my attraction to her kept growing in our short time together, it's unlikely a simple friendship would've worked out between us. But it would've prevented the invisible wall we have between us now. The hurt I'd caused. I stared up at the dark ceiling, illuminated by the flames of the fire, and cracked my knuckles for something to do. She said most of her dates did that, so I was just like all the other assholes who'd upset her. Was she really high-maintenance?

If anything, the last few hours proved how easy she was to be around. She hadn't complained about a single thing.

She hadn't said a word in over an hour, but she wasn't sleeping. Neither of us were, but she adjusted her position about every ten seconds. The wind howled something fierce outside, and the fire provided just enough heat to stave off my own shivers. I'd added more wood to it minutes ago, pretending I didn't see the way her bundled figure trembled. She needed my warmth or she'd freeze. *Would she push me away? Tell me to, rightfully, fuck off? To hell with it.*

"Becca, you're freezing." I pushed up onto my elbow and glanced down at her.

"A l-little." She faced me, her teeth chattering and terror reflected in her wide eyes. "I wouldn't mind if y-you wanted t-to come c-closer. For warmth."

"Oh, you wouldn't mind?" I teased without thinking. *Damn it.*

"C-come over here then." She gave me her back, her invitation more enticing by the second.

I smiled at her demand, glad she couldn't see it. Pressing my body against hers was certainly not a chore, but I didn't want to make her uncomfortable, either. I removed my jacket and blanket, scooted toward her back, and pulled at her million miles of comforter.

"W-what are you d-doing?"

"Body heat will spread faster without all the blankets or layers. Don't worry, I'll bundle us back up. Take off your coat."

She did, narrowing her eyes at me. Once she set it on the

floor, I slid right behind her, wrapping my limbs around hers for optimal warmth. The same delicious smell came from her neck. I bit down, preventing myself from groaning at how good she felt. The only thing separating us was our pants and sweatshirts. She moved against me, wiggling her ass against my crotch, and I used my free hand to wrap us in layers of blankets. Her chest rose faster, as did mine. After a few seconds, my body warmed.

"There, this is nice. Feeling any better?" I whispered.

"Yes."

She still trembled but not as violently as before, relieving my concern that she might have hypothermia. Her petite body fit against mine. Ignoring her curves or the way she smelled like cookies was nearly impossible.

Who the hell smells like cookies in the middle of a snowstorm?

Becca. That's who.

She adjusted her position, moving even closer to me. My arm rested over her middle, and my face tucked into her neck. For warmth. That was why.

"Jeez, Harrison. You're so warm. Good lord, how? You're like a furnace."

"I generate heat." I wrapped my arm around her tighter, imagining what it would be like to do this under normal circumstances, and I found myself enjoying the embrace. "In the summer, I can't even sleep with a sheet or I'll burn up."

"What a special talent. To just be warm."

I snorted. "Never thought about it that way before."

"Well, it's perfect for this kind of weather. My talents are useless for surviving a blizzard." Her voice had returned to normal, and relief rushed through me, easing the knots in my shoulders.

What began as a good-neighbor invitation had shifted into full-on protectiveness. The world needed more people like Becca, and the thought of anything bad happening to her filled me with rage. She was special.

A beat of silence passed, our bodies pressed closely together. After the longest time, my eyes finally grew heavy. I had no idea how I'd sleep with the blizzard raging outside, not to mention my sexy buddy pressed against me.

"So," she said, her voice holding the same nerves it did after the radio announcement, "this doesn't...we're essentially cuddling, right? It doesn't make things weird between us?"

My heart clenched in my chest. "No."

"Good. Okay. That's great. Groovy, even." She swallowed hard.

"Is this weird for you?"

Don't say yes. I wasn't ready to end it. For reasons beyond my understanding, I liked holding her like this. It had been years since I'd done this with a woman—just cuddle together without an agenda. It was...comforting.

I swore I could hear her brain whirring as she fidgeted against me.

"Um, no? Like, cuddling with a guy I don't know *isn't* on my normal agenda, but these are extreme circumstances, and I really don't want to lose any toes or fingers."

"You know me—at least a little." I said, annoyed.

"I guess that's true. Today could be like a second date, if

you think about it. We ate together, asked questions, and are now cuddling." She tensed beneath my arms. "I'm not saying this is a date. Or that I wanted a second date. Because I don't. Well, I did. But that was years ago. It's different now, I think." She cleared her throat. "Look, this is new for me, and I'm telling myself this could've been a second date to ease my mind about cuddling you. I'm not a one-night-cuddler type of girl. Which is totally fine! Some people like that. No shame. You do you. But it makes me nervous, obviously. I can't shut up. Literally, my mouth won't stop making sounds, so just toss me outside and be done with it."

My smile was so big that it hurt my face. She was cute and charming in a way that made me think of the Christmas ornaments my sister would send. Like the squirrel in underwear, or a grandma doing a cartwheel. At first, they're a bit odd and different, but then...they sneak in and damn. *I'm starting to like her.*

"Question." I ended her endless stream of chatter. "If today was the second date, then would tomorrow be the third? I heard that's the best date with you."

"I guess—" She stopped and smacked my hand resting on her stomach. "*Harrison.*"

"You're the one who said the sexy underwear comes out for the third date. Just using your words." I found way too much joy in teasing her.

She harrumphed but didn't say anything else.

I snuggled closer. "I was teasing you, Becca. Sorry if I crossed a line. You seemed nervous so I thought a joke would help."

"No, you didn't cross a line." She sighed this time, and her muscles relaxed against me. "I might be on edge about what you admitted earlier, about not wanting to put the effort into dating and about thinking I was too high-maintenance."

"Again, I'm sorry. I'm not happy about the weather situation, but it's nice spending time with you."

Pressure built in my chest, and I chastised myself for being a dick to other people when my life got hard. It was a defense mechanism that served me well with an entitled brother and an ex-wife who liked to point out my negative qualities. That didn't make it right, though.

"Mm," she replied. "You *have* made it more bearable than it would've been alone in that big house."

I grinned into the pillow. "You wouldn't have lasted half a day."

"You're right." She chuckled and let out a sleepy sigh that had no business stirring any sort of attraction below my waist. It was like the sounds she made eating—innocent, yet making me wish I knew how she sounded when she was naked. "I feel like I should give you a heads-up, I'm a wild sleeper."

Wild? I cleared my throat. "Yeah? How so?"

"Talking in my sleep, rolling around, taking my clothes off. The usual."

Taking clothes off. Her words sparked a vivid image of her in her bra, her ample cleavage I'd done my best to ignore since my hand rested inches from it. *Shit.* She would definitely feel my reaction if I didn't change the subject immediately. I'd already upset her enough. Getting a boner against her while we snuggled for survival was the worst thing I could do.

Change the subject.

Ignore how warm and soft and curvy she is.

"Uh." I swallowed hard, unable to get the image out of my head. "What are your plans for Christmas?"

"Probably heading to my parents' for a night, *if* I can get out of here." She yawned. "What about you?"

"My sister's place. It's fun with the kids."

"Mm, I bet." Her voice drifted off, and her breathing deepened.

I envied her ability to fall asleep that quickly. Some nights it took me hours, and I'd overanalyze everything in my life. Others, I'd toss and turn, thinking about the high probability this would be my last season coaching, and I'd have to hear about Hank's success for years. Or Vivian would make an appearance, and I'd remember everything I did wrong in my marriage. Tonight was different. Thoughts about Becca flashed across my mind, each one more inappropriate than the last.

The way she moaned when she ate.

The way she looked in her bra.

The way she kissed with so much passion two years ago.

Damn it. Be a better man.

Counting to four hundred didn't help, nor did thinking of plays we could run next season—assuming we had the talent. I moved to get a beer, but Becca changed position and turned toward me. She nuzzled her face against me and wrapped herself around my body, intertwining our legs.

Holy shit. She felt even better pressed up against me. She was soft in all the right places, something I'd admired about her two years ago. Most of my dates were beautiful women, but they didn't have Becca's curves. She had the perfect hips, leading to great legs, and . . . *shit I'm getting a boner.*

She nuzzled her nose against my skin and let out a little sigh. Awareness shot through my body like fire in my veins.

Deep breaths.

She's sleeping.

Don't be a creep.

I considered moving her away from me, but she might get cold again, and it wasn't worth chancing it. I had no choice. I had to tough it out, having her pressed up against me. I prayed I'd get some sleep.

A moan startled me. My watch read 3:17 a.m., and only a few embers remained. We were spooning. *Again.* My right hand had slipped underneath her shirt, my fingers lazily stroking her breasts in my sleep.

What am I doing?

Why can't I stop?

"Mm, feels good," Becca whispered.

I tensed, desperate for that husky voice again. She ground against my erection, a throaty moan escaping.

"Are you awake?" I whispered.

"Yes."

Her voice was alert. *Perfect.*

"And this feels good?" I ran my nose along her jawline, inhaling her sweet, sleepy scent as I grazed my finger over her hardened nipple. Once, twice, and then I pinched it. She trembled in my arms as her deep sighs of pleasure filled the room.

"Mm." She arched her back, rocking her hips as her breathing picked up.

That one syllable was all I needed. I cupped her full, luscious breast in my hand, already planning on licking every part of her until she cried out. She was gorgeous. Her tits were a dream.

"Tell me what you want, Becca." I bit down on her earlobe.

Instead of groaning or making that sexy *mm* sound again, she sucked in a breath and bolted upright. "Oh my *God*."

"What?" I croaked out, my brain drunk from her body.

"I thought...I thought I was *dreaming*." Her voice shook.

Shame consumed me, and my face burned with embarrassment. "I asked if you were awake. You said yes, Becca."

"No, I *know* I did. Don't feel bad." She gulped. "I can't believe you touched my boob."

Don't think about her boobs. How they felt, how she reacted.

Getting up, I ground my teeth together and placed more wood on the fire. I needed a distraction since all the blood had left my brain. My neighbor was gorgeous but *sleeping* women weren't my thing.

"Harrison."

"Hmm?" I asked, barely glancing at her because I needed my dick to settle down.

Her mouth formed a little *O* shape, and her gaze zeroed in on my bulge—my very evident bulge.

I shrugged, hoping to play it cool. "Becca, I've always been attracted to you. You're an incredibly gorgeous woman, and having your body pressed against mine is a special form of torture."

She tilted her head to the side, blinking her wide, pretty eyes. "Hmm."

"To be clear, I wanted to keep going. But I need you to explicitly say it."

"This is crazy." She ran a hand over her throat and avoided my gaze. "Right?"

"What is?" The fire crackled, and I sat back down on the mattress, not more than a foot away from her. "My reaction to your body? Your reaction to me touching your breasts? Us being stuck together during a snowstorm?"

"Yes? All the above?"

"Again, that sounds like a question." I placed my hand on her ankle, over the blanket, and squeezed it. "Look, don't be embarrassed or worried. I meant it when I said I enjoyed spending time with you today. My life is in a different place than it was two years ago, and we're both single."

"Hmm." She pulled at her bottom lip, eyeing me up and down. "I've never slept with anyone I wasn't seeing *seriously*. Well, I have, but it was one time. It was hot and fun, but I couldn't do it again. I didn't even ask his name. It was just hot, sweaty sex," she rambled, blurring her words together.

She's nervous.

"Technically, one could argue that this is the third date. It's after midnight," I pointed out.

One side of her mouth quirked up.

"Plus, we don't have to sleep together if you're uncomfortable. We could sleep, cuddle for warmth, or...I could make you feel good. Having a blizzard-buddy fling might not be the worst idea, Becs."

A blizzard buddy. I'm an idiot.

Her fingers traced her collarbone as she swallowed, loud. "Yeah? A snow-pocalypse fling. Hmm, it shouldn't sound intriguing, but it very much does. Like, just for the time we're snowed in? Hmm. It could maybe work. I wanna know, though, how would you make me feel good?"

She wants me to explain it to her? Okay.

I tended to live in a feelings-free zone, but this? Seduction and a few nights of sex? That was my equivalent of a touchdown.

I inched closer to her, trailing my finger over her ear and down her neck. "I'd start kissing you here...tasting your skin as I go. I'd ask you what you liked—or didn't like—and I'd slowly run my tongue down your neck to your chest."

She panted, and I moved my hand to her chest. "I'd play with your nipples. Licking them, biting them—gently, or...maybe a little more aggressively...you'd let me know which you prefer—leaving you ready for release. How does that sound, Becca?"

"G-good."

"Do you want me to continue?" My voice was gruff as hell. The buildup had me hard as a rock.

She moaned and nodded fast.

"I'd take my time licking your stomach while tracing my fingers between your legs. I'd make sure you're wet and ready for me, but I wouldn't enter you yet."

"No?" Her words were barely a whisper, her voice shaking.

"No." I smiled, my eyes locked on hers and my hands still caressing her breasts over her shirt. "I'd touch you, watching your every reaction. I'd leave soft kisses along the backs of your knees and bite softly along the sensitive skin on your inner thighs, before working my way up to that needy spot where you'll beg for more."

"Yeah?"

"Uh-huh." Still holding her eyes with mine, I rolled her pebbled nipples between my fingers and thumbs. "I'd take you into my mouth and suck—hard—bringing you to the very edge. Finally—when you think you can't stand it another second—I'd slide inside of you and find a rhythm you'd like, moving my body over yours and bringing you close to the edge until your body finally releases so hard it steals your breath and forces my own release to follow."

She squirmed on the mattress, her lips emitting the sexiest mews.

"Harrison," she panted, a wild look entering her eyes. "Yes-ss-s."

"Yes, what?" I tensed, prayed, and cashed in on any drop of good karma I had in the world that she'd agree.

I waited, but she didn't speak. Instead, she flung off the blankets and jumped on me, slamming her mouth onto mine in a frenzied passion and knocking me back to the mattress.

"Damn it." She wrapped her arms around my shoulders and bit down on my lip, sucking it into her mouth while moving her hips against mine. "I'm so turned on. Never...those words...Harrison. Snow-pocalypse fling. I need it right now."

The need in her voice snapped me to reality. It was hot how ready she was, and how she didn't care. She wanted it fast, but I wanted it slow. If I only got one night with her, I'd make it last. I cupped the back of her head and slowed down the kiss, sliding my tongue inside her mouth.

She matched me stroke for stroke as I finally got to repeat that kiss from two years ago.

Did she like it gentle or quick? Or slow? Strong or soft? Becca responded to each variation with gusto, gripping my hair in her hands.

"Harrison," she said between kisses, "I might explode. My body is tingling right now. The scruff on your jaw feels so rough on my skin. I love it."

"Good." I set her on the bed and then crawled over her, kissing her neck. "Think how good it'll feel when I put my mouth on you."

She whimpered, her hands going to the edge of her shirt as though to pull it off.

I chuckled at her urgency but stilled her hands. "Are you in a hurry?"

"Yes." She clenched her teeth. "You got me all hot and bothered."

"Then I'm doing a great job seducing you." I smoothed the edge of her shirt up, taking my time and running my hands over her soft skin. When I reached her breasts, she arched her back. I shook my head. "Neck first, remember?"

Her eyes held a wild expression, her pouty lips wet and swollen from our kiss. She was a dream. I trailed my tongue along her jaw, licking the pulse point below her ear before biting down on her earlobe and pinching one of her nipples. She bucked beneath me as my greedy hands explored her breasts.

"Oh, you like when I touch you here."

She responded with a groan and weaved her fingers through the hair at the back of my head.

Moving my lips down her jaw, I alternated between gentle nips and open-mouthed kisses, continuing until I reached the intersection where her neck met her shoulder. Pausing a moment, I dipped my tongue into the hollow of her throat and sucked gently at her soft skin.

"Harrison." She groaned again.

"What?" I smiled into her neck. "Are you getting bored?"

"No, *no.*" She ran the pads of her fingers along the waistband of my pants. "But I'm ready for the main event."

"Oh, you are, huh?" I moved my mouth back to hers, teasing her tongue with mine for long minutes.

Satisfied I'd tasted all of her exposed skin, I lifted her shirt over her head, tossed it to the floor and then stared down at her thin lacy bra. Her nipples poked through the fabric, making my mouth water.

She was gorgeous.

"Fucking hell, Becca." I slid one strap off her shoulder, my body tight as a coil with need. Reaching around her slim rib cage, I undid her bra, releasing the most perfect set of breasts I had ever seen. Round and full, her perfect pink nipples sent a wave of desperation through me. Unable to wait a moment longer, I leaned forward and sucked one into my mouth.

"Harrison, oh my." She dug her nails into my shoulders and wrapped her legs around me, trapping me against her.

My hands shook as I touched her, the slow and controlled pace I'd aimed for shot completely to hell. I moved fast, teasing and licking her breasts with the same fervor she'd displayed earlier. I moved down her chest, tasting her stomach, and groaned when my lips met the waistband of her pajama bottoms.

"You doing okay? You want me to stop?" I asked, praying she wouldn't ask me to stop.

"I will literally die if you stop," she said in a husky voice.

"We can't have that, can we?" I chuckled against her warm skin and dipped my fingers into her sweatpants, slowly sliding them down her legs.

My mind raced with dirty thoughts... How would she sound? Would she cry out? Shake?

From somewhere in the house, a loud, shattering crash reverberated around us. I paused, my eyes meeting Becca's wild ones.

"What was that?" she asked.

"Fuck." I swallowed so loud that it clicked in the back of my throat. I didn't want to stop. I really didn't want to fucking stop. "I should check on it."

Her gaze filled with understanding. "Of c-course. I'll come with you."

"Stay here by the fire." I stood, adjusting myself in my pants and *not* looking at her sitting on the mattress, naked from the waist up.

Bad fucking timing.

CHAPTER ELEVEN

BECCA

Flustered, turned on, and worried were a terrible combination. My poor body didn't know how to react. Harrison had revved me up until I was seconds away from the release I wanted. But with his absence, common sense trickled back in. *What am I doing? Him? Why?*

Me? A fling?

My mind cackled at my dilemma. Boy, I was attracted to him. That wasn't the issue.

Using only words to get me worked up? That was the hottest thing I'd experienced...ever. My skin still tingled from his talented mouth, but survival took precedence over orgasms. At least for today.

He'd disappeared a few minutes ago without any indication of what had happened.

I have to check on him.

"Damn it." I layered up in all the clothes I could find,

looking a tad Joey Tribbiani-ish when he put on every stitch of Chandler's clothes.

Harrison had left the basement door open, and my eyes stung as the cold air blasted up the stairs. *Dang, it's cold.*

"Harrison?"

He grunted, the sounds of metal clinking echoing up the stairs. "Yeah?"

"You okay down there? Need help?"

The wind whistled like the villain from my worst night-mares, and I shivered. *Clank.* Something heavy dropped on the floor.

Shit.

I gritted my teeth, picturing warm beaches and bonfires for imaginary warmth. "I'm coming down."

"No," he grumbled and let out a string of curse words. "Another window broke."

That's why I'm freezing my ass off.

Worry trickled down my spine, but I remained in problem-solving mode. "Okay, what do you need? Tape? Do you have a tarp anywhere?"

"I have a tarp. Can't get it to stay with tape."

"Hammer and nails?" I took two steps down the stairs. Aside from a little flicker of a small flashlight, it was dark. I sprinted to the living room and grabbed the larger flashlight and then returned and trained the light on the steps. "I can hold the light for you if that would help?"

"Sure. Bundle up. I'm freezing my balls off right now."

I threw an extra blanket over my shoulders, making myself resemble a walking burrito, and then grabbed a coat for Harrison, a hat, scarf, and a pair of gloves. With one final breath for courage, I descended the stairs.

I was barely halfway down when the first blast of frigid air hit me, almost as though I had walked outside. Taking no mercy, the wind whipped around the unfinished base-ment, bringing with it puffs of fresh snow until every sur-face had been covered with a fresh layer of powdery white. A huge gym was set up to the left, with a bench and a bunch of weights. There was a treadmill covered in snow and a large black box. My first thought was to wipe it off, to make sure it wouldn't leak into the machine. But come on, Becca, there would be no melting!

On the west side of the basement was a gaping hole. Beside it, Harrison—shaking from cold and wearing only the clothes he'd worn in bed—held a tarp up to the window. Around him, shards of glass covered the floor in every direction.

"Harrison, you need more layers!" I shouted.

He dropped the tarp to the floor and ran toward me. "I d-didn't think it would be th-this bad."

"You're shivering. Come here." I pulled him close and wrapped my arms around him as far as they would reach.

He wrapped his large arms tightly around me, his chin resting on top of my head. It was like hugging a Popsicle.

"Do you need to head upstairs to warm up for a minute?" I asked.

"No. We need to stop the c-cold before it gets w-worse."

He buried his ice-cold nose into my neck, making me jump in shock, but I held on tighter. "You head back up if you g-get too c-cold, okay?" he said.

"Let's do it together." I broke our embrace, assessing him head to toe. A slight bluish color tinted his lips. We needed to fix this, fast. "Where are your tools?"

"Here." He hustled toward an organized shelf and pulled out a nail gun. "I hope it's charged. If not, we might be shit out of luck."

"Try it." He'd been down here five minutes but it was already dangerously cold.

Please work! Oh my God, please work.

My pulse skyrocketed as the temperature plummeted further. I pointed the flashlight at the broken window as Harrison climbed a stepladder. Holding the tarp at the top of the window frame with one hand, he settled the nail gun against the vinyl and pulled the trigger.

Bam, bam, bam. The staccato of the nail gun sounded like mini gunshots.

"Thank Christ, it works." He copied the movement ten more times around the top of the tarp and then sealed the sides and bottom. "Can you grab another tarp from the green bin over there?"

"Yes." My teeth chattered, but my eyes scanned over the room.

Green bin. Green bin. There. Finding the bin, I brought him the second tarp.

Harrison attached the second tarp over the first and grabbed a roll of duct tape. Pulling out a long strip, he tried ripping it. "I can't—I can't tear it. My hands are too cold." His face fell in disappointment.

"I'll do it." We traded the flashlight for the tape, and I

ripped the pieces we needed. We sealed the tarp around the window well, our synchronous teeth chattering the only sound besides the wind. There was *so* much glass on the floor, though.

"Do you have a broom?" I asked.

"Later." Without warning, he shoved his flashlight in his pocket, took the tape from my grip, and tossed it on the floor. "Heat. I need heat."

I didn't get time to react before he scooped me up in his arms, engulfing me in his woodsy scent. He pressed his face into my neck, gripping me tighter with each step. My pulse raced in my ears, from the cold, from his proximity, from the fear of the blizzard.

It was all overwhelming.

"We need to block the air from escaping. A blanket or pillow would work." His voice still shook from the cold.

"Good idea."

Reaching the top of the stairs, he gently set me on the floor before wedging one of the blankets under the door. Once a second blanket was secured, he dove into our make-shift bed.

"I can't feel my fingers." His body shivered. "Toes are iffy, too."

"*Harrison.*" Worry etched its way down my body, my stomach tightening with concern. "Move closer to the fire. Warm up."

"I need you next to me." He lifted the covers, waving his hand in invitation. "Come on. I'll warm up much faster with you."

It took me zero seconds to decide what to do. I discarded two of my layers before sliding next to his massive body. He wrapped his limbs around me like a second skin. He trembled and I squeezed him tighter, like it would help. "Did you take your shoes off?"

"No." He snuggled deeper into my embrace and shuffled his feet around. Two loud clunks hit the floor and he pressed his socked feet against my legs.

"Aah!" I yelped. "You're freezing!"

"Told you. They're ice." His lips moved along my skin, and I shivered, not from cold this time.

He needs warmth. Not you thinking about his hard muscles.

"Next time, put on more clothes. I hope you don't have any nerve damage." I ran my fingers through his hair, telling myself it was to comfort him.

He had a great head of hair, dark brown, and thick with enough curl to give him that dreamy just-woke-up look.

He hummed against me, and my eyes drifted closed. While he might've been cold, his body still produced heat, and the toastier I became, the easier it was to fall asleep with our bodies intertwined. My last thought was about how safe I felt in Harrison's arms.

"Becca." A hand shook my shoulder. "Becca, wake up."

"Hmm?" I was so warm and comfortable. I could've lived in this moment forever. I peeked an eye open as sunlight lit up the living room. "What's going on? It's early."

"Do you know what you're doing?" The deep sexy voice asked. "You're rubbing your hands all over my chest."

"Am I?" I stilled, flushing as my nails *dug* into Harrison's bare chest. I jerked my hand out of his shirt like it was a hot flame. In my sleep, I'd wrapped around him like he was my lifeline. *Oh my God.* "Um, sorry. Sorry." I rolled away from him, my heart beating against my ribs.

"Do you know why you're here?" The blankets rustled as he rolled over onto his side.

Our faces were inches apart, and the sleep lines on his face were so dang adorable, his normally hard features all soft and lazy. My stomach swooped.

"Why I'm here? The blizzard?" I was unsure why he'd asked me that. I touched his forehead, checking for a fever. "Are you alright?"

"I'm fine." He wet his bottom lip with his tongue as he trailed his fingers over my face and down my jaw. "You're absolutely positive that you're awake?"

"Yes, Harrison." My eyelids fluttered when he began kneading my neck. The frigid air was thick with tension. His touch, the heated look in his eyes…the warmth between my thighs. "Oh, that feels good."

"Good. I need you wide awake for this." His tone dripped with insinuation and desire.

"For what?" I asked, playing with fire—I knew this was going to happen. *We* were going to happen.

He stared at my mouth, his dark green eyes hooded with lust. He licked the corner of his mouth and then cupped my face in his large hands before guiding me closer. Our lips touched, and fireworks ricocheted in my stomach. His kiss was slow and tender, his tongue teasing mine. We had never kissed like this before. Unhurried and lazy. He nipped at my lips, each bite sending goose bumps down my body.

"If another window breaks, ignore it." His dark gaze held mine. "I don't care if the fucking roof falls, I need to kiss you again."

I trembled at the fierceness in his voice, the promise in his words. I nodded and brought my mouth to his again, not caring about the consequences. I'd never felt so desired.

"You're sure you want this, Becca?" he asked, husky and sexy and patient.

I admired his restraint because I had none. Zero. "Yes," I said through clenched teeth. "Do you?"

"Without question." He laughed, his breath tickling my face and sending a ripple of awareness straight between my legs.

Harrison slowly lifted the edge of my sweatshirt and shirt, sucking in a breath as he stared down at my breasts. My tight nipples poked the air, and he groaned before pinching them between his fingers. His touch lit me up.

"I need to see your chest," I begged, my thoughts a horny mess.

"Happy to oblige." Grabbing the hem of his own sweat-shirt, he lifted it over his head and tossed it to the floor.

Oh boy. My mouth watered at the hard lines and muscles of his chest. I ran my fingers over his skin. His eyes flared, and grabbing my hand, he weaved our fingers together before ducking his head. He sucked one of my nipples into his mouth.

"Oh, *wow.*" I arched my back as he swirled his tongue around each point before gently nipping them with his teeth. Electric pleasure raced through my veins, my mind spinning as control slipped further from reach. I wanted him, desperately.

My skin prickled with heat as his lips moved from my sensitive nipples, down the center of my cleavage, and past my belly button before pausing at my waistband. I panted, burning from the trail he'd left with his tongue.

He looked up at me, his long lashes framing his strong cheekbones. "Are you wet for me?"

So crass, so hot. I nodded. Words were impossible.

"I told you what I'd do, didn't I?" He licked his lips and gently pulled down my sweatpants, leaving me in black panties. "Becca..." He made a tsk sound. "You told me sexy underwear wasn't until the third date. You lied. These are *sexy.*" He groaned before dipping down and sliding the fabric to the side.

"Oh my."

"Yup. Wet for me." Something like a growl came from his throat as he brought his mouth to my inner thighs. He licked and kissed the perimeter around my center, never quite touching the spot I needed him most.

"Perfect."

Flattening his tongue, he took one long stroke against my center.

Stars danced behind my eyes as I clutched the blankets. With each flick of his tongue, pleasure teased my core. He swirled and sucked, fast at first and then slower before slipping one finger inside me. The pleasure was almost painful, and an orgasm was building. Seconds later, he joined a second finger with the first, stretching me and adding exactly the pressure I craved. I arched my hips, rocking closer to his face. My hands moved to his head, holding him in place.

Yes. My goodness.

"More," I begged, not caring about anything besides my growing orgasm.

"Needy." We were so close I could feel his smile against me. "I fucking love it."

He took his time, speeding up and then slowing down each time my orgasm neared. His stubbled jaw rubbed against my thighs, and my body jerked as the feeling intensified. More *everything.*

"I'm so close." I moaned, grabbing his hand and pulling it toward me, ready for him to join me.

Refusing to be rushed, Harrison didn't budge. Instead he flicked his tongue harder against my core. He held me tight against his mouth, sucking with exactly the pressure I needed until my nerves caught fire. Pleasure burst through me, white-hot and bright. My body convulsed, my orgasm hitting so fast and hard my toes curled and lights danced behind my eyes.

"Harrison...*yes.*"

My heart pounded so hard I thought it might beat right out of my chest. He'd made me come with his mouth, giving me the strongest orgasm I'd ever experienced. The pleasure lingered, and my legs trembled with aftershocks.

"Whoa."

"I could eat you all damn day." He licked his lips and stared at me with nothing but hunger in his green eyes.

Holy bologna.

"Uh, well..." I stammered. "That was incredible."

"I'm not done with you." He pressed a kiss on my still-throbbing core and held my gaze. "Do you want me to stop, Becca?"

Heck no. Stop this chemistry? This absolute pleasure? I'd never forgive myself for walking away from this.

"Nope. No."

"Good girl." He smiled and trailed kisses over my thighs, along my stomach, and up my chest, teasing me with his agonizingly slow pace. The stubble on his cheeks scraped, leaving behind a slight sting, but then he kissed away the pain. He took long minutes worshiping every inch of my skin as his mouth made its way up my body. His soft lips and his greedy hands drove me closer to the edge once again. Harrison was a Sex God. I was sure of it. Another orgasm prickled at the base of my spine, but he wouldn't touch me where I needed it most.

"Harrison," I pleaded.

"Patience." He nipped my skin in rebuke.

Lifting my legs, he removed my underwear and spread me wide open before giving me a wolfish grin and teasing me again with his tongue. He made me feel desired, sexy, and dirty—a lethal combination.

His hands and tongue drove me wild until I burned from the inside. Desperation clung to me, wild and unyielding, and only he could satisfy it.

"Harrison, I need you...please, just..." I begged, reaching for him and trying again to drag him up my body.

"What do you need, Becca? Say it."

"You."

He paused his tongue and stared hard at me. "I can get you off with my mouth and fingers all day. I'd love to just do that."

I shook my head, frustration making me dig my nails into his arm. "Not enough."

"Greedy girl," he said, his tone indicating his pleasure. "You stay in this position for thirty seconds. Don't move." Standing up, he left my side and ran across the floor.

I remained like he'd asked, naked and ready for him. Normally, I'd panic and cover up. But not now, not with him. I felt alive.

"God, you're a sight." He returned with a condom, wasting no time in falling back on the mattress. "You're sure this is what you want, Becca?"

I bit my lip and nodded, pulling him closer. "I want you—I need to feel all of you."

"Damn," he groaned and removed his sweats.

He was hard as hell, and I gulped at his length. It made sense. He was one of the largest guys I knew, but I'd had no idea how much I wanted this experience with him until now.

I held my hand out to him. "Let me put it on."

He handed me the condom, his heaving chest matching my own.

"Wow, Harrison." I ran my hand over his thick shaft, drunk on power and need.

After ripping open the foil, I rolled the condom over his length and then moved my gaze back up to his. Our eyes met, and he unleashed the sexiest growl. I'd never wanted anything more in that moment than to see Harrison lose control.

He lifted me onto his lap, the hunger in his eyes matching my own. "You take your time letting me fit you, okay?"

Had anyone ever said those words to me before? Never. He gave me all the power, and damn, I loved it.

I lowered myself onto him, taking him inside me an inch at a time while I adjusted to his size. His gaze never left mine as I hissed—his cock was huge, thick, and ready for me.

"Wow." Completely seated now, I swallowed and tentatively rocked my hips.

"Yeah," he grunted. "You're tight as hell. It's...fuck, it's good."

He gripped my waist, his jaw tight as I rode him. His gaze never left mine as we found our rhythm together— slow, steady, new. His eyes darkened, and he changed the angle, hitting me deeper. Harder.

He slammed his mouth against mine, kissing me with so much fervor that dizziness washed over me at all the sensations and smells around us. The smell of his skin...the feel of his razor stubble...the taste of my desire on his tongue. It was all so hot.

"Fuck." He squeezed my butt before moving his hands over my skin, kneading my flesh as sweat pooled between our chests.

The familiar tingling started at the base of my spine. "Harrison," I moaned.

Understanding my need, he brought his fingers to my clit and added pressure. The tingling grew stronger. I gripped his shoulders, digging my nails into him. He guided me with one hand on my hip, setting the pace he wanted, and I dug into him harder. Faster.

I was so close. He quickened the pace of his finger, and a second orgasm exploded over me.

"Yes," I yelled, riding it out and loving his eyes on me as he watched me come—like my pleasure turned him on. Like it mattered.

He sucked my tongue as I moaned and rode out the spasms. I caught my breath, and his grip on me tightened. Then, flipping me onto my back, he stared down at me with hungry eyes.

"Goddamn." He pressed his face into my shoulder. "You're so fucking hot, Becca. Wrap your legs around me."

I did and held on. His control snapped, and Harrison *took* me. I closed my eyes and gripped his firm ass. Thrills shot through me as his muscles clenched. His breathing quickened. This wasn't sexy or slow, it was rough and animalistic. My body hummed, and I arched my hips, taking more of him, wanting everything he gave me.

"Fuck," he moaned, his thrusts slowing until he trembled.

"I'm coming, shit." His chest rumbled with a deep sigh of pleasure.

I wanted to bottle up that sound. It was so dirty and sexy. *I slept with Harrison Cooper.*

Holding himself up on his elbows, he pressed one kiss right in the center of my chest before rolling off and settling next to me on his back with his chest heaving. "Damn."

"Uh-huh." My heart raced like I'd sprinted a 5k.

As his breathing evened and my heart rate slowed, the high of being with him dissipated. Now my thoughts entered. *Not good.*

He reached over and set his hand on my hip, patting it. "You okay?"

"Yes." My voice sounded off. "I should clean up and put clothes on."

"Becs?"

"Yeah?" My face heated, and I had trouble keeping eye contact.

"No going shy on me." Tight lines formed around his lips.

"Okay."

"I mean it, Becca." He squeezed my forearm, his lips hinting at a smile. "This was the best morning I've had in a long time, and I don't want to assume, but I hope you enjoyed it, too."

I swallowed my doubt and forced a fake smile. I did enjoy it, but I wondered if I'd made a horrible mistake. Getting hurt again wasn't in my plan. But I kept those thoughts to myself.

"Of course." I nodded. "Yeah, me too."

"Want me to make some breakfast?"

"Sure, yeah." My face heated as I pulled my shirt over my head. There was no dignified way to redress myself. "Can I use the shower?"

"Absolutely." His tone held a twinge of concern. "There should be enough stored warm water for a quick one."

I nodded. With my clothes bundled in my hands, I ran to his shower and turned it on. I didn't want to waste any warm water, so I washed everything as fast as I could. I didn't wash my hair because it would freeze—and it was then everything hit me.

We slept together.

This was outside my comfort zone in so many ways that it scared me. No playbook could guide me through this situation.

It's just a fling. A blizzard-buddy fling. I repeated the words in my head as I braced myself to face him. I would do it. Be casual and flingy and cool. Yeah, for sure. I just had to make sure my mind, heart, and hormones all stayed on the same page. Easy-peasy.

CHAPTER TWELVE

HARRISON

The tension in my neck had subsided, and my body relaxed more today than it had in weeks. I usually worked out hard for a few hours to even feel a little bit of peace. The thought of going downstairs to lift weights didn't even cross my mind. Who the fuck was I?

Is this because of Becca? Because of getting laid? Is that all I'd needed?

Focusing on the task of cooking, my mind replayed the event, overanalyzing it like a football game. What worked well, what I could do better next time. Because, damn, I wanted there to be a next time. Smiling to myself, I schooled my features as soft footsteps entered the kitchen.

Becca wore yoga pants, bright pink boots, and a multicolored sweater and had wrapped herself in one of the blankets. "You look like a rainbow threw up."

"Thank you." She masked her face into indifference and

sat at the kitchen table, her posture too straight. "You seem to be in a good mood."

"I am." I shrugged and gave her a sheepish look. "I have a beautiful woman in my house, I'm about to eat, and I've regained feeling in all my body parts. What's there to be glum about?"

"Ah, with a cheery outlook like that, it's crazy to think I used to think of you as being a grump."

"A grump?" My interest piqued. "Care to expand?"

She blushed as she cracked her knuckles, her gaze on the tabletop. "You never really smile on campus. I used to think it was just me. You know, the whole date-that-went-wrong thing. But the girls noticed, too. If we had the game on TV, you had a deep frown on your face. Made you seem very intimidating and unapproachable."

Irritation crept over me. "Again, the date didn't go wrong. It was great, and we've established I'm an ass. And the smiling thing, do you mean in passing?"

"Yes, but also all the time. Seeing you in your truck, when you're coaching, or even a casual walk-by on the quad. You have this sullen handsome-guy-who's-unhappy look about you."

Am I unhappy?

What does happy even mean? I scratched my chin, focusing on the eggs instead of her words. This wasn't a casual conversation. This felt deeper, and it didn't sit well with me. Had anyone ever called me a grump before? Or unhappy?

My sister calls me an asshole.

My parents say I'm not as enjoyable as dear Hank.

My ex said I enjoyed being miserable.

My players said I wasn't approachable.

Huh. Grump was the nicest way to say all the above. Something Becca had said earlier came back to my mind, and I schooled my tone so it wasn't too intense. "Is this what you meant when you said I always looked down on you when you were with the girls?"

"Oh. Right." She winced. "Yeah, actually. Since the date, I've run into you with the girls probably four times. Once, we were wearing matching shirts on the way to a philanthropy event, and you had this angry expression on your face. It made me feel silly for about a second."

"Becca—"

"No, it's okay. It was only a second because I love what I do and I'm proud of who I am." She placed the palms of her hands on the table, her chest puffed out.

She really was proud, and that loosened something tight in my chest.

"You should be proud." I flipped the eggs and sighed, remembering the day she mentioned. She'd worn a hot pink tank top that showed off her curves, and she'd had the biggest smile on her face. I was jealous.

I gripped the back of my neck, kneading the stress for a beat. "My ex-wife caused me issues that morning, asking for more money. Then I saw you, so happy and beautiful with those girls who love you. It reminded me of what I didn't have. The team has had a rough couple of years. We aren't a *team* in the truest sense."

"What do you mean?"

"A team is all of us working toward the same goal." I shook my head, remembering how one captain was set on going to the NFL and didn't care about anyone else's stats but his own. Or how another junior on the team didn't give a shit about his grades. Or how two seniors cared more about getting high than working out. "They show up for practices and games, but it's like they're going through the motions. Their souls aren't in it."

She played with the hem of her shirt, a deep line between her eyebrows. "What's the goal for the team?"

"Hmm?" Tilting my head, I studied her eyes.

"You said their souls aren't in it and a team should be working toward the same goal. So, Coach Cooper, what is the goal?"

I blinked, startled that the answer wasn't at the tip of my tongue. "To win games sounds too obvious."

She flashed a quick grin. "I'm sure that's at least a subgoal."

Gripping the back of my neck, I sighed. "I got into coaching to help develop strong players who were decent humans. Winning games takes time, dedication, and teamwork, and this group of players is missing the drive. I don't...I lost it somewhere."

My stomach ached with the fact that this was on me. I was the head coach. Admitting the issue to her, saying it out loud to the world, freed me of the weight I'd carried around alone. I couldn't stop. "I'm sure you've heard rumors. This could very well be my last season as the head coach. But you and the girls...you were all a family. I was jealous at how close you were."

"Jealous? Of me?" She snorted, her brown eyes widening.

"I don't think those words have ever been said in the universe. I'm not someone to envy."

"I'm sure they have, Becca." I put our food on the plates and added some seasoning from the cupboard. "Look at you. You're living the life you want with a huge smile. You have a house full of young women who respect you. That's cause for jealousy."

She frowned and sucked her bottom lip into her mouth, her forehead furrowing as she studied me. I would've given any amount of money to know what was going through her head.

"Harrison," she said, softly. Her fingers tapped on the table in a pattern, like she was nervous.

"Hmm?"

"You can fix this, you know." She smiled.

I tilted my head. "What do you mean?"

"Leading a house full of women isn't easy, nor is it something that just comes naturally. I studied and read about leadership. A lot, actually." She sat up straighter. "We start every family meeting with our why, our purpose. Do you?"

I shook my head. "No."

"You should. Everything we do reflects on our goal, to be better citizens and the best versions of ourselves." She held up her fingers, counting. "That means being good students and setting a GPA expectation. That means volunteering in the community. That means setting personal goals and reflecting. That means being healthy. Even if we design a matching shirt that takes way too much time, it's about unity, about feeling like you belong."

Could I do that? Would the guys buy into it? Grimacing, I ran a hand over my face. It couldn't hurt to try, right? Reflecting on how I lead the team didn't paint the best picture. We worked hard, but was working hard as individuals the same as working hard together? My mind raced, grasping the different pieces of my job. The players, the game plays, the opponents, scouting, winning. When did I forget the core of coaching was shaping them into men?

I was often comfortable sitting in silence but the loudness of my thoughts distracted me. There was one simple answer from Becca's statement. "I need a team vision."

"That is more than just winning."

"Yes."

Her answering smile knocked the wind out of me. Her eyes filled with pride, and the warm sensation brewing in my chest grew. I liked seeing that look on her face. "I can work on that. You," I pointed at her, "are amazing."

Her smile grew. "That might be the nicest thing someone could say to me. I get mocked constantly for what I do."

Irritation flushed through me. This thoughtful, intelligent woman was mocked for her career? Unacceptable.

She took a bite of food and moaned.

Damn, that sound was a distraction. I forced myself to focus on the topic of conversation.

"It's easy to assume a lot about me in my role as a house mom," she continued. "Some think I'm not very bright, or that I'm easy. My least favorite assumption is that I'm an old party girl and use my job to sleep around with frat guys."

"People say this to you . . . on dates?" My skin heated with anger. "Seriously?"

"Um, yes." She shrugged. "Sometimes not in so many words. It's hinted, and I don't bite so they push harder. The guys my mom sets me up with are a little better than the winners I've found on dating apps, but they aren't the right ones for me, either. It's exhausting, if I'm honest. My mom had a bad first marriage and credits my dad for giving her the life she'd always wanted. She has that hope for me—that finding my guy is the answer. What she doesn't understand, though, is that I'm happy with my life. You know? Dating or having a partner doesn't equate to being happier."

A million questions ran through my mind. *Did she punch these dudes in the face? Who is the right guy for her? Can I make her happy?*

I cleared my throat and shoved eggs into my mouth before I said anything stupid, but I was consumed with guilt. I'd called her high-maintenance. I took her beauty and friendliness as meaning she'd be too much work. Even in the short time we'd spent together, I grew to enjoy how well she communicated, how she made her stories come to life. I'd made assumptions, just like the others, and I regretted it.

"Listen, Becca, I hope you know you're not high-maintenance. I'm sorry I assumed."

"You've apologized, and I've decided to forgive you."

She gave me a shy smile, and my chest tightened. I scratched at it.

"Plus, though you might've hurt my feelings for a bit,

you were still a gentleman the whole night. You wouldn't even rank in the top ten worst dates, Champ." She patted my forearm and went back to her food. "Enough about me. I want to know about you. Do you date? Are they awful? Why do you think you're going to get fired?"

"That is a lot of questions."

"Well, I haven't been in this position before, and I think it would be good to get to know you. Who knows how long we might be stuck together without power? Maybe we can even be friends after this *snow-pocalypse blizzard-buddy fling* we agreed to."

Friends?

We'd slept together, and I enjoyed the sounds she made when she orgasmed. That didn't seem friendly to me, but if that was how she wanted to play it, then I'd keep quiet. I'd already hurt her enough by saying the wrong things once. Plus, what else would we be besides friends?

I had no idea, but I knew I wanted more with her.

"Ah, well." I frowned, reflecting on my dating life. "I don't really date. Maybe a couple times a year, if that."

"Really? How come?" Her eyes grew wide, and her voice was pitched high. "You're such an eligible bachelor!"

"Thank you?" I laughed at her expression and arched a brow. "You did say I was a grump, though."

"Yeah, but that won't keep women away. It's part of the mystery." She waved a hand like it was no big deal. "You're a football coach and wear tight pants on the field."

"You've looked then?"

"Obviously." She grinned and rested her chin on her

hand. "So why don't you date? Are you a forever-bachelor since getting divorced?"

"I don't think so." I scratched my chest again. "It's more…I don't have time to put effort into dating someone. An occasional dinner or drinks, sure. But a commitment? All my time is spent coaching. Whether it's coming up with the best practice plans, watching old tapes to see what went wrong, or recruiting players—from summer until about now, I live and breathe football. The team will always come first. That's not fair to anyone."

"If your partner understood your passion for it, I think they'd be flexible. My mom always says that if someone wanted to make time for you, they would, no matter what their excuses were. I believe it."

"I'm not hopeless then?" I leaned closer, waiting for her answer but not sure why what she thought mattered so much. But it did.

"Of course not." She tilted her head, her eyes narrowing. "You mentioned you might get fired. Why? The girls tell me you've had a great record."

I rubbed my temples—the question stung. I slacked in building a solid team foundation, while my brother had built a winning team. He was in the bowl game, I was not. "We didn't perform as well as expected this year despite the raw talent."

"But isn't the team young?"

"Sure, but it's not a reason. We were projected to go further in our division, and we didn't." I stood, grabbing our empty paper plates and tossing them away.

I want a drink.

Leaning against the kitchen counter, I closed my eyes and found the words kept spilling out. "Last I heard, some of our big players are smoking dope and partying their faces off. That's not what you do if you're a serious athlete."

"It's what you do when you're a dumb college kid learning how to balance the fame of being on the team and being on your own for the first time, though. Think about when you were in college. There is no way you were perfect and never broke the rules. What did *you* do?"

"I went to the gym every day to get bigger, faster, and better." I pushed off the counter and crossed my arms over my chest. Becca remained at the table with her expression cheery, and the bitterness crept up my throat. "I took it seriously because I had goals."

"Then you're not the norm. College boys are stupid, and I mean that in the nicest way possible. You're saying you never let loose on the weekends with a couple of drinks? You didn't hook up with girls who gave you flirty looks? I bet a dollar you did, Harrison."

"Sure, I hooked up with chicks and drank a bit, but never enough to affect my game. Our coach would've benched us."

"Then why don't you bench them?" She crossed one leg over the other, putting her colorful boots on display. "Set your team vision and make expectations clear. Invest in who they are as people, Coach Cooper. That means meeting them where they are. I won't pretend I know anything about sports; I always tried to get out of PE class. But if the girls in the house ever acted up and went against the contract they'd signed, I'd revoke any and all privileges. No question. Can you do the same on the field?"

I sighed at her sound logic. "These guys get full rides. They expect to play. The talent is there. It's just..." I stopped, unsure how to describe the missing piece.

"I understand football is the biggest moneymaker for the school and all, but don't you get to decide who plays and who doesn't? Who else will help form these athletes into decent human beings?" She scrunched her nose and released a nervous laugh. "But what do I know? I think I'm going to try to read while we have some natural light."

I didn't respond before she left me in the kitchen. The conversation was a ping-pong game. She had a solution for my problems, and it irked me that I didn't think of this before. Was I so caught up in jealousy over Hank that my head was in my ass? She said invest in people, in my players.

In the beginning of my career, I made team outings mandatory. They were a pain in the ass to plan and took so much time, but looking back, they worked. When was the last time I did that? Years? Groaning, I pinched the bridge of my nose. The truth of the matter hit me in the face like the wind hitting the windows: I had to be the leader I wanted my players to become.

My neighbor with a body of a goddess was full of surprises, and for the first time, I wanted to talk more when she wanted the silence.

For as loud as her colors and personality were, Becca was quiet as the day went on. I was used to stillness, so every little sigh or crinkling of pages turning reminded me that she was very much here. The temperatures still rocked forty below. Thankfully, the fireplace was large and kept the first two rooms in the house warm.

"Hey, Harrison?" Becca asked a couple hours after breakfast.

"Yeah?" I looked up from the book I'd been reading. She suggested one of her books, *Factfulness*, which showed how the world really wasn't as bad as the news suggested. I tried not to take the recommendation personally.

"Do you think the sorority house is okay? I keep imagining windows breaking. The girls probably didn't clean their rooms or remove stuff near the windows. I'd hate for them to lose anything." She looked at me over the spine of her book, concern etched on her face. "I know we shouldn't leave your house for any reason, but do you think it'll be safe tomorrow?"

"It seems like the wind is settling down a bit. We can listen to the radio this afternoon and get an update. If it starts to clear up, we can take a trip over there to check."

"Okay, good." She stared out the window and clicked her tongue. "It's insane how white it is. Do you have a snowblower? Would that even work? Would shoveling even help? It seems too high."

"Great question." I glanced out the window and studied the snowdrifts that had piled up. Some were easily over six feet high and completely covered the fence in the backyard. "Might take a good week or so for it to melt. Damn good thing this hit after most of the students left."

She paled. "Holy moly, you're right. Could you imagine all the dorms out of power? The girls in the house?" She winced. "It would be awful! I'm so glad they aren't here."

"I'm assuming the school has emergency generators or would move everyone into the library or something." I shook my head, imagining how much of a disaster it would've been if the storm hit a week ago with campus at its highest population.

Becca stood and walked over to the window, her gaze now focused outside. "I have a shovel that I could use on our small sidewalk, but I don't think it'd help much."

"Becca, I can help you get the house ready for when the girls get back, if that's what you're worried about."

"You wouldn't mind? Really?" Turning back toward me, surprise registered on her face before it transformed into a warm smile.

"I wouldn't mind at all." I returned her smile and had an inexplicable urge to make more promises to her. "We can barter a couple cups of your hot chocolate for payment."

"That I can get behind! Thank you, Harrison. It takes away a little of my anxiety. Well, except the fact the snow-drifts could be six feet high and block the doors."

She rubbed her bottom lip with her pointer finger, drawing my attention to her mouth. My blood headed south. *Am I a damn teenager?*

"We can try different points of entry." Joining her at the window, I placed my hand over hers. "Don't worry, okay? We'll figure it out."

She gave me that warm smile again—the kind of smile very few people directed my way—and I craved more. There was no pity or disdain in her eyes. Just...happiness. No wonder the girls liked her so much. After spending one day with her, I'd do anything she asked of me.

She placed the back of her hand theatrically against her forehead. "My dear sir! Why the ladies would just fawn all over you if they knew how kind you are," she said, faking a Southern accent.

My lips quirked. "Yeah? Are you one of them?"

She blushed and then dropped her gaze to the ground for a second before lifting her head and flashing me a playful smile. Her eyes glinted with mischief. "Do you want me to be?"

Yes. Maybe. I don't know. Before I could decide, my phone blared from the counter and the moment was broken. *Damn it.*

I let out a frustrated sigh before picking up my phone and sliding my finger across the screen. "Hey, Mom."

"Blair said you two are celebrating the holidays at her house in Illinois. Is that true? Don't you think it's a little selfish? You should at least try to be with family to celebrate your brother's success."

CHAPTER THIRTEEN

BECCA

It was fascinating how fast the walls around Harrison reconstructed themselves. The second he answered his phone, his demeanor did a one-eighty. Gone were the relaxed shoulders and half-smile I loved, and instead, his entire body went taut.

Is it me?

His mom?

My book didn't provide the distraction it should've as I eavesdropped on one side of a clearly heated conversation.

Harrison paced the hallway, each footstep echoing across the wood. "Take it you haven't heard about the weather we're getting here?"

A woman's voice crackled over the phone, and he clenched his fist against his thigh. "I'm going to Blair's. There isn't more to say."

His voice changed, now holding a bitter and angry tone

I hadn't heard before. I sat up straighter. *Have I ever spoken to my mother that way?* Probably as a teenager, but this was a grown man who had strong feelings. I desperately wanted to know why.

"Go be with Hank. We all know you'd rather see him, so cut the bullshit and stop trying to guilt me into something I physically can't do." He disconnected the call and stood with his back toward me.

"You drink whiskey, Becca?" he asked, his voice hard and angry. "I'm getting one."

"Uh." I thought of ten different reasons why I should say no, but none of them made sense. He wanted a drinking buddy, and I liked the taste of whiskey. I rarely drank so this could be fun. "Sure. I'd love one."

"Great." He bustled around the kitchen for several minutes before bringing me a small glass with amber liquid and two large cubes. His eyes held the same sad and angry expression they'd taken on during his phone conversation. I wanted to ask what had happened, but that crossed the line. He'd either share, or not. I bit my tongue to prevent the question from slipping out. Not probing went against every gene in my DNA.

Harrison dropped onto the couch and then took a long sip without a single wince. *Impressive.* I smelled the rich liquor before taking my own tiny sip and cringing at the strength of it, setting my glass beside me on a coaster.

"Don't like it?"

"No. No. I do. It's strong." The tension in the room made me tense. Though I knew it wasn't directed at me, as an empath I absorbed the feelings of everyone around me, and I hated it. My gut yelled at me to *Fill the silence!*

"I don't drink often. You know—with the girls, I'm always on call. Could you imagine me showing up at the hospital drunk? It would make the news!" I swallowed another sip like a badass, refusing to wince. "When I do let loose, I like a nice margarita. A little fruit, a little salt, and a few tingles down my body. That's my favorite."

"Are you nervous? You talk a lot when you're nervous. I'd hoped we were beyond that." He frowned before holding my gaze and taking another long drink. "You also don't have to drink it if you don't like it."

"I'm not nervous. Well, maybe a little." I held the drink closer to my chest. "You can't drink alone. That's a rule. I'm drinking with you and totally not thinking of the millions of questions I have."

"You can ask me anything." He slung his arm over the back of the couch, his attention solely on me. "What's on your mind?"

"Uh, how's the family?" Flustered by his complete focus, my voice pitched way too high and my words tumbled out like a squeak.

He bared his teeth in something resembling a smile before taking another long sip. "Ah, yes. My mother." His gaze roamed over my face, lingering on my lips for a second, before he let out a sigh. "She wants me to feel bad for not flying out to California tomorrow."

Wait, what? "That makes no sense. The airports are shut down for the weather."

"Yeah." He let out a bitter laugh.

"She doesn't like the fact you're going to your sister's?"

"Correct. I mentioned Blair and I are close, and my mom isn't a fan because that leaves her youngest son out. Hank is..." He stopped and pinched the bridge of his nose. "Hank isn't a bad guy. We have different definitions of what hard work is. He's an entitled prick, and my parents enable that behavior. But Blair and I see through his charade and call him out."

"Surely, they all understand why you can't go visit him, though? The blizzard has knocked out half our state."

He made a *no shit* face and shrugged. "Doesn't matter. He coaches university football, too, and his team made it to the bowl championship next week. Instead of my parents traveling to see my sister and her three young children for Christmas, they want us all to fly out a week early to support Hank."

Harrison Cooper had layers. I would need six blizzards to figure them all out. I took a bigger sip, this time not wincing, and enjoyed the slight numbness it gave my throat. Maybe there was a reason for a drink this strong. Hmm.

I refocused on his strained shoulders. "Okay. I'm confused. They didn't want to spend the holidays with their grandchildren?"

"Correct. They sent presents, which they felt was enough. Because Hank did something on his own for the first time in his life and the world should stop and celebrate him." He downed the last of his glass and slammed it on the side table. "I know you're thinking I'm a grown man and shouldn't have parent issues. It's pathetic. But you know what my parents did when I played in my first bowl? Nothing. They didn't fly out because Hank was still in high school and had a baseball game. A *rec-league* baseball game."

"No." I scooted closer to him and patted his thigh. "I don't think it's pathetic. I'm sorry you've had these experiences."

He stared at my hand for a beat before relaxing. "I get in a real shitty mood whenever I talk to my mom. She has this unique talent for making me feel like everything is my fault. Catholic guilt is real."

I smiled. "Parents must learn that skill in parenting school."

"Parenting school?" He laughed, scrubbing his palms over his eyes. "This is embarrassing."

"No, it's not." I took another sip and found the taste not so bad anymore. "I would feel pretty awful if those things happened to me. My parents might view finding the perfect guy as the only way to find happiness—which is annoying—but they've never made me feel like I wasn't a priority. Thinking about them doing something like that hurts."

"You're lucky."

"I know I am." I frowned, thinking about his situation. "I still don't understand why they wouldn't want to see you or your sister before flying out there, especially if the game isn't until next week. They could've stopped here for two days at least."

"Story of my life, Becca. I invited them, and they said it was too much. I stopped trying to understand their actions. I'd probably stop talking to them if it weren't for Blair. She's by far the best child they have."

His phone rang, and glancing at the screen, his face relaxed into a smile before he swiped his finger to answer. "Speaking of you," he said into the phone while keeping his eyes on me. "Yup, she called me too and laid it on thick as hell."

He nodded a couple of times and then laughed. "Oh yeah, I forgot to mention my next-door neighbor is staying with me until this snowstorm passes."

He glanced out the window, agreeing with whatever she said before his tone changed. "You wouldn't mind if she came along for Christmas, would you? No? Great!"

My stomach bottomed out. I usually spent the holiday with my parents—just the three of us. Did I want to go with him to see his family? Maybe? I took another swig and coughed. *Rats.* There went my cool points.

Harrison hung up and patted my back a couple of times. "You okay, Becca?"

His eyes are so pretty. Like an evergreen forest. Oh, I love forests.

"Becca?" He lowered his voice. "Hey, do you need anything?"

"Sorry, I choked on the strong libation." Feeling idiotic for using the word *libation*, my face heated.

Harrison smiled and shook his head. "Glad you're okay."

"Listen…" I began, hoping the words would naturally come to me. It took a second, but I found them. *Whiskey messing with my mind, eh?* "Uh, the holidays. I can't go to your sister's. Because of reasons."

"What reasons?" He furrowed those dark brows,

I wondered if those brows were soft or not. I bet they

were soft. If I reached over, I could find out for sure. Like a caterpillar.

Focus, Becs!

"I can't," I said again.

"We're paired up this week, though." His voice held a hint of worry.

"But my parents—I always spend it with them." I chewed the corner of my lip, anxious at the turn of conversation.

Seeing his family was totally outside the blizzard-buddy contract. Oh, we should've made one. That would've spelled out the rules, making it easier for me to keep things straight. Dang.

I studied my neighbor, admiring his strong jaw. His two-day beard growth gave him a rougher and sexier look than the man I'd known as my neighbor. His lips moved but I was too focused on his beard, or his eyebrows, or both to understand what he'd said.

"Hmm?" I hoped I sounded flippant and cool and not spacey. Was I spacey? No. Why are my thoughts like snow-flakes then? Just blowing around without patterns?

"You said your parents live a couple hours out of town, right? Not sure you can make it there this week."

I nodded, and his gaze went to the window. *The weather.* "I forgot about the roads."

"Yeah. It wouldn't be safe driving beyond town. My sister is fifteen minutes away max, and we can take it real slow with my truck. But no pressure. I realize I asked her without inviting you first. You don't have to go. Hell, I can stay here with you if you're uncomfortable."

The insides of my belly did the swoopy thing again, and I blamed that on the alcohol. That had to be the reason my thoughts were incoherent. "You need to visit your sister, Harrison. I can hang out here."

"Do you like cookies, chaos, and carols?"

Of course I freaking did. "Yes? I am a human."

"Then come. You'd like my sister and her three hooligans. It'll be relaxing, and she's a hell of a cook."

He wiggled his brows and I couldn't stop myself from giggling. Cute Harrison in his Henley was dangerous in all caps. HILARIOUS-HOT-HENLEY HARRISON.

I had to tell the girls.

Wait, no, I couldn't. Well, maybe. I'd think about it later when my brain wasn't spinning in circles.

"So is that a yes?" He smiled as his gaze moved across my face.

We're talking about Christmas, not his nickname. "Assuming I can't drive to my parents', then yes."

"Great!" He clapped his hands, smiling with so much joy on his face that I grinned hard.

"I don't want you to miss time with your family, but I'm looking forward to spending the day with you at Blair's. You'll fit right in." He stood and pointed to my glass. "Another? It's going to be another cold and long night."

Cold meant snuggles, and snuggles meant touching, and touching meant getting naked. Butterflies erupted in my stomach, and I nodded. "What the heck. Sure."

"I do appreciate a positive attitude."

I snorted and studied his bookshelf as he made more

drinks. Maybe it was the extra layers I'd worn all day or the whiskey, but my body was much warmer than the day before. I took no shame in watching his butt as he put more wood on the fire. It was firm, like Captain America's, and my fingers itched to squeeze it.

"Oh lord, am I tipsy? Is that why my mouth tickles?"

"Are you?" He gave me a goofy grin. "I didn't know one drink would go to your head. Let me get you some water."

I brought the glass to my mouth again. "I was thinking about warmth and your ass, and I realized my mind feels great."

Once again, I'd lost my filter—this time thanks to the whiskey. It was nowhere in sight, and words flowed straight from my brain to my lips. "You were grumpy earlier. Is it always because of your family? You shouldn't put too much stock in their opinion if it upsets you. If you're happy with yourself, then screw the rest of the noise. To hell with them, I say!"

"Are you always this bold after one drink?" He cupped my face with one of his hands.

I beamed at him.

He chuckled, the sound deep and wonderful. "It's kinda cute."

"Ah, yes. A woman's favorite word." I jerked out of his hand and collapsed onto the mattress faceup.

"*Cute.*" I scoffed. "I'm *cute*, like a button. Not sexy, or alluring, or someone you take home to parents—because I'm a glorified babysitter for a sorority. I'm the girl who buys the Jell-O for wrestling when we're fundraising or need money for matching shirts. *Cute*, as in the girl you take for happy hours and pity dates."

A boulder lifted from my shoulders as I released all the locked-up words. Sure, he wasn't one of the horrible dates who used *cute* like an insult, but unleashing my anger at him was invigorating.

I narrowed my eyes and pointed a finger at Harrison. "You, sir, probably don't date the *cute* ladies. You date the va-va-voom ladies."

"I have no idea what the hell a *va-va-voom* lady is." He covered his mouth with his hand. "But you are incredible."

"Does my face feel hot to you?" Sitting up, I grabbed his hand and placed it on my forehead. "I don't know if it's because I was thinking about squeezing your butt, or if it's the fire, or the whiskey. I'm not sure how to figure it out."

"You can squeeze my ass if you want, but I get a turn, too. I'm an ass-squeezing equal opportunist." His eyes twinkled with amusement.

"Stand up and turn around," I demanded.

"I will, but first, you should drink water and eat." He patted my knee and twisted the cap off the water bottle. "I had no idea you were a lightweight."

"We learn something new every day, Champ. I tell you what, I found out the other day that yonic is the female version of phallic. One of the girls put on some weird show and *Bam!*—they were talking about vaginas. Who knew *yonic* was a word? It sounds like sonic." I shrugged and took the water from him, gulping it down and spilling a little on my chest. "Those flower vagina paintings...one could say they were yonic. Remember that if you ever need to impress someone."

He smiled, showcasing two beautiful dimples, and I reached out and put a finger in each one. "You might be the handsomest man, Harrison Cooper."

"You, Becca, are most definitely the most entertaining person I know. Most beautiful and least boring are up for grabs, too." He placed his hands over mine and held them like that for a good ten seconds.

My throat closed up, and my head spun. I wanted to confess that I liked him. Like it was seventh grade and I wanted Matt to know I had a crush on him. But this was different. And weirder. We weren't in junior high anymore, and he'd ghosted me once. He'd apologized but he didn't date. He dated football, he'd said.

Liking him was out of the question. It didn't align with my head or the blizzard-buddy plan.

"I'm gonna prepare some food. You keep your cute butt here." He released me and gave my wrist a light squeeze before heading into the kitchen.

Food sounded great after getting what the girls called *the spins*, and I scowled at the whiskey glass. Whiskey was the real villain of the story.

Jerk face.

"You're dangerous." I glared at the glass.

"You talking to the whiskey or...?"

"Yes." I nodded, unashamed. "He's dangerous with his smooth taste and honey-colored looks. He's a lot like you."

Harrison arched a brow and handed me a bunch of

crackers. "I don't recall you getting this buzzed from a glass of wine."

"Wine is in my blood. Whiskey is not." I shoved a couple crackers into my mouth, making sure I kept my mouth closed as I chewed. Loud-mouth eaters should be banned from eating, and I refused to be one of them. "Thanks for the snack."

"Eat more."

He watched me as I ate more crackers, finished an entire bottle of water, *and* an entire bag of chips. It wasn't my sexiest moment. But to be fair, the bag was only half-full.

"Wow, I feel like my brain is back in its rightful place." I relaxed onto the mattress and snuck a glance at Harrison. His hair had fallen over his forehead and one dimple teased the side of his face. God, he was so pretty and rough. But it was the playful smirk that had my heart racing.

"Did I entertain you?"

"Wildly." He trailed his fingers down my jaw and over my neck before resting them on my shoulder. "Hate to say it, but you're officially cut off from the whiskey."

"That's fair." I laughed, but regret was already setting in as my buzz disappeared. *The things I said! How horrifying!* "So about the ass thing…"

"What about it?" He practically bounced with amusement.

I shoved him, and he fell to the mattress, yanking me with him so I landed on his chest. Gliding his hands from my arms to my waist, he teased the waistline of my sweatpants before slipping his hands inside and grabbing both of my butt cheeks. "You're sure you're feeling okay?"

"Yup." I ground into him as he kneaded my skin.

Blizzard buddy. No feelings. JUST SEX. I mentally yelled the words to myself in all caps.

Heat spread to my core, and without discussing our expiration date, I wanted to take advantage. "Don't get too carried away yet. I want time to explore *you*."

"Yeah?" His lips moved toward mine, the hint of whiskey on his breath enticing me. "How about this? I get ten minutes massaging you, and if you haven't come by then, you can take a turn on me."

I gulped, my body burning hot at his words. "I go first."

"That is my intention, Becca. I want to make you come first."

CHAPTER FOURTEEN

Harrison

Becca's back was sexy with the perfect combination of muscles and curves. When had I ever been this fascinated by a woman? It wasn't just her body though; her personality and insight were incredible. I trailed my fingers over her bare spine, continuing toward her ass, and pressed lightly on the two dimples at the base. She squirmed beneath me, and I chuckled. "Does this feel alright?"

"Yes," she said, her words muffled by the pillow. "Eight minutes left, buddy."

Buddy? Oh, hell no.

While I appreciated her desperation to touch and explore my body, this was about making her feel good. She had no idea what her positivity and advice did to me. It woke up a part of me that had been dormant for a while.

"Eight minutes is plenty of time to make you feel good." I brought my hands back up to her waist and teased her sides.

Biting down on her earlobe, I massaged her neck. "You

respond so well when I kiss you here and touch you there."
I teased the sides of her breasts, licking and biting her neck
until she whimpered. "What happens if I slide my fingers
inside you? Will you be wet?"

She moaned into the pillow, arching her back as I slid
a finger inside her. Finding her wet, I smiled and nipped
my way down her back. I trembled at the thought of being
inside her again. *She's so hot. So sweet.* "Goddamn it, Becca."

"What?"

"You're driving me wild." I slid two fingers inside her,
finding a rhythm. She matched it by rocking her hips.

With my lips, I admired her strong and curvy body, trailing my kisses over her soft skin and stopping momentarily
when I reached the small tattoo on her hip. Bending low, I
sank my teeth into the tender flesh over the ink.

She yelped. "Did you just...bite me?" Her eyes wide, she
gazed at me over her shoulder. "You did."

"Yup." I moved my fingers—in and out, in and out—
until she clenched around them. Stimulating her clit with
my thumb, I swiped my tongue over the mark. "I fucking
love this tattoo."

"I...I forgot about...that." She panted.

I loved how she couldn't focus or straighten out her
thoughts when I touched her. I slowed down, damn well
intent on using every second of my remaining time wisely.
"You're so sexy right now. Your muscles get all tight when
you're seconds away from orgasm, and you make these little
sounds in the back of your throat. I could watch you like
this for hours."

"*Oh my God.*" She bucked against me, her ass moving up and down as she ground against my hand. "Harrison...yes."

It was deliciously hot, and I wanted nothing more than to bury myself inside her. But right now, she came first. "That's my girl...ride it out."

She did. She rocked fast, her muscles spasming and her pussy tightening around my fingers. Just like in everything else she did, Becca was a passionate woman. She writhed on my hand for another minute before spinning onto her back and looking up at me with hazy eyes. "I'm tingling again."

"From me, I hope, and not whiskey."

She grinned up at me, her cheeks red and her eyes heated. She twisted her finger, signaling me to turn around. "My turn."

"You get five minutes before I take you."

"Five minutes, huh?" She crawled toward me and removed my shirt. My pants followed, and I was completely naked before her. Reaching toward me, she wrapped her fingers around my shaft and gave it a couple of light pumps. "Five minutes is plenty of time to make you come."

I stopped her wrist. "I want to be inside of you when I come."

"Oh?" She moved behind me, and wrapping her right arm around my waist, she adjusted her grip and stroked my dick from base to tip. "You're so hard and big right now."

"Because watching you come is a turn-on." My words were rough, the urge to not come early taking priority. Her hands were so small, and the way her tits rubbed against my back...*fuck.* I wasn't in control anymore.

"Get on your stomach, Harrison."

"Uh, how about—"

She shoved me to the bed and straddled me from behind. Digging her nails into my skin, she held me down with a thigh on each side of my hips, teasing me with light touches.

"Becca..." I swallowed hard. "I'm barely holding on here."

"Good." She bit down on my ear, sucking the lobe between her teeth. "Mm. You taste good."

"Goddamn it." I fisted the sheets as more blood left my brain and traveled straight to my throbbing dick. I would have blue balls soon if I didn't switch our positions. I shifted my weight, intent on flipping over, but she stopped me.

"Uh-uh," she tsked. "I have three more minutes."

Three more? Damn.

She rubbed and teased every muscle on my body. Reaching my ass, she dug her nails into it and released a moan as she bit down—exactly as I had done to her. "Your ass is perfect. I'm not even an ass girl, but holy crap I want to keep it."

"Thirty seconds, Becca." My voice came out strained.

She giggled, taking her time while working her way back up my body until she sank her teeth gently into my neck. "You're impatient, Harrison."

"You drive me crazy, Becca."

Unable to wait another second, I flipped over and pulled her underneath me. Her hair spilled out over the pillow in every direction. Her lips parted, and she reached behind my head, yanking me down until our mouths crashed together.

We rolled around, grinding against each other and tasting every bit of each other's exposed skin. When I couldn't last another second without being inside her, I stopped, my heart racing. "I need a condom."

"Well, hustle."

I hustled to my bedroom and retrieved a condom. I rolled it on in record time. As I returned to the mattress, she opened her legs, baring every inch of herself to my gaze.

"God, Becca...you're beautiful." I slid inside of her, our mutual sighs of satisfaction filling the air. I moved inside her for several moments before moaning into her hair. "You feel good."

"So do you." She arched her hips, letting me go deeper, and I lost it.

I pumped into her, my pace fast and relentless as I pistoned in and out of her body. She egged me on—scratching my back and begging me to go harder, deeper. I kissed everywhere my lips touched—her mouth, her neck, her chest—but it wasn't enough. I moved her legs high, bending them over my shoulders and sinking more still until I found the deepest part of her. *Heaven.*

I licked the salt from her skin, my heart hammering in my chest and matching the same frantic beat of hers. I wanted more. No matter how much I filled her, it wasn't enough. I *needed* more. I pounded into her, gripping her legs and kissing her so hard our teeth clashed together.

She reached around, squeezing my ass, and whimpered but still met my pace. "Don't stop...I'm going... going to—"

Her body stiffened, and she let out the sexiest sound I'd ever heard, setting off my own orgasm like fireworks exploding inside my veins. Sweat pooled between our chests as I thrusted into her a final time.

My heart beat so fast it physically hurt my ribs. I pulled out and fell to the mattress beside her, completely spent and confused. "Damn."

"Ditto to that." She panted, her voice holding the same awe as my own. "It's all because you bent over to put more wood on the fire. This is your fault."

Propping my head in my hand, I gazed down at her. I was strangely content just lying with her. "I'll do it really slow next time."

She snorted. "Just don't let me near the whiskey."

"No objections there." My stomach growled, ruining the post-sex moment. "Didn't realize I hadn't eaten in a while. Want to eat real quick before going to bed?"

"Sounds perfect. Crackers did their job sobering me up, but those orgasms made me a hungry lady."

She sat up, patted her stomach, and dressed herself. The normalcy of the situation plucked at my heart. We joked, laughed, and talked with the ease of longtime lovers. She should've been out of place in my bachelor pad but Becca wasn't out of place at all. Even as we sat down for a make-shift dinner of sandwiches and pretzels, she seemed like she belonged here with me.

"Depending on how we feel in the morning, we can check on the house." I took a large bite and swallowed.

"I hope it's okay." Her shoulders sagged, and she pushed

her hair out of her face. "The house is old. There's insurance for the structure, but I'm worried about the girls' stuff."

"Not yours, though?"

"All replaceable. My laptop is the most expensive thing I own, but everything is saved in the cloud."

"Huh." *What is not replaceable here? Photos? Trophies?* "Impressive."

"That's a stretch." She made a goofy face and took both our plates to the trash. Returning, she yawned real loud and dove headfirst onto the bed. "Don't even know what time it is, but it's dark and this bed is comfy."

"I agree with you." I added another log to the fire, smirking when I caught her staring at my ass. "Feel free to cop a feel if you want."

"My hands were out of my control. It isn't my fault."

I joined her on the bed, and she moved into my arms. She fit perfectly against me, and it hit me—I liked her here.

"Good night, Harrison."

Before I could stop myself or overthink it, I pressed a kiss on her forehead. "Good night."

My niece would love Becca. The thought kept repeating in my mind as I stared at her mismatched, brightly colored winter gear the next morning. She bundled the scarf around her face three times, only a sliver of her eyes showing.

"You want a pair of sunglasses? That would help with the wind."

"Yes!" she responded with way too much enthusiasm. "Then I'll be protected head-to-toe."

"That's the idea." I handed her my favorite pair, my lips curving up at her ridiculous outfit. She was totally endearing and needed to be protected at all costs.

"Do you need more layers?" Her voice came out all muffled from the scarf. "You should, Harrison. I heard the radio this morning. The temperatures are still reaching negative forty with the windchill. You almost lost a toe in your basement, remember?"

"Yeah, yeah, okay." I mollified her by adding another scarf and a hat. "The snow stopped but the wind is wicked. Stay close."

"Yes, sir." She saluted me.

I chuckled. She was a damn hoot.

We held hands once we stepped outside and, holy shit, it was cold. Drifts were three or four feet deep, and each step took all my strength. *Get to the street.* Making sure Becca was behind me, I gripped her tighter and forged a path toward the sorority house.

Managing the snow was easier on the road, but my face stung from the cold, and worry lodged itself into my chest. Was Becca okay? I tried blocking the wind from hitting her, but she was accident prone. I grunted and guided us toward the front of the house.

The large front door was situated inside a nook, and thank God, there wasn't a drift blocking the entrance. "Key?"

"Here!" She shoved something into my hand.

It took a couple of tries to get the small metal device into the lock, but finding it, I turned the knob and nudged her inside before following her.

"God, it's not much warmer in here than it is out there, huh?" I said.

"At least we have a break from the wind."

I pushed down my scarf so I could speak easier. I marched into the living room, checking for anything out of place or broken. Seemed fine. Cold, but safe. Something did catch my eye though: the stack of presents under the tree. "Are the presents from you to the girls? Could they be ruined from the cold?"

"Oh man. I forgot about them in my haste to survive!" She walked toward them and bent down, all her colors clashing with the beige carpet. "Those dang girls didn't listen."

Her voice took on a different tone, and I joined her as I eyed at least fifteen small gifts with her name written on them.

"When you care about someone, you show them. This is their way of doing that." I put a hand on her shoulder and squeezed.

The girls loved her, and while a little sliver of jealousy weaved its way into my spine, I ignored it. She deserved the adoration of the girls, and my issues with the team had nothing to do with her. I could be happy for her, while planning to be better for the team. Becca inspired me, plain and simple.

"Let's check the rest of the house, and we'll grab them before we head back." My voice was tighter than I intended.

"Okay." Her eyes glazed over as she stared at the gifts. "My heart feels eight times its size right now. Do you ever feel like that? Overcome with gratitude and love?"

No. "I'm sure I have. Probably with my niece and nephews."

"I can't believe they'd do this." She put a hand over her heart.

"I believe it." I smiled at her and ignored the warm feeling rising in my chest. It was foreign and weird, like drinking really hot soup too fast. I scratched it, hoping the sensation would go away. "You're easy to like, Becca."

She scrunched her nose, and her watery smile shifted into joy. "Thanks."

"It's the truth."

Becca threw her arms around me and pressed her lips to mine, squishing them in a hard, not-sexy kiss before jumping back.

"Uh, Becca, what was that?"

"I wanted to kiss you." Her face flushed, and she winked before walking past me. "Now let's scan the premises and get back to that fire. I go up, you go down?"

"Sounds good."

I ran my lips together, warm from her surprise kiss. The last time someone had kissed me for no particular reason was...so long ago that it stunned me. I stood there, frozen, touching my lips like it was my first time.

Kissing was a means to an end, a promise of pleasure. But hers was not that. Her lips had been cold, and the peck was too quick; but the gesture stayed with me long after she'd taken off upstairs, leaving me on the bottom floor. If I didn't get busy, I'd think of all the reasons why I wanted another blitz-kiss.

I found a duffel bag in the closet and gently placed Becca's gifts in there.

I got it. I understood why they loved her so much. I imagined what each gift might be and how she would react to it. She struck me as someone who would find joy in anything given to her, yet she would prefer something handmade over a gift card any day of the week. I chose gift cards because they were easier. The final box barely fit in the bag, but I zipped it up just as her footsteps thudded downstairs.

"How are the windows up there?" I asked.

"Still intact! I can't believe it. I mean, it's colder than a witch's tit up there, but no more shattered windows. You find anything down here?"

"Nope." I paused and almost snorted. "A witch's tit, huh?"

"It's an expression my dad always said. It's weird, I know, but I can't help it. Every time I asked the time, he would always say it's *half-past a freckle*. One of those dumb dad-isms. Don't your parents have sayings you adopted unwillingly?"

"Ah, not that I know of."

"Doubtful. Think about it." She eyed the bag in my hand and tilted her head. "What's in there?"

"All your gifts. It's Christmas Eve, so you'll get to open them tomorrow. I don't have a tree, though."

When was the last time I cared about having a tree? Years? Decades? Vivian had bought a live evergreen for the one holiday we were together as a married couple, but I couldn't even picture what it looked like. I didn't help her decorate it. Never cared to. Huh, maybe I was a grinch?

"We could steal this one?" She pointed to her decorated tree filled with brightly colored ornaments, garlands of popcorn, and pictures of girls. "The girls won't care."

"We're not taking that thing across the yard in this weather."

Her face fell, and I felt like a real schmuck for not decorating at all this year. Blair even gave me crap for not putting up lights.

You're a real scrooge, Harrison.

Scrooge, grinch, grump. That was me.

She sighed before nodding. "You're being the rational one. Good call."

"We'll Christmas the shit out of my house when we get back." I needed to rectify her frown immediately.

"Yeah? What does that even mean?"

"Not sure, but we'll decorate, drink hot chocolate, and make the place more cheery."

I couldn't believe the words escaping my mouth. My ex had said I didn't have the holiday gene, and my family complained about my obsession with football. But Becca's grin stretched across her face, and her eyes widened with joy.

Worth it.

"Let's Christmas the *shit* out of your house! I already have so many ideas!" She ran toward the door, barely waiting for me to follow her.

A bubble of excitement washed over me as I thought about the holidays. It was a feeling I hadn't experienced in years off the football field, and even the wind couldn't put a damper on my sudden good mood.

CHAPTER FIFTEEN

BECCA

Instead of a tree, Harrison found a two-foot-tall Snoopy wearing a Santa outfit. He stood in the center of the room with a red blanket around him while I dug through the one measly sized Christmas storage box containing two plain red stockings, a weathered wreath, garland, and a snowman candle. That was it.

I held up the odd candle, my brow arched. "Um, what is this?"

"Who, you mean. That's Ballsy."

"Uh, what did you say?"

"Ballsy." He got up from his job—sorting through the red and green yarn I'd given him to string around the tree—and took the object from my hands. "My niece gave him to me a couple years ago. She named him Ballsy."

"No one discouraged her from the name?"

"In hindsight, we probably should've." He smiled and

picked up the battered garland and gently placed it on Snoopy. "I'm not one to decorate."

I motioned around the living room and stifled a laugh. "I couldn't tell by the plain walls."

"Sarcasm isn't a good look on you." He frowned again and huffed as he went back to sorting yarn.

Watching a large man untangling balls of yarn did some sort of thing to my heart. It was almost like it skipped a beat, seeing two things I'd consider complete opposites joined together. I set a hand on his shoulder and patted it.

"Why don't you hang up pictures of your niece and nephews? Or some football accolades? No one should have bare walls."

He opened his mouth but closed it before settling on a grunt.

"That's the spirit!" I teased and earned a semi-smile from him. "After the holidays, I will force my way back in here and hang up pictures with or without your permission."

His posture straightened. "Planning a break-in already?"

"I do know about a crappy window downstairs. Just saying, I could get in if I wanted to find a way." I wiggled my eyebrows, hoping he'd give me the rest of his smile, and it worked.

His momentary grumpiness subsided, and he flung a pillow at me. "When my ex and I broke up, I threw everything into a box including all the pictures. It was cleansing to not see her face or have any memory of her in my space. I never got around to redecorating."

"It's been a couple of years, right?"

"Yeah. I know. Terrible excuse. My priority has been football. It's my escape—my solace." He ran a hand through his thick hair. "I didn't take care of the house because one bad season meant I could get fired. But coming home each night, I craved silence and nothing. That doesn't make sense to someone like you, does it?"

"What does that mean?" I was unsure if I needed to defend myself or not. It was nice to hear him share about his past but not at the cost of making fun of me. "Because I'm so loud?"

"Not at all," he said softly. "Because you're so colorful. I might have the respect of my players and coaches, but my job is to win at the end of the day. That isn't the business of making friends, which means very few attachments to things or people."

Unsure how to respond, I pursed my lips and returned my attention to decorating. A couple of minutes passed before Harrison's large frame appeared behind me. He set his large hands on my hips, and my heart raced at his proximity. Butterflies partied in my stomach, and I urged them to settle down. They seriously needed a curfew.

"I didn't upset you, did I?" His voice was husky and filled with concern. "I meant it as a compliment, and you've been silent since then."

"No. I appreciate you asking." I smiled up at him.

Catching me off guard, he kissed me. It was a sweet, just-because kiss, and my face burned red.

"Ah, well, the kiss distracted me," I said.

"Good." Amusement danced in his eyes. "That was a blizzard-buddy kiss."

"I'm a fan of them." I ignored the pang in my chest at the reminder of our temporary arrangement. *Blizzard buddy.* I pushed him away and went back to the box before I spoke. "This might seem like prying, but your breakup sounds like it was pretty bad. What happened?"

"It is prying."

"I'm a nosy person. But more importantly, you seem to carry a smidge of anger about it still. That *can't* be healthy."

"You sound like my sister." He grumbled something else but I didn't catch it.

"I can't wait to meet her."

"Yeah, might be regretting that decision already. I can picture the two of you ganging up on me."

"Poor Harrison." I earned another smile from him. "Enough stalling. Tell me about the breakup. You've already heard about my disastrous and lackluster dating life. It's only fair you have your turn. We're together for this snow-mageddon, so spill it."

He stared at the fire for a full minute before his features settled. "What it came down to was she expected a different life as the wife of a football coach. I think, in her mind, she assumed it would be like being an NFL wife, with fame and traveling together."

"Surely you talked about how different college football is?" I said without thinking.

"Yes, Becca. While Vivian was hard to please, I'm not

innocent in this, either. Football is an obsession. Winning is the means to my livelihood, and I couldn't provide the lifestyle she wanted or give her the attention she deserved. The fights started early on and got worse each season. We were married just under two years before she'd had enough and walked out. We had a big game the following week, so I didn't stop her. Leaving me was intended to spark me to life. She wanted me to fight for our relationship, and I failed." He blew out a long breath, deep frown lines covering his handsome face. "We divorced soon after that, and last I checked, she was engaged to some guy who plays for Chicago."

It was a lot of information to take in, and I weighed my response carefully.

"I'm an asshole," he continued. "It's not something I'm proud of, but shit happens." His shoulders slumped.

So much of what he'd shared bothered me, but I couldn't describe why. Was it because I understood how he felt since none of my dates understood my passion for my job? Or was it because someone had hurt Harrison?

He looked at me, waiting for my response with a line between his eyebrows.

I set the decorations down and gave him my full attention. "I don't think you're an asshole. I'm no relationship expert—hell, I'm the complete opposite of one—but I think it's safe to say it takes two people for a relationship to work. You each had different expectations and priorities, and they didn't line up. Your drive for winning and coaching a good team isn't worse or better than her desire for living the high life. But those individual goals probably should've been discussed before getting married. Just saying…"

"No shit." He laughed.

We worked in silence for the next few minutes until Harrison let out a loud whoop. Holding up two different balls of yarn, he began hanging them over the Snoopy. "Look at me, Christmas-ing up the place."

"Proud of you," I said sarcastically, but he missed it.

Harrison's grin grew the more he dangled the yarn around the living room in his own disorganized hot mess of a way. The green tangled with the red when he moved from the Snoopy to the bookshelf, but I didn't say a word. This large man getting goofy over yarn, even though it was uneven and chaotic, was endearing and sexy as hell.

"I would hang it over the fireplace, but the last thing we need is to start a fire, huh?"

"Probably a good idea." I found some tape and helped him secure the yarn in the farthest corner. "Where do you want to put up these measly stockings?"

"I know!" He took the plain red stockings and tucked a corner of each under a heavy book on his bookcase, hanging them at an angle. He puffed out his chest. "Father Christmas over here."

I snorted. "You've really outdone yourself, Harrison." I placed my hands on my hips and admired the living room and its weird combination of decorations. "Can't say it doesn't feel Christmas-y."

"And wait." He unzipped the duffel bag and placed the

small gifts around our Snoopy. "Look at all the gifts for you. You can't open them until tomorrow, though."

He seemed so happy for me with his Cheshire cat–like grin plastered on his face. I'd brought him a secret gift, its contents remaining safely hidden in my bag. "Well, you can't open your gift, either."

"My gift?" His voice went up an octave. "I have a gift?"

"Yep." I pulled the box from my bag. It was a half-assed wrapping job I'd done in a hurry, but it was worth it to see the surprise on his face. "Tomorrow morning you'll see."

His expression froze somewhere between bewilderment and fear, and my cheeks burned. Regret and embarrassment flooded my body. *What was I thinking?*

"It's not a big deal. Really. I found this . . . thing. It's not a big thing, but also not a little thing. It . . . it reminded me of you, and I thought, what the hell? It's not even a real present. I mean . . . it's like a knickknack, really. It's stupid."

I busied myself by picking up the little pieces of dust and debris that had escaped the storage box. Startling me, Harrison placed one large hand on my lower back, making my entire body taut.

"Becca," he said, his voice low and sexy.

"Hmm?" I didn't meet his eyes. Instead, I focused on the lopsided Snoopy.

He moved his hand up my back, over my shoulder, and then under my chin to force me to face him. "You're rambling. Why in the hell are you nervous?"

"Uh, because your face got all twisted, and I felt silly for getting you a gift."

"I've woken up alone, without gifts, on Christmas morning for three years. Your thoughtfulness caught my grinch-ass off-guard."

Lines appeared around his eyes as he offered me a real smile, and my embarrassment drifted away. He cupped my face, his fingers caressing the apples of my cheeks. "I'm stoked to wake up with you tomorrow *and* to have a gift."

"It really is stupid," I mumbled.

"Doesn't matter. I'll like it." He continued touching me, his strong fingers kneading the muscles between my shoulder and neck before pressing his lips to my forehead. "Do you want some soup? I'm craving it."

"Uh, yes." I almost laughed at the complete change of topic. "Soup sounds perfect."

"Good." He moved to the kitchen, taking his body heat and intensity with him, and I welcomed the moment of solitude. The change from intense to light and flirty gave me whiplash, and I wasn't buckled in for the ride.

It was still unclear what we were. Neighbors? Friends? A fling for sure. But I dang well knew I couldn't go back to pretending he didn't exist. Not after everything we'd shared. We had to be at least friends. We'd figure that part out, though the thought of never kissing him again made my heart ache.

My phone rang, jostling me from overthinking. I swiped my finger across the screen and brought the device to my ear. "Hello! Happy Christmas Eve, Mom!"

"My dear Becca. Are you surviving this tundra? Seriously.

I can't wait until we retire and move to the Southwest. I'll take sunshine and heat over this insane cold any day of the week!"

"I hear you. You still have power?" I couldn't decide whether I preferred the power on or off. Off meant cozying by the fire, sharing the bed, and being near Harrison. That would all end when the power returned. Plus my phone had 20 percent battery left.

"Yes, honey. We have generators. Plus, we're having the Conways over for dinner tonight, and the Davids tomorrow. They're all disappointed you can't be here, but they'll obviously understand."

"Tell them hi for me, and I'll catch up with them as soon as I can."

"Well, that's why I'm calling. The New Year's Eve party on the boat—the black-tie big gala event raising money for the underfunded schools. I know you wanted to stay in and read during this break, but it would do you good to have one night out. We can go shopping for a dress and, oh—a date! I know three very handsome gentlemen who would just cut off their arm to take you!"

"Mom, slow down." I rubbed my temple with my free hand, already regretting I'd answered the phone. "I do *not* need you to set me up with a date."

"You'll need a plus-one to a gala, darling. The tables are set up in pairs, and it would look silly if you came alone."

"Then I guess I shouldn't go to the gala, huh? I don't mind sitting alone. Plus that way I can sneak out early after I taste all the food and champagne."

"Nonsense!" She covered the phone and shouted something to my dad.

"Ugh," I mumbled.

Harrison appeared, his expression concerned. I waved my hand in the air in the universal sign of "it's nothing." He furrowed his brows, and tight lines formed around his mouth as he rested his hands on his hips. "I'll take you."

"Wh-what?"

"Whatever your mom is trying to rope you into, I'll be your date." He shrugged, his posture stiff and rigid.

"My date?" I took my pointer finger and slammed it against my chest. I couldn't possibly have heard him right.

"Yes." He grinned and squeezed my shoulder before heading back into the kitchen. "Tell your mom you have a plus-one."

Uh, what just happened? What are words? Where am I?

"Mom…" I said, trying without luck to regain her attention. "Mom! Call off your dating shenanigans. I have a plus-one."

"You have a date? Oh! Sexy neighbor, huh? Did the cute underwear work after all?"

I groaned. "I don't want to run down my phone battery even more, but send me the details so I can pass them along to my plus-one."

"You better not be pulling my leg, honey."

"I would never," I lied, because she and I both knew I would. "Tell Dad I love him, and I'll call you tomorrow, okay?"

"But Becca…"

"Love you! Bye, Mom!" I hung up and tossed the phone onto the couch.

The dating conversation exhausted me every single time. Why was she like this? My life was fine without love!

But Harrison? Volunteering? It had to be guilt or something. *A date with him?*

The idea wasn't horrible. If anything, my smile almost hurt my face picturing it. It had to be the Christmas spirit. Only explanation.

CHAPTER SIXTEEN

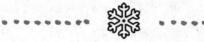

HARRISON

A high-pitched whirring sound woke me. I lazily removed my arms from around Becca's body and rose from the bed to check it out. *If it's another broken window...*

Only it wasn't. The lights were on in the kitchen, the digital clock above the stove blinking at me. A heavy combination of joy and disappointment took root in my gut. If the power worked, then Becca would return to the sorority house. That meant our time together was over, and I wasn't ready for that.

Because she's dynamite in bed?

Because I'm sick of being alone?

Because I want her around all the time?

I reset the clocks and the temperature in the house. The food in the fridge was edible and the furnace worked. I made my way back to the mattress, each step feeling heavier than the last. Disappointment usually stemmed from football—the long sighs, the heavy weight on my shoulders—so it was uncomfortable experiencing these same sensations at the thought of Becca leaving. If I only had a couple hours left with Becca, then I wanted to spend every second of them next to her.

"Morning." I pulled her into my arms and kissed the top of her head.

"Something wrong?"

God, her voice was cute and sleepy.

"The power came back on." I was already irritated with myself for being annoyed. I should be happy my life was going back to normal. I could watch football, drink beer, and not worry about my pipes breaking. Instead, I thought about going to sleep and waking up alone. About the lack of conversation or color in my house. But more, I thought about how things would surely change with Becca, and I had no idea how to stop it. Living in this temporary bubble, just the two of us, had been so easy.

"It did?" She bolted upright and brought the blankets to her chin, her face lighting up in a smile. "It's a Christmas miracle."

"Must be." I wished it was still dark and I could lose myself in her warm body. Have her stroke my face or put her freezing toes against my calves.

She leaned over to me and looked up with a tender expression on her face. "Merry Christmas, Harrison." She smiled and rested her head against my shoulder.

Tightness formed in my chest. "You too, Becca."

"I never would've guessed I'd be waking up with you on Christmas morning, but life has a funny way of working out, huh?" She laughed, the sound joyful and pure.

"I guess so." I stretched, hoping to rid my body of the negativity plaguing her happiness. Sure, our time together was almost over, but I needed to chill.

"Presents!" She moved across the mattress toward our Snoopy tree, and the blanket fell, exposing her bare back and the two dimples right above her ass. I bit my knuckle at the pretty picture she made, forcing myself not to initiate something again. I wasn't sure if it was the promise of being her date or the fact it was Christmas Eve, but sex with a woman hadn't meant this much in a long damn while.

Just thinking about it is sending all my blood south.

"Harrison, you can open your gift now." She threw on one of my extra-large plaid shirts before handing me a small box. "Remember, it's stupid with a capital S."

I fought a grin at her worried expression and removed the ribbon. Inside was a small wooden log about four inches in length. On one end, a Santa hat was glued above a set of googly eyes, an itty-bitty peg nose, and a painted-on smile. At the bottom, a pair of tiny peg legs were attached with glue and stuck out on each side. The remainder of the length was covered in a small piece of red and green plaid fabric resembling a blanket.

For the life of me, I had no idea how to respond. Was it a joke? Did she... make it? It looked like something my niece would create.

At my silence, Becca burst into a fit of giggles, confusing me even more. She clasped her hands over her belly and snorted at least five times before wiping under her eyes. "Your face... oh my. This was so worth it."

"Is this a...joke of some sort?" I asked carefully, hoping I didn't insult her or make her frown. Her face was meant for joy and smiles, but what the fuck was this thing? And why did she give it to me?

"It's called a Caga Tío." She stared at me, her expression somewhere between amusement and worry.

Those words meant nothing to me, and I cleared my throat. "Oh."

Obviously.

"It's a Christmas tradition in Barcelona. I learned about it in a class and thought it was the most interesting thing. See, you have this log—well, this one's a miniature version. The families there use a real log, like the size of the ones in your fireplace, and they set it up with legs and eyes—like the miniature you opened."

"Okay?" I enjoyed how animated she got when she spoke about Barcelona, but this thing sounded weird. "It's a tradition?"

"Yes." She took the small log from my hand and set it on the ground, propping it up on its front legs. "The night before Christmas, they don't actually have Santa come deliver gifts. Instead, they get gifts on Three Kings' Day, which is in January. But that's not the point. On Christmas Eve, they get sticks and hit Caga Tío. They beat the log in the hope he will poop out presents the following morning."

I opened my mouth twice, closing it each time.

Becca pointed to the end of the log with no eyes and smiled. "They don't get big presents. They are more like stocking stuffers."

"Thank you?"

"I told you it was stupid." Her joy disappeared, and a sad smile replaced it. "You'd said you didn't have a lot of decorations, and I figured, heck, I have a million. I thought I'd give you my weirdest one to commemorate our holiday together. You don't have to keep it."

I'm an asshole. I cupped her face in my hands, gently guiding her to face me. Her eyelashes fanned over her red cheeks, but eventually, her eyes met mine. "Thank you."

"You don't—"

I brought my lips to hers, taking all the time in the world—telling her without words what her gift meant. Yeah, it was an odd gift, but it was one of the things that made her...her. She opened her mouth and deepened the kiss, her tongue swirling against mine until I groaned. "I appreciate the thought behind your gift."

"You sure?"

"Yes." I ran the tips of my fingers down her neck until I reached her collarbone. Everything about her was delicate and special. But instead of running in the opposite direction, I wanted to learn more about her quirks. "It is by far the strangest gift I've ever received, but it doesn't mean it's not one of my favorites."

She shrugged, and her face tinged red. "You're lucky you're such a good kisser or I'd probably be more upset."

"Good to know." I grinned and pressed another quick kiss on her mouth.

Her phone buzzed, and she glanced down, rolling her large brown eyes.

"What is it?" I asked.

"The girls. They think it's hilarious to do a group text wishing me a good holiday. They know how I feel about group texts. They're the worst. One night, I put my phone on silent and woke up with seventy messages. Seventy!"

"Are they messing with you?"

"No. They really do think they're being nice. See?" She held her device toward me and scrolled through warm wishes and pictures. "But instead of texting me separately, they do it as one message."

"That's nice."

I couldn't recall the guys on the team texting me, or any of the coaches, about anything other than excuses. A dull flicker of irritation threatened, and I swallowed it down. Maybe I should reach out to them? No. That wasn't my leadership style and would likely cause a state of alarm. But if one of our shared goals was better communication, it wouldn't worry them. I'd think about it, once my time with Becca ended.

"It is. I shouldn't complain." She bit down on her lip, her face twisting in concentration. "It does make it easier to send them all good wishes. Hold on, let me come up with something."

She typed out a couple of different messages, talking to herself before deleting them. I glanced at my own phone, not expecting to see anything.

Two notifications from two captains. Dexter and Jack. It was simple and to the point, but it felt like so much more than just a simple **Merry Christmas, Coach.**

"Huh."

"What?" She set her phone down and glanced at me. "Get some news?"

"No. Two players texted me happy holidays."

"Aw." She bumped my shoulder with hers. "Things can't be too bad if they're reaching out, right?"

My surprise at the small gesture of good wishes confirmed that I was part of the problem. A simple message shouldn't have been a big deal, and yet it made my brain race. I typed out a **thanks** and hit send on the text. "It's time for you to open up your gifts."

She chewed her bottom lip, her teeth grazing the plumpest part of it. "Don't we need to head to your sister's soon?"

"Nah, we can take our time. They'll want to do their own morning routine with the monsters. Plus, I'm a selfish man, and I want to see what the girls got you."

"Okay." Her normal smile returned. "I seriously told them no presents. They don't listen."

"I bet you're real stern with them."

She snapped her gaze to me, her eyes holding a spark of fire.

"What?" I held up my hands in surrender.

"I'm stern with them, thank you very much. We've had almost zero incidents with the law since I've been their house mom, and they wouldn't dare break the rules."

"Becca Ratched, huh?"

"Oh, shut up." She threw a pillow at me, and I caught it with a huge grin on my face.

I could picture her trying to yell at one of the dumb teen-agers, her hair all in her face and red splotches on her cheeks. It was a pretty picture.

"You said *almost* zero incidents," I teased, enjoying myself more than I had in weeks. "Why not zero?"

She ran her fingers through her hair a few times, her shoulders slumping a bit. "My first year, we had a pair of party girls who needed to rethink their priorities. One night, they decided they'd do a naked run for charity."

"Shit." I shuddered.

"I know." She nodded. "They didn't get enough buy-in from the house so they decided to do it on their own. Shock-ing no one, they received public nudity tickets. As house mom, I was written up for not laying down the law. Oh boy, I was fumed."

"I'd love to see you fumed." I pictured it in my head: her soft features hardening…her eyes narrowing…Refocusing, I cleared my throat. "I bet you were upset."

"I was. I learned a lot about leading and listening. Some days, I think about going back to school to be a counselor. One of the best conversations I've had in this position was with those two girls after it happened. It was hard—emotional—and it took maturity from all of us to get through it, but it really changed my style of leadership."

"That's impressive, Becca. Seriously." I cupped her chin again and nodded to affirm my words. "You're a hell of a woman, and a leader."

She blushed and turned away from me.

In the comfortable silence, I passed her the gifts, and a weird sensation of pride struck me. She cultivated respect and a healthy atmosphere in a house of fifty college girls. *Something I can't figure out with the guys in my program.*

Taking her time with each present, she opened each gift carefully to avoid ripping the wrapping paper.

I fought the urge to roll my eyes. "Are you one of those people who saves all the wrapping paper? Do you fold it and keep it color coded underneath your bed?"

She made a goofy face and burst into another fit of giggles. "Uh, no. I'm not that organized. But it's interesting you seem to know people do that. Do you have color coded things under your bed, Harrison?"

"Hell no. But my aunt used to save every scrap. I had a smart mouth, so I'd get assigned to sort the paper once present time was over."

"Mm. I don't believe you." She smirked before opening the next gift. "Oh oh, how sweet!" She held up a mug with a picture of some girls on it. "These girls know I love my hot chocolate a little too much. I know it's cheesy, but sometimes they feel like my younger siblings."

The joy and simplicity of her words sparked an uncomfortable truth in my gut. *I have issues with my brother.*

Distance. I needed some distance from the conversation, so I stood and slapped my hands together. "Speaking of that, let me go make us some mugs to celebrate Christmas. We can finish up with gifts, shower, and head to my sister's. Sound like a plan?"

"That'll be great, Harrison! Thank you!" She smiled so big that it almost cured the weird nostalgia—or whatever bullshit it was I was feeling about my family. Almost, but not quite.

"Truck has gas, we have extra jackets, and our phones are charged. You're ready to drive across town?"

"Yup." She double-checked her seat belt and wrapped her fingers around the oh-shit handle above her passenger window. "Totally ready."

"My truck is completely safe and has four-wheel drive." I patted her knee before backing out of the parking space and turning onto the road. My tires slid twice but gained traction within a couple seconds. My stomach bottomed out in fear, but I plastered on a calm smile and forced myself to relax. "See? No big deal."

"Yup. Yup. Totally fine," she said, her voice coming out more like a squeak.

She was not totally fine. I would've reached over and offered comfort, but removing even one hand from the wheel would've been idiotic. Luckily, there was no traffic in sight, probably because the roads were dangerous and it was horribly cold. The streets were an ice rink, and we were nothing more than a hockey puck. I voiced none of my concerns, though, because Becca was already tense—really fucking tense.

Distract her. "Hey, so your parents—"

My phone blasted through the Bluetooth speaker, and I winced. "Shit, that's loud!"

"It's okay." She clutched her hand to her chest. "You can answer. Maybe it'll be as embarrassing as my mom calling."

"Doubtful." I hit the talk button and regretted it the second my brother's voice came through the speakers.

I knew better than to just answer. Who else would call on a holiday but family?

"Hair ball." His tone was irritatingly bright and cheerful. "Merry fucking Christmas."

I tightened my grip. "Yeah, you too, Hank."

"What's this bullshit about you not flying out to see your baby bro? I'm in the bowl, man. I could win it! I know that would just grind your gears, huh bro? Me in the bowl, you not. How mad are you, for realsies?"

Hank loved taunting me when our parents weren't around, and he had the unique ability to piss me off more than any other human. My pulse pounded around my temples, and every muscle in my back hurt.

Deep breath.

"We had a blizzard." I swallowed hard before continuing. "I've been snowed in for three days without power. Have you seen the news?"

"Too busy getting ready for the game. Mom and Dad got here a couple days ago, and we're hitting a resort. Blair bailed, too, but I guess it's not fun traveling with those three demons. Am I right? Those kids are a shit ton of work. We got it made, huh? No kids. Decent income. Well, I do at least. My season kicked ass."

Jesus. He's a dick.

I blew out a breath. "Again, we're snowed in. We didn't have a choice. Enjoy the resort with Mom and Dad."

"Why're you rushing me off the phone? I know you're home alone, and no offense bro, but you're not the best company. You should thank me for calling you. Who knows how many days it's been since you've seen a human? If you would've won some games, you could've gotten a piece of tail. But that ship sailed, bro." He cackled, and I wanted to punch the windshield.

"Harrison, come back to bed." Becca cupped her hands over her mouth, making her voice sound muffled. It was perfect, and I damn near proposed then and there.

"Dude. You're with a chick? What the fuck? Who is she? She hot?"

"Bye, Hank." I hung up, mortified at my blood relative and thankful for Becca's quick thinking. "That was my wonderful brother."

"What a . . ." She paused a long second as she gathered her thoughts. ". . . Self-absorbed, pompous man-child. Oh! I'm so mad." She shook her head and held her fists in the air. "I would've slapped him if he were here. Right in the face, and I wouldn't have felt bad about it."

"I wouldn't have stopped you." I grinned.

"Is he always like that?"

"Yep. Has been since we were teenagers. And my parents, well, they didn't care. He's the golden child. Plus, he's smart and only does that crap with me when our parents aren't around."

"You would think with Blair giving them grandbabies, she would be the favorite."

Becca was on my side. I appreciated her company more than I could express in words. Even if it was for just for a few days, having Becca on my team felt...right.

"I am quite flipping glad I'm not meeting him today. I don't care if it's Christmas, I'd ruin his holiday without question."

"You and me both."

Family had the ability to build you up or tear you down, and my family fell into the latter category because Hank was a jerk. I rolled my shoulders, hoping to ease the knot there, but the stressful drive didn't help.

"You want to talk about it?" she asked after a minute of silence. "I can be a good listener. The girls talk and talk and talk, and I'm skilled at giving advice to others—even if I'm not good at taking my own advice. I'm here, if you want."

"No. I'm good." I focused on navigating the roads to my sister's house. "Look, I should focus on getting us there safely."

"I understand, really. Trust me."

Becca sat silently beside me—unlike my ex-wife who would've sighed or said something to imply that I was over-reacting. Guilt and anger at my own reaction to her offer washed over me. I gritted my teeth, trying to understand why I was in such a bad mood. It was more than Hank, my parents, and the blizzard. No—I was confident it was because the power had returned. But how did I explain that to Becca? My thoughts raced, and before I could come up with an explanation, Becca reached out and placed her hand on my arm.

"Harrison," she said in a kind, soft voice, "I really do understand. No explanation needed. I'd like to think we're precious cargo, so I prefer to arrive in one piece." She squeezed her tiny fingers around me for a second before letting go.

In all of my life, no one had ever simply accepted my desire not to talk. No one. Not my friends, my assistant coaches, my family, or my ex-wife. But Becca did, and I had no idea why my chest tightened at her acceptance.

CHAPTER SEVENTEEN

Becca

We will *not crash. Everything is fine.*

I held on to the side bar so tightly that my knuckles hurt. Harrison's face was etched with worry lines, and I swore sweat pooled on his forehead, which was not a good sign. Plus it was *freezing.* The roads were the devil's version of an obstacle course, and it was a dumb idea for us to drive to his sister's. We should've bunkered down and stayed warm and cozy in his house.

"Almost there. Promise." He clenched his teeth, his tone not easing my worry.

"Cool, great." I swallowed hard as the truck slid a few feet to the right. The radio crackled with Christmas songs, and Harrison exhaled loudly every thirty seconds. Even though my nerves tended to make me more talkative, this called for silence. Instead, I tapped my toe along with the holiday music rather than focusing on the weightless feeling in my stomach. His truck had to be at least three times the size of my Camry. *Thank goodness Harrison drives this beast.*

After what felt like an hour, Harrison pulled onto a neighborhood street with high snowdrifts lining each side. White was everywhere. Endless. Like we were stuck in a snow globe that had way too much power in it.

"Holy balls." I blew out a surprised breath.

"Looks like they haven't plowed this street yet," Harrison grumbled, irritation lacing every word. "Hell, where is the actual road?"

Excellent question, blizzard buddy.

"Can your truck make it through those drifts or do we stay here until the gas runs out and we freeze to death?"

He snorted and silently studied the road ahead.

I blinked a few times, hoping the vision of the blizzard-hit street was an illusion, but it remained the same. Tall white walls of snow led up to the second stories of some houses. "Please tell me your sister's house is the first one on the right."

"That would be too easy. She's seven down." He let out a curse and wiped his hands over his face. "I'll take it slow, and I guess we'll see if this four-wheel drive is good for anything. If I feel even a little bit stuck, we'll park here and walk."

Be brave.

"You got it, Coach."

He smiled, just for a second, before his face tightened with absolute focus. He pressed down on the gas. The truck roared and made a high-pitched squeal I'd never heard before. About five seconds later, the truck lurched forward and climbed over the snowdrifts.

"This is wild," I gasped.

"Four-wheel drive, baby. Whoo!" Harrison cheered, sounding absolutely manic. I couldn't blame him. We were in Santa's sleigh, cruising over these huge drifts.

I let out a relieved laugh. "I'll never make fun of a giant truck again."

Harrison's dark brows furrowed, confused at my statement.

"You know? Large trucks mean a small... *you know*."

"Not true." His smirk grew. "At least, not with me."

"Don't look overconfident, Truck Boy. I said I'd never make fun of them again. Unless they have truck balls. I'm not a fan of those dangly sacks, and nothing will convince me otherwise."

"Truck balls?" His voice rose an octave. "What the actual hell are you talking about, Becca?"

"You know what I mean. Some guys actually spend money and hang a ball sack from the back of the trailer hitch. There was this guy in high school who had one, and he parked next to me all year. I hated him. I took a black marker and drew pubes all over it to piss him off, but it backfired. He liked it so much all his friends did it, and I've never regretted anything more in my life."

"You... you are the most interesting person." He took his gaze off the road for a brief second and gave me an unguarded smile. "I can assure you I don't have *truck* balls."

The sweet, brief look warmed my frozen toes, and I

smiled back at him. "Well, you don't need them. You happen to have a great dick, so no need to overcompensate."

He laughed hard in reply, and I'd never heard anything so joyful. It was a deep, loud bark of laughter that came from his chest. And oh, baby! The way his lips curved up had me grinning like a fool. It was probably a good thing the power had returned. I needed to get back to the sorority house and put some distance between me and my blizzard buddy, because the fragile lines I'd drawn in the snow had definitely blown away.

I liked him more than I should. My heart pitter-pattered as I stared at him, taking in his profile and wondering so many little things that I had no business asking. Like, had he enjoyed being married or did he hate it? What would he do if he couldn't coach? Did he like me, too?

Yeah, no asking questions, I scolded myself as the truck pulled to a stop.

Harrison jutted his chin toward the brick two-story house on my right. "This is Blair's."

"It's a nice house."

"She's done really well for herself. Her husband is a great guy, and I'm thankful they live so close."

"I'm thankful for you. If I had your brother for a sibling, I'd probably sabotage every family holiday. I know you don't want to talk about it—and this is me *totally not* bringing it up—but if you want ideas on how to really mess with him, let me know. I was really good at pranks when I was a kid."

He smiled, and his dimples popped, just for me. "I might take you up on it, but not today."

"It's a date." I foolishly tried flirting and immediately regretted using the word *date*. "Uh, promise. Rain check. It's penciled in. That's what I meant. I'll add it to my calendar for us to chat about mean Hank. That's all I said."

"Wow, Becca. You're even cuter when you're flustered." He leaned toward me, his full lips curving up in amusement and his eyes crinkled on the sides. Cupping my face in his large hands, he traced his thumb over my ear, sending goose bumps over every inch of my skin. He took his time bringing his lips to mine, giving me the sweetest and most gentle kiss I'd ever had in my life. "Thank you."

"Uh, you're welcome?" I had no idea what he was thanking me for, or even what day it was, because that kiss was so out of character. He tasted like mint, and I had no idea how. Did he have a candy cane that he hid from me? That would've been rude. I loved candy canes. Why was I thinking about candy canes when the guy I was crushing on looked at me like maybe he liked me, too?

"I'm not the most skilled at expressing myself, but I'm glad you're here with me today. Really fucking glad, Becca."

The look in his eyes matched his intense tone, and I could only nod.

Fling. Fling. Flingy-fling. That's what this was. I had to remind myself when he looked at me like this, all warm and fuzzy, making me question why we weren't together and doing this all the time.

Because I deserve a real relationship and he doesn't do those.

"Now, let's go inside before the kids run out into the cold. I can already see their little heads in the window."

He nodded toward the large bay window at the front of the house.

I followed his gaze and grinned at the outline of three kids staring back at us. They each had a mop of brown hair and large smiles. Harrison grabbed our bags from the back and then, taking my hand, rushed toward the house. We barely cracked open the door before three little humans barreled into Harrison, each one finding a limb and wrapping themselves around the giant man so tightly that he couldn't walk. My eyes stung with emotion, but the wind blew really strong, so winter allergies were an easy excuse. For sure. Not at all seeing the grumpy guy get love from three kids.

"Blair," Harrison shouted into the hallway. "Your monsters are preventing me from entering your house. Control them."

"Uncle Harry! You have to see what I got from Santa!"

"Uncle Harry, you brought me a present, right? Mom said you wouldn't because I ate all the waffles this morning, but you promised."

"Uncle Harry, Mom said we can play outside for five minutes. I got my snow pants on. Did you bring yours? We can make an igloo and live there."

Three little voices were filled with so much joy and pummeled him with question after question. Moving toward a chair, he maneuvered the kids onto his lap, and it was a full five minutes before the littlest one pointed a finger at me. "Who are you?"

"I'm Becca. I'm a friend of your Uncle Harry's."

"Uncle Harry has friends?" Her eyes grew wide.

"He sure does." I laughed and stood as a beautiful woman bearing no resemblance to Harrison walked into the room. I offered her a smile and extended my hand. "You must be Harrison's favorite family member. Hi. I'm his neighbor, Becca."

"Ah, you've heard of Hank then?" She met my hand and smiled. "Nice to meet you. I must say, it's a surprise to have a guest of my brother's."

"Oh, you're not alone in being surprised. This is a shock for me, too."

Her eyes warmed, and she ran a hand through her light brown hair. She looked tired, and after seeing her three kiddos, I could imagine why. "Well, my offspring don't introduce themselves because they're monsters, but the oldest is George, followed by Brodie, and the little one there is Gabby. Children, say hi to Uncle Harry's friend."

"I thought I was his best friend," Gabby whined. "You pinky-promised me!"

"I can have more than one friend," Harrison said, but her big blue eyes pooled with tears. "Gabs..."

"Want to know a secret?" I asked, gaining her attention. She nodded, and I lowered my voice. "Your uncle told me you were his best friend and that I would always come in second. So don't worry, he kept his promise. He said Gabby is always number one."

The little girl glanced at her uncle, and he nodded. She wiped her eyes, and in less than a second cuddled farther into his lap. Harrison met my gaze over the children's heads, and his eyes warmed. He looked so natural with the kids—so happy. For one stupid half-second, I wondered what his children would look like. Would they get his green eyes and strong jawline? Would they be stubborn like their father?

Whoa. Take a step back.

I swallowed the knot in my throat. I was being level-ten extra, thinking about Harrison having kids. We were barely friends, and this thought crossed a line. I wasn't even sure I wanted kids, so I had no idea why it even popped into my head. I mentally scolded myself.

"Becca's been keeping me company during the blizzard. What did you monkeys do?" Harrison asked, and I focused on their answers and not him.

"We used all the old cardboard boxes to build a spaceship! Want to see?" George jumped up from his uncle's leg and faced me. "Come on, Ms. Becca. You and Uncle Harry need to try it out. It has buttons!"

"I'm game if you are," I said as George took my hand and dragged me to a door just off the living room. "I love boxes. They're the best toys. I used to build entire cities with them and pretend I was mayor."

"You don't have to if you don't want to." Blair wore the same expression toward her children that my mom always had when I did something irritating. "Just tell them no."

"I don't mind. I've been cooped up with this guy for a while. I could use a new friend."

"Great!" George exclaimed and led me down the hall to a large door where a flight of stairs descended into a massive playroom.

The number of toys all strewn about the floor was a lot

to take in, but I was pleased it had all the markings of being used often. Kids should be free to play and use their imaginations, not made to behave in ways based on their parents' expectations. Knowing Blair raised her children to explore and be creative made me happy. I smiled when she and Harrison followed with the other kids.

"Uncle Harry! You get in first." Gabs pointed her little finger at him and tugged on his pant leg.

There was no way Harrison would fit in the cardboard box. His broad shoulders alone would barely fit, but he didn't seem concerned. Crouching down on all fours, he followed Gabby into the small spaceship.

Footsteps pounded down the stairs, and a tall, handsome man appeared next to Blair. "Don't you want to open more presents?" Blair's features held an exasperated expression. "I swear. I buy them all the gifts in the world, and they only want to play with the box they came in."

I laughed and offered her a shrug of my shoulders. "Kids, I guess?"

She smiled then jutted her chin to the man beside her. "Becca, this is my husband, Ben."

I shook his hand before turning my attention back to Harrison and the three kids on the floor. Together they filled the room with the sounds of beeping and fake explosions as they played. *Kind of like my ovaries watching him with little ones.*

No. I stopped that train of thought as quickly as it appeared and then focused on the cardboard spaceship taking over their floor and the beast of a coach acting silly with his young niece and nephews. I cleared my throat, hoping my face didn't give away my embarrassment. *Do his players know how silly he can be? How fun he is?*

Did he only let his guard down with Blair and her children? I studied his hard angles and more gentle facial expressions. Who knew this big man had such a soft side?

"You look deep in thought." Blair stood next to me and brought a chipped mug to her lips. The scents of coffee and vanilla wafted my way.

"His athletes probably don't know all the sides to your brother."

"I don't know all his sides." She laughed. "But I see what you mean."

"It wouldn't hurt for them to see him acting like this. Carefree and fun, rather than the hard-ass most people think of him as. Because he's not."

Blair narrowed her eyes and studied me. I recognized the look—she was curious. Harrison disappeared farther into the spaceship, and Blair jutted her chin toward upstairs. "Want some coffee?"

"Yes, please." I followed her back to the main floor as playful sounds carried from the basement. She putzed around, grabbing a mug with pictures of her kids and filling it with coffee before sliding it across the island counter to me. She set a carton of milk and a jar of sugar next to it and then handed me a spoon. I sighed in relief—people who drank black coffee had to be psychopaths. "Thank you."

"I've been trying to come up with a line that would assure you I wasn't prying, but I got nothing." Blair shrugged, not appearing the least bit ashamed of herself.

I smiled. "Naturally you are curious about me. I'm an open book—too open, sometimes. In fact, you might regret asking me anything. But ask away."

She chuckled and released a long breath, a smile toying with her lips. She had an easy, unassuming presence that complimented Harrison's tough exterior. "You're so different than his ex-wife, who was the last woman he brought over. I don't think she acknowledged the kids with more than a half-assed hug in all their years together, let alone mention the fact that Harrison isn't the toughie he portrays himself to be. I've always known what was under the surface, but most people don't care to look."

"I can't really speak about his ex since I never met her, but from what I can piece together, she wasn't a good fit for your brother. She could've been lovely and wonderful, but they clearly weren't compatible long-term." I blinked away the thought of who would be a good fit for him—someone tenacious and willing to call him out when he was being a jerk; someone soft where he was hard. *Kinda like...*nope.

Fling. Flingy-fling.

Blair snorted and released a long cackle that sounded a bit like a goose. It made me like her even more. "She was a pill. I tell ya, I know Harrison can be a real crank-ster, but there's a lot of good under there, and she didn't want to work hard enough to find it."

"I can relate to that."

"What's that? You? I've known you a whole sixty seconds, and I know not a single soul thinks you're cranky.

Literally, the word doesn't even belong in the same sentence as you."

I blushed. "No, I meant...well, I'm definitely not *cranky*. I meant, a lot of the guys I date or get set up with never care to work hard enough to get to know me. They see bits and pieces and assume I'm different or odd. What almost thirty-year-old wants to live in a house with college girls?"

"Different is so much better than boring."

I held up my mug and touched it to hers. "Thank you. Can you call my mom and tell her that? I'd appreciate it."

We laughed just as Harrison came back upstairs with little Gabby on his shoulders. She had his same dark, messy hair, and another unwelcome thought of him with kids intruded. His kids would surely have dark hair and big smiles. He'd teach them to play football, too.

He deposited Gabby onto a large blue couch and headed toward our bags. "What room should we be in, B?"

Blair blinked, her expression nervous. "You're in the computer room with the air mattress, Becca is in the guest room."

Harrison's entire face went from joyful to unamused so fast that I bit down on my knuckle to prevent giggles from escaping. He pretty much just told the world we were sleeping together, and instead of being embarrassed, I found it pretty dang funny.

"Blair," he scolded.

"Harrison."

He hardened his stare at his sister, but she was unfazed. "I'll put our stuff in the guest room."

"Can't have you do that. What kind of message would it send my innocent children? You're their uncle, and he can't be sharing a room with a *friend*."

Oh my goodness. My face burned at her insinuation, and I began counting tiles on the floor instead of watching his face. We were friends. Maybe. Well, we had to be. We'd slept together. *Oh, snap. I'm sweating.*

"Becca, want to help me?" His tone was too playful.

Did I miss a joke?

"Hmm?" I said.

"Walk me upstairs."

"Why are you smirking like that? Did I miss something? Your face looks funny." I set the mug down as Gabby and Blair laughed.

"He does look funny. Is that a smile, Gabs? What do you think?" Blair teased, and her daughter laughed harder.

"It is! He's smiling!" I gasped. "Take a picture!"

"Okay, enough." Harrison took my hand and dragged me upstairs. "First them, and now you? All the jokes. I swear...am I that damn grumpy?"

"Maybe?"

He tossed our bags into a bedroom containing nothing more than a large bed and two side tables. Then, shutting the door, he pressed me up against it. Suddenly, I wasn't feeling amused.

"Tell me, Becca." He leaned in, breathing the words into my ear. "Do you want to share a room with me tonight?"

"The children!" I lost my motivation to tease him when he dragged his lips down my neck. "Oh. Oh my."

He grazed my earlobe with his teeth, pulling on it while gripping my sides with his large hands. "I've been a little spoiled lately, and we're—technically—still in our *snow-pocalypse fling*."

"Hmm?" I moaned, arching my back and giving him more access to my neck. Every part of my body tingled at his touch—and after seeing him with kids, I wanted to climb him like a tree.

"I'm getting used to having your fine ass next to me every night, where I can do this." He slid one hand up my shirt and cupped my breast before tweaking my nipple.

"And this." With his other hand, he rubbed my sex through the outside of my clothes. "Do you want to spend the night alone?"

"N-no." My voice shook, and the desperate need to be naked took over. I gripped the edge of his shirt and pushed him back. "I want you."

"God, your eyes are gorgeous when you're horny." He cupped my face and brought his mouth down on mine for a long, deep kiss. "We need to head back downstairs. My sister will know exactly what we are doing, and I can't have her bringing that up all year."

"You devil." I huffed. "You got me all worked up to walk away? I'll remember that, Harrison. I'm keeping score."

"If we're keeping score, babe, you're way ahead on the orgasm count." He grinned, looking all sorts of sexy and naughty. I felt the heat of his stare in my core. "But I'm a good sport."

"Whatever." I rolled my eyes and swatted at his chest.

He caught my hand and held my gaze for more time than I was prepared for. It was an intimate look—one that had meaning beyond friendship or a fling—and I broke it by glancing at his crotch.

"Oh boy, you might need to cool off before you head downstairs," I teased. "Seems like you have something in your pants."

"I'll be sneaking into your room tonight." His eyes lit up. "That's a promise."

"Can't wait. Now, I'm going to go talk more with your sister and learn embarrassing stuff about you."

"She wouldn't dare."

"I think she might." I felt confident and bold, something I hadn't felt with a man in a long time, and waltzed out of the room. "Take your time up here."

Something resembling a growl came from Harrison, and I couldn't stop the smile spreading over my entire face even if I'd tried.

CHAPTER EIGHTEEN

Harrison

I had to hand it to Blair—she had a better bullshit face than I did. The tight lines around her eyes and mouth didn't fool me, but they did her kids. Parents should make sacrifices for their kids. But this is how I found myself sitting on the couch, nursing my third beer while talking to our family on FaceTime.

"Tell me about your presents, Gabby," my mom said in a nicer tone than I was used to. It pleased me when they were kind to Blair's kids, even though they were never as involved with us. Kids were messy and loud, and my parents liked a quieter life. "You look adorable in your pj's. Oh, I wish you were here to snuggle!"

"Grandma, you know we can't fly. It's snowy out. I wish you were here with us!" Gabby moved the iPad and showed the room. "Everyone is here, see?"

"Your Uncle Hank isn't, though."

"Yeah, Gabs. Your *favorite* uncle has a big football game

to coach, unlike your other one." Hank joined the conversation with his annoying, teasing voice. I gripped my beer tighter at his reminder that my team had a losing season while he got lucky. "Tell me who's your favorite. Come on."

"Hank, don't do that," my mom said without any real effort. "It isn't fair to your brother."

Poor Gabby looked at me, her expression worried.

I picked her up, hugging her tightly in my arms. "I think Uncle Hank's ego can take a hit, sweetheart. It'll be good for him."

"Harry! My dude." Hank's voice grated on my last nerve. "You drinking yourself into oblivion after your horrible season? Still think you should've flown out earlier, but whatever. Hey, is that chick still there with you? I thought I spied someone outside of our family."

"Chick? What chick?" my mom asked.

Great.

I pulled at my hair and mouthed *I'm sorry* to Becca. "My neighbor runs the sorority house next door, and some windows blew out. She's staying with me during the storm, and I thought it'd be rude to leave her alone on Christmas."

"A sorority house? That's a little young for you. I know you're trying to get over Vivian, but she was your age. Don't be an idiot, Harrison." My mom's voice grated on me.

I ground my teeth together. "I think Blair wanted to talk to you. Wish you well and all."

I tossed the iPad at my sister. While I appreciated my parents providing a home for me growing up, I didn't enjoy chatting with them now. Every muscle in my body tensed, and I wanted to go for a run.

Great idea. Run in sub-zero temperatures.

My negative thoughts ran rampant, but a small hand landed on my thigh. I glanced at Becca's sweet face, her large eyes softening the longer I looked at her.

"Want to help me find ingredients for some hot chocolate?" she asked. "Maybe we could sneak something harder into yours?"

"God, yes."

She'd given me an out, and I'd snatch it up. I led us out of the living room and into the hall toward the kitchen. Blair's sly smile did not go unnoticed.

"Man, I don't think I can complain about my parents ever again." Becca shook her head, and a line formed between her brows. "Yours are kinda awful. No offense."

Her *no offense* had me chuckling, instantly easing the tension around my shoulders. "Literally, not a single ounce taken. It's become a chore to talk to them and maintain the façade that we're a happy family. The only reason Blair talks to them is to make sure her kids know their grandparents."

"Why are they so..." She trailed off and bit down on her bottom lip, drawing all my attention to it. *How long has it been since I kissed her?* Hours. That wouldn't do.

"Hey, come here." I pulled her against my chest and wrapped my arms around her shoulders, cradling her head against me. She smelled so good and fit so well. The same heavy disappointment hit me, knowing our lives would return to normal the next day. She'd go back to the house and had no business being with a guy like me. I closed my eyes and hugged her. "Thanks for giving me an escape."

"You're welcome."

I lifted her body so her face was even with mine, and she offered me a goofy smile that jumbled my thoughts into messy, emotional nonsense.

"I like your size, Harrison."

"That's what she said." Instead of chastising me, she giggled. Thank God, because I could be immature.

"Well that, too." Red traveled all the way up her neck. "I meant your muscles, your body. I've never dated—uh, been with—a big dude before. Not like you. It makes me feel petite, and I'm not a small woman."

"You're small to me. It's cute." I moved her legs until they wrapped around my waist. "I like *your* size."

Her grip tightened on me as her brows drew together. "I'm sorry your family makes you feel bad about yourself, but I'm glad you have Blair. I tell the girls all the time that it doesn't matter your age, families are tough. Relationships can still be toxic even if you're related to them. Sharing blood doesn't guarantee a relationship. I know they're your parents and brother, but no one should purposefully make others feel that way. No one."

Validation. The tension ebbed and flowed through me, but for the first time in ages, I didn't want sympathy. Vivian had told me to get over it. So having Becca validate the emotional turmoil I'd shoved down felt like a revelation.

"You're right."

"I often am. I tell the girls all the—"

I kissed her. It was a soft, thank-you kiss that started slow. She opened her mouth just enough for me to get a taste of her. The wine from dinner remained on her tongue, and I savored how the rich flavor mixed with her. She kissed me with as much patience and passion as my own, and it wasn't until she ground her hips against me that I stopped.

"Damn, Becca." My breath came out in uneven pants, the blood leaving my head and going to my dick. "I might need to hang out back here a minute."

"You started it, buddy." She pointed her finger at my chest and raised one brow. "I was telling you all the ways your family kinda sucks, and you were telling me how amazing and right I am when you planted those sexy lips on me."

"Sexy lips?"

"I said what I said." Her gaze moved from my eyes to my mouth. "I know what they can do."

"You enjoy teasing me."

She shook her head, running her fingers through my hair. "Nope. I'm just trying to take your mind off that call."

"It's working."

"Success tastes sweet." She adjusted her plaid shirt and blue jeans, giving me a long look before nodding to herself. "I'm not one who condones confrontation, but I think you should just unload on them. Don't take their guilt and nonsense. Tell your brother to suck his own dick and hang up the next time they act like assholes."

"Whoa, I didn't realize sweet Becca had this mean side."

"Not mean." She ran a hand through her messy hair.

She was always pretty, but knowing how she was on

the inside? She was gorgeous with a heart of gold. Strong. Fierce. Unapologetically herself. I couldn't believe I'd passed on two years that I could've been telling her how amazing she was.

She clicked her tongue. "I tend to get defensive for those I care about. It doesn't happen often, but I can if provoked. I went off on one of the girls' friends who stole from her last year. I tell you, that little thief was scared."

While I wanted to hear all about how she'd scared someone, her words about caring for me stood out like flashing neon lights. *She cares about me.* My chest tightened, and the urge to kiss her again was overpowered by worry. If she cares about me, then that means feelings, and feelings mean a relationship. She looked at me expectantly, and it felt like a balloon was growing inside my lungs. Did I want a relationship with her?

Maybe?

I could get fired and have to move, and she lived in a house with all the girls. It would never work. But also, not seeing her or kissing her again wouldn't work, either.

Say something. Anything.

I must've been quiet too long because her face fell, and the familiar blush graced her skin.

"Snap." She gulped. "I care about you like I do all my neighbors. Like, *friendly* and 'thanks for saving me from the blizzard' care. That's what I meant. Don't get all panicky. It's fine. It's no big deal at all. For real. I swear it." She backed away.

It took her movement to snap me out of my little mind

freeze, and I intertwined our fingers and halted her retreat by placing our hands together, palm to palm. I could panic later, after she was asleep. Right now, I needed to ease her mind. "Hey now. I care about you, too. Not necessarily just in a *neighborly* way, but also in an 'I like getting naked with you' way."

A small smile played on her lips, and the hesitant look in her eyes evaporated. "Okay, good." She released our hands and moved toward the kitchen, but not before adding a little sway to her strut. "Glad that almost embarrassing moment has passed. Now, I really do want a hot chocolate. I'm going through withdrawal, and that's not good for anybody."

"You have a chocolate problem." I entered the room and found her already rummaging through Blair's cabinets.

I grabbed the ingredients and handed them to her as Blair walked into the room with my parents and brother still on the call. Hank was blabbing about football with my parents encouraging him. My shoulders tightened, and I cracked my knuckles so loudly that Blair shot me a concerned look. "Sorry."

"Is that Harrison again? Let me have him," Hank said.

I shook my head, but Blair ignored it and passed me the iPad. Becca's face hardened as I met her gaze. No more sympathy. No more letting Hank be an asshole.

"What, Hank?" My tone was short.

"What's with the 'tude? If you're getting laid, I figured you'd be in a better mood. Well, maybe not since you sucked ass this season."

"Well, bro, with you somehow making it this far with

your team, I figured you'd have better things to do than behave like a dick to us. But we can't all know everything."

Becca snorted, her reaction encouraging me. Hank's expression turned wounded, and he looked over his shoulder at our mom. A thirty-year-old man was getting his mom involved.

"Harrison, don't talk to Hank in that rude tone. He has enough to worry about with the game coming up. Be a better brother."

"Nah, I'm good. I'm a fantastic brother to Blair and uncle to her kiddos." I waited as my mother stuttered and blinked. *Had I ever spoken out to her? Is this the first time?* The realization was like a bolt of adrenaline, and I kept going. "You're a man–child, Hank. Don't bring Mom into this. And by the way, if you want to even be considered in the running for favorite uncle, try showing up for anything. A birthday, a dinner, hell, even a random drop-in. You can't buy your way for the kids to like you. They're better than that, and smarter. Now I'm going to enjoy the rest of this holiday with people who care about me. Bye."

I hung up and handed the device back to my sister. The milk sat in the fridge, and I passed it to Becca, ignoring the look on my sister's face. I wasn't sure if my stomach swooped because it felt good or if I regretted what I'd done. "Can you make me a cup, too, Becca?"

"Hell yes, I can. You deserve more than this after that little showdown." Becca moved toward me with her hand raised. "High five, man!"

Pride warmed me as I smacked my hand to hers. "God, I have a high right now."

"I cannot believe you just did that. Finally." Blair's shocked expression changed to joy as she joined the mini celebration. "I know they're family, and Ben wants the kids to have all their grandparents since he came from a small family, but damn they annoy me. Good for you, Harrison." Beside her, the iPad chimed. "Uh-oh, they are calling back."

"Ignore it." Becca stood and hit the red button on Blair's device. "I'm about to make hot chocolate for everyone. Let's put on a holiday movie, enjoy the drinks, and relax. You all go sit down, and I'll serve."

"I can help," I offered.

It was cute the way she bossed us all around. I could imagine, yet again, why the sorority girls liked and respected her so much. She took care of those around her, supported them, and never lost her cool.

"Nope, I've got it. Enjoy time with your family, Harrison. It's important. I'll be in there in a minute." She reached over and squeezed my wrist with her fingers, making her eyes go all buggy.

"What the hell are you trying to tell me right now?"

"Ugh, way to make it not discreet. Go hang with your sister. This is a bonding moment."

"We don't need to bond." I rolled my eyes, but Becca flicked me. "Hey!"

"No funny business later if you don't go."

"Whoa." I held up both hands in surrender. "I'm going."

"I knew that would work." She gave me a smug grin and mumbled *horndog* under her breath as I walked away. We had a couple hours until nighttime, and I couldn't wait to get in bed with her.

Blair knew Becca was more than my friendly single neighbor and still made a point to put us in separate rooms. The house was silent, and it was like I was a teenager again, sneaking around. It wasn't like Blair would ground me for going into Becca's guest room, but she would give me shit.

The guest room sat three doors down from the makeshift room I'd been forced into. I tiptoed past the kids' rooms and the sitting area without any issue. *Score.* Then, as I touched the handle to Becca's room, something shuffled behind me.

"I knew it." Blair grinned.

"Were you—are you waiting to see if I snuck into her room? Are you shitting me?" My heartbeat raced.

"I did what I did to find out the truth. It's like pulling teeth. One-word answers are bullshit. She's more than just a neighbor." She pointed a finger at me. "She encouraged you to stand up to our family, didn't she?"

"Christ." I ran my hand over my face and laughed. "You're the same nosy punk you were growing up."

"So? Dish it." She smiled so widely that she looked insane, like the Joker without makeup. "Are you dating? Do you like her? I like her a lot. She's great with kids, and she doesn't buy Hank's act."

"She's the sorority house mom I went out with two years ago." I sighed, hating how I ended things based on assumptions. She was more...everything. She deserved the absolute best.

"You've dated her before?" She arched her eyebrows. "That's right. The high-maintenance one. I remember. I have no idea why you'd think she's high-maintenance. She seems chill."

Yeah, I fucked that one up. I ran a hand over my chest, pulling on my shirt to get some air flow. This conversation had me sweating. "Not everything has to be something, okay? We've enjoyed being locked in together during the storm. We're two consenting, unattached adults who know what we're doing."

"Enjoyed, huh?" She made another stupid face, and a part of me expected her to start humming *Harrison and Becca sitting in a tree, K-I-S-S-I-N-G.* "You must've since you're sneaking into her room while my innocent children sleep down the hall."

"Blair..." I warned, my patience already thinning.

"You like this girl. Good for you."

I ran my hand over my face, trying to find the right words so she'd leave me alone. "Yeah. I guess I do. There, happy?"

She wiggled her eyebrows and made a fist in the air like she'd scored a touchdown with ten seconds left on the clock. "Yes. I am. I love her. She's like a breath of fresh air."

She's not wrong. "Is this interrogation done or what?"

"Ugh. Rude. You're disobeying my rules in my home

and are giving me the brush-off. Just tell me—is this gonna be a thing? Will we see her again?"

I just want to get Becca naked. So I said the first thing that came to mind, not really thinking about the truth because the truth meant feelings. It meant chancing another screwup and hurting Becca.

"I don't know, Blair. No? Maybe? It's been a couple days, and the storm forced us together. If the power hadn't gone out, I don't think we'd even be on speaking terms."

That didn't sit well with me. It had only been a short time, but it felt like Becca had been around longer. *She knows me better than Vivian did after the four years she knew me.*

Blair frowned. "You're different with her. She's nothing like your ex-wife, and I know the kids like her already. I'm saying, Harry, if anyone can break through the twenty-foot-high walls around your heart, it's her."

A second thought of Vivian in ten seconds. No thank you. I shuddered at the reminder of my failed marriage and had to end the conversation. I had a beautiful woman waiting for me on the other side of the door.

"I'm not about to have a touchy-feely conversation in your hallway in the middle of the night. Sometimes, it's sex. That's it. Nothing more or less." I glared at my dear sister.

She flipped me the bird. "Don't be an asshole. It's nice seeing you with someone. That's all. Now I'm going to go put headphones on and pretend I don't know what your intentions are right now."

"Blair!" I shooed her away, but not before she gave me

a wink and thumbs-up. She was a pain in my ass but I loved her.

Finally. Becca. I knocked on the door with two knuckles, and the door flew open. Her face was bare, her hair up in a bun, and she wore an extra-large rugby shirt that went to her knees. She was fucking adorable.

"Oh, hello." She smiled, her cheeks already pink. "Fancy seeing you here."

"May I come in?"

She sucked her bottom lip into her mouth and glanced down the hallway. "Will we get caught? Is it safe?"

"Do you want to get caught?" I lowered my voice, taking a step into the bedroom. Her light vanilla scent enveloped me, calming and enticing me. "We'll have to be real quiet."

Something flashed across her face. Concern, worry. Something I couldn't pinpoint. I wanted to ask about it but never got the chance.

She fisted my shirt and yanked me closer to her as heat entered her eyes. "I can probably manage to be quiet. It depends on what you do to my body."

"Mm, I love doing things to your body."

"Were you talking to yourself out in the hallway? Giving yourself a pep talk? *I, Harrison, am sexy. I'm the man. I'm the best in bed, oh yeah.*"

The way she lowered her voice had me laughing, and I wasted no time kissing her. She giggled against my mouth, and I backed her up until her knees hit the bed, causing both of us to land on the soft mattress. "I do not sound like that."

I moved my lips down to her neck. She always smelled so damn good. She squirmed beneath me, and I bit down.

She moaned, arching her back and pressing her body against mine. "I bet you were talking to yourself, building yourself up with all sorts of stupid pickup lines to impress me. I mean, I am a pretty intimidating woman. Everyone is afraid of me."

The audacity of this woman. I paused and positioned myself on my elbows so I could look down at her. For the briefest of moments, I fantasized about a life with her: playful, happy, sunny. Laughter, and chocolate, and a teammate who was rooting for me through rain or shine.

Kissing and cuddles, memories. Joy.

Total opposite of my ex. She was along for the winning, not the losing side of life. Relationships required both.

That's why Blair and Becca were so important. Something plucked in my chest, a quiet want making me think about asking for more, but I ignored it. I studied her, content with being with her in the moment.

Her eyelashes were crazy long, and the night-light showcased the shape of her face. I pressed my lips to her forehead, not quite able to express what I was feeling. "You are a marshmallow. Not intimidating."

"Lies." She must have had no idea of my inner turmoil and tickled my sides. "Admit it. You're scared of me because I'm so awesome."

"You do scare me, a little." My throat dried up when she moved her hands from my sides up to my chest. I loved how she touched me like she wanted me, cared for me.

"I've been wanting your hands on me all damn day," I growled.

"Are you always so insatiable?" Her voice dropped, all low and husky. Becca was gorgeous on any given day, but throw in that deep voice and she owned me. "I'm not one to have a sex drive this high, but you've turned me into this...fiend."

"I'm glad I have that effect on you, Becca." I slid my hands beneath her shirt, groaning at all the soft, bare skin under there. "Were you waiting for me, thinking about my hands on your naked body?"

"Yes." She arched her back when I found two pebbled nipples, teasing them with my fingers until she let out a strangled cry. "Mm, that feels good."

"Your skin feels so good." My voice cracked. Her breasts were the perfect size. Her reaction to the slightest touch was enough to get me hard. Just a brush of my palm over her pebbled tips sent her arching off the bed. "So sensitive."

"So good." Her eyes slammed shut, and her chest heaved.

I followed her curves down to her hips, loving how smooth her skin was beneath my calloused hands. She parted her legs for me, not hiding a damn thing about her body. I trailed the sides of her legs and inside her thighs, just barely touching where she needed.

She reached out and gripped my arm, digging her nails into it. "Harrison."

My name was all she said, but it was loaded with need, want, and emotion.

"Please," she moaned.

How could I not give her what she wanted? I slid down the bed, my knees hitting the floor with a slight thud. "I want to make you feel good."

I planned to taste every inch of her again and again. If tonight was our last time, I would make it count. It was selfish, but if she thought back to this time together, I hoped she remembered our chemistry.

Pleasuring her was the only way I could show her how much I cared about her. I went slow—tracing my tongue along each of her thighs, teasing the sensitive skin I knew so well. "Do you know how sexy you are, Becca? Every part of you."

"Shh. More licking, less talking." Her voice came out strangled. She gripped the sheets and thrashed back and forth.

"Bossy Becca. I love the idea of you bossing me around the bedroom." I slowly licked her, focusing on her clit for a full minute before sliding two fingers into her. Very slowly, wanting to drag this out and make her pleasure more intense.

"Tell me what you want."

"Ke-keep doing…oh." She panted.

I quickened the pace, curling my digits inside her as I sucked her swollen clit into my mouth. Nothing mattered besides her pleasure. Her sounds, her scent, the way her skin felt against mine. It was a dream. A fantasy. I loved how she lost control, flung her head back, how she moaned my name and gave me every part of herself.

I flattened my tongue against her, slowing my pace until

sweat covered her entire body. Her stomach trembled, and her thighs tensed. She twitched with need, and only then, I matched my thrusting with my tongue and gave her the pressure she needed.

Her legs tightened around my head, a deep guttural groan escaping before her orgasm hit. She bucked, throaty sounds escaping from her closed lips. I licked harder.

"Damn, you're sexy." My cock was hard as a rod, and I wanted her more than my next breath. I kissed along her stomach, up her chest, and removed her rugby shirt. "I need to feel your skin on mine."

"Then why are you wearing clothes?" Her eyes widened with heat, and my heart skipped a beat. She was perfect.

She yanked my pajamas off with hungry fingers, giggling when my dick slapped against my stomach. But her humor quickly faded as she propped herself up on her elbows, completely naked and open for me. I scrambled for the condom in my pocket, and dropping the wrapper before sliding it on, I positioned myself over her.

A quick expression on her face made me pause. Her eyebrows pinched just a little, and a shadow of concern crossed her eyes. "Hey, you okay?"

"Yes," She gripped my ass with both hands and pulled me toward her. "Why are you stopping, you insane, beautiful man?"

"You had this look on your face. Are you sure? I can go down on you as long as you want." And I would. Happily. I just needed that frown to never return. Ever.

"Shh." She grabbed my face, dragged my mouth to hers,

and kissed me with so much energy that my body tingled. She bit down on my lip, sucking it into her mouth, and my control snapped. She captivated me. No way around it.

She sucked on my tongue as she wrapped her fingers around my dick. I hissed against her mouth, the feel of her velvety fingers enough to make me thrust into her fist.

"Becca," I warned. "I want to be inside you."

"Then get in there." She pushed me onto my back and then crawled over me and positioned my dick at her entrance.

I pulsated with need. The need to take her, to be closer to her. Her hair fell around her shoulders, her perfect pink nipples erect and delectable. My heart hammered against my ribs as she lowered herself onto me, sliding my dick deep into her warm body. Her mouth formed an O as she groaned.

"So thick, so good." She rocked her hips, her teeth biting down on her lower lip as she stared at me. There was something about her large brown eyes that made everything *more*. Like she saw past all my bullshit and liked me anyway.

I let her take control, loving how she took charge. Her eyes were half-closed, and sweat dripped down her chest. Dark shadows highlighted her curves, even giving me a glimpse of her adorable freckles. I could stare at her body for days.

She rocked faster, her cheeks growing redder. I gripped her ass. It was so firm and perfect. She fell forward, our chests squishing together. Her heart beat against mine in the same wild rhythm.

"Yes," she cried out before slamming her mouth onto mine in a wet kiss. "Harrison...yes!"

Her muscles tightened, and I massaged her clit. Her body trembled around me and I kissed her harder, just as she came. She clung to me like she needed me, and I tried not to let that get to my head.

Her post-orgasm look was a punch to the gut. Her gaze so clear, open, and honest, and filled with emotion. The pressure in my chest grew double in size, making an uncomfortable ball form in my throat.

She gave me the sexiest, coy smile before squeezing herself around my cock. Losing control, I flipped her over and thrust into her. She locked her legs around me and ran her tongue over her lips, clawing at me. I cupped the back of her head with one hand and took what she gave to me. Our ragged breathing and my thrusts were the only sounds in the room, and I fucking loved it. She arched her hips, taking me deeper until I came hard and fast.

"Damn." I moaned into her hair, the lingering effects of pleasure flowing through my veins causing feelings and emotions to bubble up. I wanted to tell her how good she smelled and how I could sleep with her a million times and never get bored. That maybe I wanted to see her all the time and *not* as neighbors.

Discarding the condom in the bathroom, I slid back into the bed, completely spent and satisfied—a feeling I hadn't experienced in a long time.

"Damn. Come here, woman." I patted the spot beside

me but she hesitated, making me nervous. "I like you here. Come on."

She ran her fingers over her lips a few times before sliding right next to me, her sides touching mine with no space between our naked bodies.

She fit with me, and not just in the bedroom. Her personality and compassion, the easy way she supported me and shared a passion for her job. It all made my brain fuzzy.

She adjusted her position, tucking herself into my side, and I held her there, tracing my fingers up and down her spine. We had dynamite chemistry and seemed to understand each other.

Tomorrow couldn't be the last day. There was no way.

I had to do something to prolong this time together. I'd talk to her, see if we could make it work. This was too good to pass up, and it felt right knowing we could stay in each other's lives.

CHAPTER NINETEEN

BECCA

Waking up with Harrison's arms around me was a special form of hell. He was warm, beyond sexy, and *not mine*. The words echoed around my brain repeatedly since I'd accidentally heard his conversation with his sister. It was great sex, but that was it.

It was a good thing I'd happened to walk by the door just as he'd admitted what the thing between us was. It was fine. It was a holiday fling, and my love life needed some spice to it. It sucked that my heart forgot she wasn't supposed to involve herself. She usually stayed in her own lane, but, alas, she fell for Harrison.

I catalogued everything about him as he held me—his strong arms, the woodsy scent that would always remind me of Christmas. I could look back on this year and remember our time fondly. Maybe not soon, but eventually. Right?

I should get up. Make a clean break.

I moved to the left just a bit, but before I could step on

the floor, he tightened his hold and yanked me back to bed. "Where you goin'?"

Even his sleepy voice is sexy. "Uh, to the bathroom."

"Come here." He pulled me tight against his chest and kissed the top of my head. "I shit you not, I've never slept better since this storm hit."

My stomach swooped at his words, but I rationalized it. "Maybe you sleep better when it's freezing outside? You could crack a window at night. That'll work."

"It's you." He laughed into my hair. "How much would it take for you to stay in bed with me all day? Those kids wore me out, and I'm more interested in you being naked."

"We're at your sister's house!" I swatted at him, but butterflies exploded in my gut. While he might not have feelings for me, maybe we could continue sleeping together? *I can totally pretend I'm okay with that. For sure. Totes cool, Becca.*

Not.

"Later then." He ran his hands up and down my back, massaging me in various places. Succumbing to his touch would've been so easy, but I forced myself out of the bed. It was better for the both of us.

I didn't respond to his comment. Correcting him made no sense since I'd be returning to the sorority house. There was so much to do before the girls returned. My escape from reality was slowly coming to an end, regardless of whether I wanted it to or not. The house and the girls came first, not my love life, and it would be better if I focused on that instead of the inevitable goodbye that was building. The one date from two years ago had been hard to get over, so this? It would be way worse.

Plus his comment to his sister and the fact we'd agreed to a blizzard-buddy relationship. Blizzard buddies who boned for a bit. The tagline wrote itself, and I chewed on my already chapped lips, hating how my shoulders slumped with sadness.

Being sad was tough for me. I preferred thinking of silver linings and that the glass was always half-full. But this…I needed a distraction from myself and the onslaught of feelings. *The house!*

"What time did you want to leave today?" My words slurred together. "I'm good with whatever you want to do, but I'd like to get started with everything at the house. The window needs to be repaired, and I doubt that's the only thing wrong with the place. It's ginormous. The lack of heat could've messed with stuff, and I should take inventory of the girls' rooms and the kitchen and furnace. Oh, and the pipes! I hope they didn't burst. We didn't think to turn on a faucet. Snap." I rubbed my forehead, overwhelmed with everything. Feelings, the to-do-list, saying goodbye to our temporary situation. "I need to get to work ASAP."

He coughed. "Sure, right."

I glanced at him, taking in his furrowed brow, before stepping into the bathroom. But duty called, and I shut the door before asking him what was wrong. It was silly to get all nervous and uncertain about how to act with him. We'd survived the storm together, celebrated the holiday with his family, and slept together multiple times. Orgasms didn't equate to feelings, no matter what I thought. People did casual stuff all the time. *Look at the girls and all their casual hookups. If they can do it, so can I.*

I splashed water on my face a couple of times and almost didn't recognize myself with the rosy cheeks and wide eyes. *Must be the orgasms.* It was the only explanation. It couldn't be Harrison and the way he relaxed once I got to know him, or the way he was with kids, or even how much he loved his sister. His kindness and humor were subtle, but definitely there.

Knock it off. I scolded myself for letting my mind wander into dangerous territory. It wouldn't do me any good to think about what-ifs with my sexy neighbor.

After brushing my teeth, I accepted I'd have to fake it until I got back to the house. I preached to the girls they should enjoy the good things and live in the moment. So I'd do just that. Harrison and I had a great couple of days together. End of story. We could wave when we got mail and smile if we crossed paths on the quad. Well, I would smile. Harrison would probably give a slight lift of his chin.

Content with my decision to act strong, I left the bathroom and found Harrison half-dressed and throwing his clothes into his overnight bag. He must've gone to his room and grabbed it. The hard-earned muscles on his back shifted with each movement, and it was a fist-biting visual.

Sex. I can do sex with him, just not feelings.

"Have I told you how sexy your back is?"

He turned, one brow raised and a smirk forming. "Doesn't hurt to hear it multiple times."

"Well, it is very sexy." I walked up to him and dragged my finger up his spine, tracing the outlines of his angles. "Didn't realize I had a thing for backs until I saw yours."

Turning toward me, his eyes warmed, and he tipped my chin up with his fingers. "You're cute."

The words and his gentleness had my heart hammering against my rib cage. "I do what I can." I closed my eyes as he brought his lips against mine in a brief kiss. "Shall we brave the small army your sister birthed?"

"I guess." He pulled me against him in an entire chest-to-chest, full-armed hug that felt like home and Christmas wrapped up in one gesture. I squeezed his torso, resting my head on his chest.

Instead of confessing how much I liked him, I said the next thing that popped into my mind—the never-ending place of random and useless facts. "Did you know hugging someone produces dopamine in your system, essentially causing you happiness? There are people who cuddle others for money. It's basically getting paid to hug strangers. Seems kinda weird, but it wouldn't be so bad if you could demand they shower beforehand. Maybe I should look into that during breaks. I don't know. I'm not strapped for cash, but a little extra moolah is always nice, right?"

"Are you nervous, Becca?" He pulled back from the hug and narrowed his eyes, assessing me with his tongue pressing against the inside of his cheek. "It's been a while since you spat out random, yet super-fun, facts."

I broke out of the hug and organized my things into the bag. "I'm not nervous. Just anxious, that's all. It's like whenever we went on vacation when I was a kid. I could never enjoy the last two days because all I thought about was getting home and returning to normal life. My brain is wired to think about all the things I have to do, and I've already lost four days of my break to clean the house. And who knows how much the window will cost to repair."

I took a breath, hoping I didn't sound as erratic as I felt. My emotions were out of control and downright embarrassing. If I kept talking and planning, then I could avoid the feelings I didn't want to deal with. It wasn't like I could tell him I liked him. Not again.

Not after that date and ghosting two years ago.

Not after I heard what he told his sister. I had a little bit of pride and dignity left.

I straightened my posture. "Aren't you anxious?"

"Not really."

His tone was different than earlier, but I couldn't place it. Like he wasn't happy, nor sad, nor angry. Resigned, maybe? I wasn't sure. He slipped on a shirt before turning back toward me. His muscles flexed against the cotton material.

"I'm going to get coffee. Come and join me when you're ready," he said in the same stoic tone.

My gut exploded with worry.

"Okay. Sure. Yeah." I nodded.

He gave me a brief smile before leaving the room, and for the life of me, I couldn't figure out why my body shivered.

I couldn't imagine what I might've said to upset him, yet I could've sworn he was mad when he shut the door.

Stop acting weird and be cool.

Yes, that's what I'd do.

I packed the rest of my stuff, put on a warm sweater and jeans, and made sure my hair wasn't too crazy before heading downstairs.

"It was wonderful to meet you, Becca. Seriously. I hope we see you again soon." Blair hugged me as we said goodbye, and I avoided Harrison's stare as he tried communicating something to me with his green irises alone. A huge mistake on his part—I wasn't fluent in straight eye contact.

Instead of agreeing with Blair, I thanked her. "It was wonderful spending the holiday with your family. Thank you. It would've been very cold and lonely by myself in the huge house."

"Our pleasure." She motioned with her chin to her kiddos, and each one came up and hugged my legs. "What do you say, loves?"

"Nice to meet you!"

"Merry Christmas!"

"I like your sweater!" Gabby made us all laugh.

It was a rainbow sweater with a unicorn wearing a lime green scarf. It matched my winter coat. "Thank you! I love super bright shirts."

"I do, too!"

I bent down and gave them all hugs, and my chest tightened. This family was real and kind, and it was easy to imagine fitting in with them.

"Keep Harrison in line for us, would you?"

Ben earned a grin from me. "I'll do my best."

"I can hear you." Harrison put a hand on my shoulder, and I tensed. It was such a boyfriend thing to do.

Oh, honey, it's time to go! Say goodbyes!

"We should get going, but it was great seeing you. You guys are all my favorite." A genuine warmth came from the hard-ass football coach.

The world really didn't know him. It saddened me because they were missing out.

"You, too." Blair hugged her brother.

"Ready Becca?" Harrison flexed his jaw as he shouldered the bags.

"Yup. Lots to do today now that the ice age is over." I waved at Blair and her family and headed toward the truck.

Each step brought more sadness. It was the same melancholy I'd get at the end of a vacation, only this time it was rooted around my heart.

Harrison loaded the back of the truck without a word, and an awkward tension filled the cab once he joined me. He gripped the steering wheel, swallowing so hard his Adam's apple bobbed. "You buckled in?"

"Yes." I motioned with my finger as though checking it off a list.

He didn't react. Instead he nodded and started the drive home.

A million thoughts raced through my mind—like how much I liked his sister and her family, how much I liked him, and how much I hated that the temporary arrangement was coming to an end. Do I thank him after I get my stuff from his house? Do I kiss him before leaving? Do I give him a high five for a great time? I didn't know. This was out of my element, and I couldn't risk asking for more. I'd have to follow his lead.

Goodbyes were awful.

He said he would be my date, though!

A thrill shot through me knowing I'd see him again. He wouldn't back out of that, I was sure. But what else did that mean? Did he regret agreeing to it?

My heart raced as I thought about him showing up to the damn gala and putting a stop to my mom's shenanigans. But I wouldn't bring it up yet. There was an obvious finality in the air. The ball of nerves and anxiety grew in my gut, and I snuck a glance at him. His shoulders were straight, and his jaw was tense, like he had ten pieces of gum in his mouth holding his teeth together. Was he wondering, too, about how to end this without hurting my feelings? Or was he simply focusing on the icy road? *Good lord, this is why I don't date.*

"You're squirming over there. You good?" He flicked his gaze to me for a second.

"Uh, yeah. Just thinking."

He let out a pent-up breath, like he was annoyed with me. "I'm sure the house is doing fine. We checked it, remember?"

"Right." I didn't tell him the house was the furthest thing from my mind. But he'd given me an out, and I had welcomed it. *Coward.*

"There's so much to do." I pulled at a hangnail.

"It'll be quicker if we tag-team it." He gave me a tight smile.

"Tag-team?"

"If you want." He spoke fast, and I swore the man stuttered. "If you want an extra set of capable hands, I mean. I'd be happy to help you."

He's being nice. That's all.

"Yeah, that'd be nice. I'll do a quick assessment and let you know what needs to be done."

"Got it." The smile disappeared, and he turned on the radio.

Holy moly, things got uncomfortable fast. The drive that lasted almost thirty minutes to his sister's house was cut in half now that salt trucks were working. We pulled into his driveway after I almost tore off my whole nail. My entire lower back was a muddle of sweat, and I couldn't do a damn thing about it. This was it, the end of our blizzard-buddy shenanigans. He stopped the car, put the gearshift in park, and unbuckled. I undid my seat belt, too, slowly chewing my poor lip until it stung.

"Wait here. I'll grab the bags and get the door unlocked first. It's still cold outside." He didn't wait for a reply.

Minutes later, he signaled for me to join him at the front door, and I ran. He narrowed his eyes at me. "Be careful, Becca."

"I made it fine." I brushed past him into his house and welcomed the familiar scent. It was warm, cozy, and pure Harrison. Woodsy and clean. The daylight shined through the windows, showcasing all the decorations we'd put up. It was like another hit to the stomach, and I said the first thing I could. "Your heat came on!"

"Yup. Thankfully. Much better than a fire."

Memories of that fire would stay with me for years—the smell, the picture Harrison made bending over as he placed more wood on it, and the fact it had kept us from freezing to death.

The bed we'd shared was unmade and messy from our last time together, and a pang of hurt hit me as I stared at the wrinkled sheets. I cleared my throat and tried to keep the conversation going. This inevitable goodbye hurt more than it should. Nervous, desperate laughter took over, and years of faking it 'til I made it helped me form words even though I wanted to cry.

"It worked well enough, though. We survived even though my hair will smell like firewood for a week."

He didn't acknowledge my comment, and instead walked farther into the house and began pulling things out of the cupboards without looking in my direction. "Want to get your stuff together? The bowl game starts in about an hour, and I plan to drink beer and watch it." He set a single dish and a bag of chips on the counter. One bowl, not two. *Time for me to go.*

He placed his hands on his hips and stared out the window, an unreadable expression on his face. Embarrassment and regret threatened to spill over, so I ducked my head and grabbed the few items I'd left around the room. I tripped over the carpet but righted myself.

"Right. Of course. The bowl. Hank." I nodded hard even though he wasn't watching me. "You've been more than gracious sharing your home and family with me."

He exhaled before walking down the hallway that led to his bedroom. My mind was torn between feeling his pain at the knowledge his brother was coaching in the game he'd worked all year to be included in, while also mourning the fact something had shifted between us the moment the sun came up and the town thawed.

I smiled at the Snoopy decorations as I zipped my duffel bag shut. My books and yarn didn't fit so I had them in my hands.

I hated this moment. We were freaking adults, and I'd had a great time with him. Sure, it hurt knowing he just wanted sex and someone to keep warm with for the week, but it had been more than that to me. It was almost like we'd formed a friendship. A really hot friendship where I could be myself and he could peel back the layers he was too afraid to show others. We fit.

It wasn't pride that stopped me—the one thing age had taught me each year was that admitting the truth, even if it was tough, was always better. I needed to tell him that without a single expectation of him feeling the same way. No regrets, and I could move on. I'd say how I wouldn't be opposed to hanging out together. No commitment. I'd keep it casual. Super cas. The chillest. That didn't scream *relationship*.

Proud of my decision, I had my bags in my hands, balancing the books and yarn on top of them, and went in search of him. I poked my head into the kitchen and then the hallway. "Harrison?"

No response.

I moved closer to his bedroom, but there wasn't a single light on or movement.

I saw him come back here, though. Was he hiding from me? Hoping to avoid ending our fling?

He did ghost me two years ago.

My eyes stung at the possibility that he might ghost me again, and I waited a full minute before calling out to him.

"Harrison, I'm leaving. I don't...want to, okay? I liked this time with you. I like you, actually. I'd prefer to say this to your face." I waited for his footsteps that were so familiar to me now.

Nothing.

Maybe he went to the basement?

I moved toward the door with the blanket shoved under it and cracked it open. "Harrison?"

Nothing, again.

One more try. His truck still sat in the driveway, so he didn't drive away...which meant he was in the house. *But why is he hiding?*

Maybe he's in the bathroom. Oh, snap—that would be weird. I chewed my lip again and checked the guest bathroom. The door was wide open. "Harrison?"

"No, it's over." His voice came from the back of the house. "Don't say anything more."

My stomach hollowed, and I blinked back the sting in my eyes. *It's over?* Just like that?

"Wow, uh, okay. Yeah." I cleared my throat and rushed toward the front door. I couldn't get out of there fast enough. He said something else, and I stopped, desperately wanting him to explain himself more, but it was just a quick bye.

I thought there'd been something between us, even if it was brief. He'd felt it, too, I was so sure. But this... I sighed, my shoulders slumping as I stomped out of his house and his life.

He'd said it's over, which was better than ghosting me. Message received.

The wind whipped at my face, and my tears stung, but I pushed forward. A part of me hoped he would realize his mistake and run out, but it never happened. I checked every ten yards because, though he could act tough all he wanted, he had a huge heart under all that flannel. I'd felt it.

The walk alone was uneventful and cold. I glanced at his house one last time, and my heart jumped into my throat when he ran out his front door.

He's coming over here! Thank goodness!

Only he was running in the wrong direction. He sprinted to his truck, his phone against his ear, and sped out of the driveway without a single look in my direction.

Cool. Great. I'm fine.

The wind howled, and the arctic temperatures knocked sense into me. I ran inside the large house, vowing to never let Harrison Cooper upset me again. It was stupid. He'd never promised a single thing—it was my expectations and hopes that caused the pain racing through my body now that our blizzard fling was over.

CHAPTER TWENTY

HARRISON

Son of a bitch. Dexter shouldn't have gotten behind the wheel after drinking. I sat in the hospital waiting room, clutching my head in my hands, a mixture of anger and despair combining into a dangerous thought that leaned toward saying words I shouldn't.

I told you so. I fucking told you so.

"Coach, I'm going to get a bottle of water. Need anything?"

"No thanks, Brian." I gave the sophomore a tight smile before he retreated down the hall to the vending machines. It had already been eight hours, and my stomach growled and my throat hurt. The thought of eating anything made me want to vomit, though.

The text on my phone from one of my captains flashed in my mind, and I gripped the back of my neck, worry wedging its way down my spine.

> He ran off the road and slammed into a house. He
> went through the windshield and is in surgery. We
> don't know anything more.

Dexter might not make it. Words like medically induced coma and brain damage were whispered, and every time I glanced at his parents, my stomach hollowed out. The kid partied too hard. He knew better. On Christmas Day. In the middle of the afternoon, he got hammered. If he survived this, he was still an idiot.

He should've made a better decision. That was the root of my anger, and I bounced my knee up and down at a rapid pace, hoping to relieve the boiling emotions. Ten other members of the team lined the waiting room, each wearing a worried expression. All the townies and guys who lived close by had showed up for their teammate. For the first time all year, they were united. Would this have happened if we had more team unity? If we had a collective vision, like Becca talked about, would he be more focused? Could I have been a better coach and mentor for these guys?

Dexter's two best friends sat next to his parents, one holding his mom's hand while the team said a prayer. It smelled like coffee and antiseptic, and no one spoke louder than a whisper. Someone turned on the bowl game, and I welcomed the noise.

Things had shifted into a different perspective when one of my own players might not make it through the night. It was insane to think just hours ago, I was sulking because

Becca wanted to go to her house and my brother was coaching the biggest game of his life.

Now Dexter and my team deserved all my attention. These were *my* guys. Through the good, bad, frustrating, and challenging moments, they were my team, and I was their leader. It was time I owned up to the difficulties.

"Alice, Chris, do you need anything from your home?" I asked Dexter's parents. "One of the guys or I can run to get it."

"Uh," Dexter's mom stuttered before looking at her husband. "Our dog is home."

Greg stood up, all six feet six of him, and nodded. "Can I have your keys? I can watch him until we get news. I love dogs."

"I'll go with," another player said. "Want us to grab any clothes?"

Alice and Chris thanked them before pulling them into a hug.

Pride filled me. Two other guys asked how they could help. A meal train was formed, and an hour later, a doctor pushed through the doors. It was exactly like the movies: the solemn expression, the almost deafening silence that exploded in the room, and the breath-stopping moment before he spoke.

"Parents of Dexter Smith?" he said.

"That's us." They stood; Chris's arm wrapped tightly around Alice. "Is he...how is Dexter?"

"Come with me."

Fuck! My stomach felt like it was full of acid. I reached

out and grabbed the guy next to me. The two minutes Alice
and Chris were gone from the room felt like a lifetime. My
brain tried analyzing their expressions in the seconds before
they spoke. Alice's eyebrows were drawn together and lines
danced on her forehead, and Chris's lips were turned down
on both sides.

"He's stabilized," Alice said. "They're waiting for the
brain swelling to go down. Then, they'll assess him for any
brain damage. They're . . . hopeful."

Relief flowed through me because the diagnosis could've
been worse. Dexter wasn't in the clear, but he was alive.
More prayers were said, a couple of guys cussed under their
breath, and Dexter's parents disappeared into their son's hospital room.

"Coach, can I talk to you?" Dean looked nothing like
the cocky guy I'd known for the past two years. The overtalkative, charismatic flirt with easy smiles now appeared
broken, his eyes watering and his hands trembling as he ran
them through his hair. "Please?"

"Sure." I led us to a private nook, away from the growing crowd. The fact they all left their families to be here
meant . . . everything. Maybe there was more loyalty in them
than I'd thought. It shouldn't take an accident to bring
everyone together, but this was a good sign. Maybe I hadn't
totally failed them.

"What's going on, Dean?"

Dean focused on the ground, shuffling his feet back and
forth. "I was with him."

"With Dexter?"

"Yes." He blinked, his face blanching before he sniffed. "It's my fault."

"What is? The accident?"

"I let him drive. I shouldn't have. I knew he was probably over the limit, but I didn't stop him." His voice shook, and his entire body sagged. "This is all my fault. The holiday party, the booze. What if he doesn't make it, Coach? I can't...I just..." He stopped and sobbed.

I pulled him into my arms and hugged him tight. I couldn't imagine the guilt he carried, and his cries made my chest ache. It wasn't Dean's fault that Dexter chose to drive drunk. How many times had they partied? A hundred?

"Listen to me, Dean." Keeping my hands on his arms, I pushed him away just far enough to make eye contact. "You can't think like that. It's not productive. Be strong for the team."

"I didn't stop him. I—"

"Shh." I waited until his eyes met mine. "Dexter made his own decision. He's his own person. No one is blaming you, and you shouldn't put this on yourself. Tell me you understand."

He nodded, his lips trembling. "I-I understand."

"Good. Let's head back, but you call me anytime, alright?" I squeezed his shoulder, leading us back toward the waiting room.

We needed to stay together as a team. To support Dexter and his parents, to support each other regardless of what happened. But more importantly, to use this moment as a learning opportunity. The team needed a redirect.

The cackle of the TV filled the room. I cleared my throat, rocking back on my heels as I scanned the faces in the room. We needed to do something.

"I'm officially inviting everyone over to my house." I raised my voice so everyone heard me. "We'll have food to eat, places to sleep, and ears to listen if you need to talk. I'll reach out to the other players, too."

A couple of the guys nodded, but most of them looked at me with wide eyes, like I'd announced I hated winning. I shouldn't have taken it personally, but I wasn't that naïve. My reputation preceded me, and Becca's words about me being grumpy echoed through my mind.

She would be so pleased.

If she wants me.

No. It wasn't the time to think about her urgency to return to her house. The second I got the call, I'd raced to the hospital with nothing more than a shouted goodbye to her. Even now, I scanned my phone, desperate to find her number from two years ago. I'd deleted it, her name nowhere to be found. I ran a hand through my hair, a desperate need to talk to her making me jittery. My team had to come first. She'd understand. She had to.

"Coach, there's something taped to your door."

I squinted at the door, and sure enough, there was an envelope right in the middle. "Huh. Thanks. Grab it for me, would you? I'm going to bring in the supplies."

"You got it."

Dean had shadowed me since our conversation hours earlier, and for the first time since meeting him, he had a humbleness about him. Dexter's accident aged every one of the guys, and I knew our lives would change forever.

"I'm glad you're having us all over here, Coach. The thought of going back to my place alone or bringing the mood down at my parents' house...I can't do it." Dean hung his head.

"We're a team, and that means family. Family belongs together through the good times and the bad."

Ironic I can't follow my own advice.

I hadn't thought of Hank or his game once since going to the hospital—I had no idea who'd won, and I didn't care. I'd follow up with Blair later or check out highlights once things settled down. My guys mattered more.

"I'm going to put all the drinks in the cooler. You set the food out and try and find as many pillows as you can in the closet by the door." I pointed down the hall.

Dean did as I asked as I unloaded all the water bottles. As I made a trip to the garage, I glanced over at the sorority house, imagining what Becca was up to. It had been over a day since we'd returned from my sister's, and we hadn't spoken since. I missed her.

I missed her smile and her warmth, the way she listened with her whole body and offered advice. She'd know what to do for the team right now, and my heart thudded faster at the possibility she didn't feel anything for me.

"Coach, you good?" Dean tilted his head as he eyed me. "You have an odd expression on your face."

"Just thinking about my holiday."

"I'll never forget this one, as long as I live." He rubbed his palms over his eyes and sighed.

"Hey, we have to believe he'll be okay." I waved at the three cars parking on the street near my house. *More guys.* "He's a stubborn son of a bitch. Remember when he refused to let you have a better record in the gym? Or when he twisted his wrist but didn't tell anyone because he wanted to practice? He might be a party animal, but he's tough."

"He is." Dean nodded, his shoulders relaxing a little bit. "I'll think of those memories."

"You do that."

Everyone parked, food was set out, and fifteen guys sat in my house. It was a tight fit, but it felt right. I took it in, watching as two players I'd never seen interact before joked around. I smiled. This was a proud moment.

"Hey!" Dean stood up, and the room fell silent. "Dexter's mom just texted me."

My pulse raced in my ears. We all leaned forward.

"He's showing signs of brain activity, and they're thinking about waking him up tomorrow. All of his tests came back good so far."

Cheers and sighs of relief echoed through the room. I sat at the kitchen table, thankful that his progress continued in the right direction. Dexter had a long road ahead of him, but I'd take baby steps. *Thank God.*

The thought of Dexter...no. I wouldn't think about alternatives. He'd be okay.

It was then I noticed the letter on the table.

HARRISON.

My name was scribbled in purple sparkly pen. *Becca.* A smile formed on my lips as I opened it. Knowing her, it could be anything. A poem, a song, a picture she'd drawn. A dumb quote about yonic things. Hell, she was full of surprises. I flipped the paper open, desperate to read it. To get a piece of her.

Harrison,

I realized I don't have your number, otherwise I would've texted you. It seems silly I don't have your number after everything we went through, but here we are. I wanted to thank you from the bottom of my heart for this week. From helping with the window to being my blizzard buddy, I will remember this holiday with great fondness.

We didn't exactly part on good terms, and that's okay with me; I know you had an important game to watch, and we eventually had to go back to our normal lives. Please don't feel bad about wanting to avoid "the talk." I'm okay. We can smile at each other if we cross paths on campus, and I am not holding any resentment toward you. We never made any commitments or false promises. If you were worried about how to tell me it was over, please don't.

This week was one of the best of my life, even though we could've died in the cold. So thank you.

Becca

PS The window guy is coming tomorrow. Yay!

What the actual fuck?

Was she...breaking up with me? I read the letter again and determined that, yup, this was how Becca broke up with people. In adorably awkward letters. If I wasn't so upset and confused, I would've framed this. It was so heartfelt, so her.

"Coach, you okay?" One of the younger players arched his brows until they disappeared into his hairline.

"Why?"

"You just cussed."

"Shit." I didn't mean to say that out loud. "I think I just got dumped."

He laughed and leaned toward the letter, but I snatched it out of his view. "You got dumped in a letter? That's hilarious."

"No. It's not." I stood, torn between demanding an explanation for the absurd note and wanting to rip it into a million pieces.

If you were worried about how to tell me it was over, please don't. What bullshit was that? When did I say anything related to us being over? I'd yelled at her that I had to go, and that was that. Sure, not a good move, but she'd understand once I explained.

Maybe I could've explained why I sprinted out of the house. Did she think I'd ghosted her again? My stomach tightened, the chance of being with her again slipping away. I scrubbed my face with my palms, pushing on my eyes until white spots appeared. If she wanted to break up with me, it wasn't a good sign.

I glanced out the window toward the house, almost laughing at how much had changed in a week. Well, how much I'd changed. Maybe the guys would be okay if I took off for an hour.

"Coach, we're going to watch *Remember the Titans*. Figured we could all enjoy a movie about teamwork. Want to join us?"

Shit. "Of course."

Explaining myself and convincing Becca we'd be great together would have to wait. My job was here with the guys. I just hoped Becca was patient.

Talking to Becca didn't happen the next day, either. Dexter woke from the coma, and we took turns visiting him. More players traveled from their hometowns to see him, and I remained the point person. In a whirlwind of phone calls, dodging social media, and organizing dinners for over twenty players, I thought about Becca. Often.

She became my beacon of hope at the end of the shit-storm. Dexter wouldn't play football again. That was certain. His neck and collarbone suffered too much damage, and rehab would take months, if not years, before he regained normal movement. From a coaching standpoint, it sucked because he was one of our best running backs. But the way his accident brought the team together was undeniable. He'd be our motivation.

I hated that it took them almost losing a teammate to have a wake-up call, but it served as one, and a new focus settled over the team. It wasn't until the end of day three that Dexter passed the critical stage, and I had a moment alone.

I smelled like fast food and the hospital, and I hadn't shaved since before Christmas, but I didn't care. "I'm running home for a couple hours, but text me the second anything happens, okay?"

Ferguson, one of my assistant coaches, clapped me on the back. "Will do. You deserve some time to yourself."

"Seriously, text me the second you hear."

"I will, man, don't worry." He smiled, the odd expression making lines appear around his eyes. I'd never seen him grin at me before, and I took a step back.

"Why are you happy?"

He snorted. "It's been great seeing you be a leader. You know I'd follow you anywhere, but right now, this is a new side of you. Damned if I don't respect you more."

"Holidays got you feeling mushy, huh?" I ignored the tightness in my chest at his compliment.

"Damn family watched five Hallmark Christmas movies.

I should put on some action or shoot-'em-up, bang-'em-up movies to get the feels out."

"Nah, it's good for the team." I laughed. "I appreciate you saying that. Now I have something I gotta do."

"I hope it's a shower—no offense, dude."

I waved goodbye with one place in mind: the sorority house.

CHAPTER TWENTY-ONE

BECCA

Window replaced, check.

Floors vacuumed and Swiffer-ed, check.

Kitchen scrubbed, check.

I eyed my to-do list and sighed at all the check marks. Staying busy was key. It helped not to think about him or the fact it had been three days. Plenty of time to think about everything, like the New Year's Eve date he'd said he'd attend. I either had to fake an illness or find a new date.

Ugh, that was a headache.

Clean. Don't think.

It worked for about another hour until all the cars parked on our street distracted me. Was Harrison suddenly Mr. Social and having friends over? Did he read my note? Did he think about me? Was he upset that his brother's team won the game?

Enough.

Straightening my shoulders, I reorganized the dishes. It helped a little, before my emotions grabbed ahold of me, the sting of his goodbye causing my eyes to water. I'd thought he was different, that he saw me for me and liked it.

Not true.

My phone buzzed, my mom's name flashing. Great. Just who I want to talk to. With a resigned sigh, I answered. "Hey, Mom."

"Becca. The party is in three days. Have you gone shopping for a dress yet? You haven't sent me any pictures of potential outfits, and you know how much I love that. The theme is *New Year, New You*, which is really cliché. But nonetheless, it's easy to find a dazzling dress. Just glam yourself up!"

She didn't breathe the entire time she spoke, and despite the dreaded topic of conversation, her mom-ness made me smile.

"I haven't found a dress. Listen, I'm not sure I'm going to make it."

She clicked her tongue. "Honey, you don't have a choice. I already RSVPed, and you know how serious they are about those things. Wasted food, extra chairs and tableware. Now why wouldn't you go?"

Harrison doesn't want me anymore.

I traced the line of the tile with my finger. "I'm tired from the blizzard, and the house has so many things that need to be fixed or cleaned," I lied, hoping I sounded convincing. "The girls get back soon."

"Even if what you're saying is true, which we both know it's not, you deserve a night out."

Okay, I couldn't lie for anything.

"Fine." My stomach hurt at the chance I'd upset my mom, but I was sick of it. Just done. "My date can't make it anymore, and I'm sick of being set up by you or your friends."

"The thing with the neighbor didn't work out? You sounded so smitten on the phone. I looked up pictures of the coach, and honey, he's handsome."

"He is handsome." *And kind, thoughtful, and funny when he wants to be.* I made a raspberry with my lips and continued. "It didn't work out. No hard feelings or anything from either one of us. We had a great time together, but life will go back to normal now the blizzard is over."

"Hmm, well, you sound sad. If you just let me—"

"No. *No.*" My voice came out stronger than I'd intended, but it didn't sway my mother's interest in my dating life.

"If you put yourself out there, honey, you'll find the right person. The internet is no way to meet people. You need church or friends to set you up. You stay in that house with the girls and are too afraid of making a connection."

"You're wrong, Mom." My temper flared. "I do put myself out there. I date, but it's kinda hard to find a prince when all the guys you set me up with are frogs. I'm different, and I'm okay with who I am. It takes a special person to accept me, and I'm not going to settle until I find someone who understands me. Your doctors and lawyers and sons of friends, they laugh when I tell them I like to knit, and they think my job is glorified babysitting. They're boring and stiff, looking for wife material to fit their vision. I'm not that person. They are all one-daters. They wine and dine me until, *Bam!*—they realize I'm different. I'm sick of acting like it doesn't sting."

Silence greeted me on the other end of the line, and instead of feeling guilty, I felt empowered. "I love you, Mom. I do, but no more setups. If you ignore my wishes, then I'll stop showing up for dinners. Can you promise me you're done?"

"Yes." She whimpered. "I'm sorry I upset you."

"You have great intentions, and I appreciate your dedication, but I'll figure it out myself. My life is not lacking in any way. I love my job, my friends, my *crazy* parents, and if love is on the table, it'll happen when it happens."

She paused a long moment. "So the neighbor didn't call back or what?"

"No more talking about my dating life. We can discuss politics, or the weather—hell, even Dad's new hobby of trying to build stuff—but ixnay on my love life."

"Will you still come over for dinner tomorrow?"

"Yes, Mom, I will." I laughed at the hesitant tone of her voice. She had never been so passive.

The doorbell rang, and I thanked the stars that it gave me an excuse to end the awkward conversation. "Someone's at the door—probably my Amazon order. I found these adorable mugs with stupid sayings for the girls. I should get it."

"Okay. I love you, Becca."

"You too, Mom."

I set the phone on the table and thought about grabbing a snack before the doorbell rang again. *Amazon deliverers ring twice now?* Fine by me. I loved opening new packages, and I already had a smile on my face picturing how the girls would react to the new mugs. I could stack them in the kitchen or surprise them by putting one in all their rooms. Oh, they'd love that!

Someone pounded on the door, and I frowned. In all my orders, the delivery person never knocked that hard. *Hmm.*

Curious and hesitant, I opened the front door, and my heart jumped into my throat. Leaning against the door-frame was Harrison. He looked better than I remembered. His dark hair was ruffled like he'd just woken up, and his gorgeous eyes had a myriad of emotions swirling through them. His stubble was longer, and a line appeared between his eyebrows. He wore a gray-and-green plaid shirt under his jacket, and the hues brought out the color in his eyes.

Man, I've missed him.

But aside from my physical reaction to him, my chest tightened the more I studied him. Dark circles colored the skin below his eyes, and his jaw was set in a hard line. I wanted to say a million things and none at the same time, so naturally, I blurted out the first thing.

"You haven't shaved."

He ran a hand over his jawline, blinking too fast. "Can I come in?" His voice was raspy, as though he hadn't had anything to drink in days.

I backed out of the way, allowing him entrance.

Was my neighbor nervous? I hoped so. He'd told me we were over without facing me. I stood straighter and crossed my arms in a battle stance.

He paced the foyer, stopping every two seconds to look at me.

Flustered, I let out a tiny laugh. "You look like a lion right now. You know, hunting for prey."

He ignored my awkward comment and pulled out a piece of paper from his pocket. "A note. You left a damn note taped to my door to break up with me?"

"Break up?" My voice came out shrill.

Me . . . break up with him? No way. How dare he! Was he pretending he hadn't heard my confession? And excuse me sir, ghosting me twice was the ultimate crime.

He shook his head. "A note might be worse than ghosting, Becca."

"What? No!" I put my hands on my hips and faced him. "Ghosting is rude and leaves the other person worried about what they did wrong, which you did to me. Again. My note cleared anything like that up because I'd never want anyone else to feel how I did two years ago. It was supposed to relieve any awkwardness between us since you'd said it was over." I motioned with my hand, pointing from him to me. "I see it isn't working. This feels awkward."

He snorted. "Leaving a letter doesn't allow the person to ask why." He walked closer to me, getting in my space so much I backed into the hall closet.

"You never let me ask why!" I yelled, holding my hands

up. "I replay everything in my mind, Harrison. That date two years ago? I felt so self-conscious after that, and then we spend this amazing holiday together and you don't even say goodbye to me?" My voice cracked. "*You* don't get to be angry right now."

He blinked and stepped closer to me. "When did I say it was over?" he asked, his voice low and serious.

Shit, he smelled good, and his lips were barely a foot from mine. "Uh, before I walked out."

"Hmm, I don't recall that happening." He frowned hard and narrowed his eyes. "And baby, missing out on two years with you is a regret I'll carry with me for a long time."

I refused to let him off the hook. He'd heard me. And he couldn't smooth talk me with *baby* and his sexy tone.

"Well, you said that to me, and that was it." My face heated, and my poor heart worked three times as hard. Being around him was too much. We couldn't be just friends.

Harrison sighed and lowered his voice to a whisper. "Becca, why do you want to end things?"

"Uh." Nerves exploded in my gut, and I fought the urge to pull him against me. His lips quirked up a bit on both sides like he was laughing at his own joke. I wanted to kiss away the punch line. *He turned me down! He said it was over!* "Because it was just sex?"

"Your voice went high. You don't sound sure." He cupped my chin and gently angled my face toward him. "Tell me, Becca, was what we experienced together *just* sex?"

"Um, maybe? Also, for survival purposes?" My throat

tightened, and I forgot why I was upset with him when he touched me. His minty breath hit my face, and my skin prickled with electricity. All from his dang fingers.

"Did I *not* tell you I would take you to the New Year's Eve party?"

I nodded.

He shook his head. "Yes, or no?"

I swallowed and tried to stop my heart from beating erratically against my rib cage. His words...they could change everything. "You said you'd take me, but—"

"Then why in God's name did you think it was just sex? We're good together, you and me." He rubbed his fingers over my earlobe, and his grin grew when I let out an involuntary shudder. "We have incredible chemistry. Your body responds to my touch, and I love the feeling."

Yes. Chemistry isn't the issue.

"You and your sister were talking outside the guest room. I heard you say sometimes sex is just sex. And when I tried to say goodbye to you..." I swallowed hard. "I told you I liked you. I asked for more, and you told me *it's over*. What else was I supposed to think?" I pushed out of his grip and walked farther into the living room, putting the couch between us. It was better that way—yes, my body reacted to him, but I needed more explanation. "I left you the note so you'd know not to be weird around me. I can be professional when I see you around."

"You like me." His tone changed from curious to playful.

"That's what I said. Making me repeat it is rude, and you

know it." My entire body turned as red as the Santa Claus ornament on the tree.

"I don't want to be professional around you. Not at all." He stalked around the couch, so I went in the opposite direction. "Did you hear my entire conversation with my sister, or just the sex part?"

"I don't know." I moved to the right. He moved faster.

"Eavesdropping can be dangerous." He took a couple large steps as his grin grew. "You missed the part where I told Blair I liked you."

Hold the freaking phone. *What?*

"You like me?"

"Hell yes. I can write you a note and ask you to go steady if you'd like. We could make it a tribute to junior high." He pointed his finger at me, using his coach voice: "Stop moving away from me."

I froze, torn between laughing and asking him to repeat the words. "But you said it was over."

"Trust me, that's the last thing I want."

"But the blizzard is gone." My voice shook, and my resolve dissolved. He said he *liked* me.

"You sound confused." Instead of going around the large blue couch, he stepped over it, his long legs making the movement look easy. He now stood a foot away from me. The couch made a loud thud on the floor, and his green eyes twinkled. Which was weird because he never looked so playful, giddy even. I swallowed so hard my throat clicked.

"We fit together, Becca, and I'm going to tell you why, so listen carefully."

His words made me grin, and his shoulders relaxed as I moved closer to him. His wonderful lips curved up.

"Go on." I prompted.

He held up his fingers and wiggled them. "Your girls will come first for you, just as my team does. We both have unique roles in helping younger generations. You would never be upset if I had a team obligation, just as I would never come between you or the girls at the house."

"Okay, that's all true."

He smiled—a full grin on his chiseled face—and my stomach swirled with butterflies. "You're full of colors, where I'm all the darks. You ramble when you're nervous and know so many random facts, whereas I tend to stay quiet. Yet, I want to listen to you talk all day." He cupped my face with both hands, caressing my cheeks with his large thumbs.

I almost whimpered, and my knees trembled. This guy . . . I had it bad.

"You made my house, and my Christmas, feel different. I can't describe it, but it was in the best way, and I'm a selfish man. I want you in bed with me every night you can."

"This is all . . . wonderful to hear but, Harrison, why wait three days to tell me this?" I covered his hands with my own and tensed, waiting for his answer. "What was I supposed to think? You disappeared on me after telling me we were over."

"I never said we were over, Becca. I don't know what you heard, but I'm nowhere near done with you."

"You said *it's done, we're over.*"

"Baby, I don't recall a single thing I said when I got the phone call about Dexter. My soul left my body for a few minutes but I guaran-damn-tee that you and I aren't over. If you heard that, I'm sorry."

I gulped, my heart racing. "I thought things were different this time between us, but three days...I'm scared to get hurt again."

He winced before lowering his mouth to mine and then waited for me to complete the kiss. I stood on my tiptoes and pressed my lips against his, breathing him in as relief and happiness spread through my body.

"I missed your mouth."

I giggled. "I forced myself not to think about yours."

"Were you successful? Because I can spend the next hour reminding you of all the things I can do with it that you seem to like." He wiggled his brows and gave me another quick kiss. "I'll admit I was a bit of an immature dick on the drive back. I didn't know how to handle what I was feeling. You were so focused on getting back to the house, and I assumed it was because you wanted to go back to how things were."

"What?" I raised my voice and pinched his side. "You idiot. I was talking about the house because I was sure you were going to try and let me down gently or something, since I'd overheard the *just sex* conversation."

He closed his eyes with nostrils flared. "We're no better than the kids, are we? It was all a misunderstanding. I never wanted you to go back to the house."

I rested my head against his chest and replayed the conversation in the truck that day. "We both assumed the other wanted to end it. That's funny."

"I wouldn't say funny, because I've been stewing over this fucking note you left."

"Well, I didn't have your number!" I defended my decision, but my quick temper disappeared when he held out his phone just inches from my face.

"Give me your number right now." His face was set in serious lines again. "I wish I could've called you and kept you in the loop about everything."

"You can always mail a letter, Harrison."

"I'm not going to mail a letter." He rolled his eyes. "Here, come sit down. I need to tell you what's going on."

"Is Blair okay? Your family?"

He pulled me into his lap on the couch, and I snuggled into his chest, inhaling his delicious scent. Laundry, wood, *mine*.

He rested his chin on top of my head and took a deep breath. "Minutes after we returned from Blair's, I received a text that one of my players, Dexter, got into a serious car accident. He drove drunk, crashed into a house, and flew through the windshield. I called my assistant coach who updated me. Between the hospital visits and the team dinners at the house, I haven't had a second to come here. Until now."

"And Dexter?"

He tightened his embrace. "He'll never play a sport again. I'm thankful he's alive, though. That wasn't a given."

"Holy shit."

Poor Harrison. My stomach bottomed out. I could only imagine the stress, worry, and anxiety running through his body. Just thinking about that happening to one of the girls filled me with an agonizing dread. "Are you okay?"

He sighed, and his muscles relaxed. "The fact you asked me that means a lot."

"You didn't answer the question, though."

"I will be. You'd be shocked with the guys. Everyone is coming together, supporting each other, and helping out. I hate that this happened to Dexter, but the team unity? The dynamics? They are there for each other in a way I've never witnessed."

"Tragedy can do that to people." I rubbed my hands over his shoulders, hating the pain and worry etched on his face. "Do you need anything from me? Food? Cleaning the house? I can get stuff for the guys, too. Hey! The girls come back soon, and we can do anything you need."

He smiled and squeezed his arms tighter around me. "This is why we're perfect together. You aren't mad or annoyed I had to be there for the team."

My mouth fell open. "No, I'm not mad at all. What type of person would be?"

"People from my past, but that doesn't matter. We cleared the air and can be together, yes?"

"Yes."

He positioned me so my back lay flat on the cushions, his

arms caging me beneath him. "Damn, I've missed you." He bent low and ran his nose along my jawline up to my ear. "You smell so good."

I clung to him, my heart hammering wildly. "I missed you."

He kissed my collarbone. "I like hearing you say that."

He gazed at me with so much warmth in his eyes that emotions caught in my throat. There was no confusion now, not with the way he stared at me like I mattered.

He kissed me slowly, nipping and teasing my lips like we had all the time in the world. Which we did now.

"Top five." I smiled at him. "Kissing you is in my top five favorite things."

His grin stretched across his entire face. "You're my favorite thing."

I flashed him a naughty grin, my thighs dampening with need. It had been too long since our skin had touched, and I craved him. To be touched, loved, taken care of. I reached for the end of his shirt, but he stopped me.

"Fuck, Becca."

"I don't like the sound of that." Disappointment hit me in the gut.

He kissed me once more, softly on my forehead, as tight lines formed around his eyes. "I gotta get back to the hospital. I'm so sorry. I told them I was running home to shower and eat."

He looked sorry, too, with a frown and worried eyes. I ran my fingers over his jaw, understanding his situation. "Well, I have an idea where we both win."

"Yeah? What's that?"

"Let's shower, and I'll feed you after." I intertwined our fingers and pulled him off the couch. "You never said you had to shower *alone*."

"That's true." His grin grew, and soon enough, he showed me exactly how much he'd missed me the past three days.

CHAPTER TWENTY-TWO

HARRISON

Roses seemed too obvious. Becca didn't strike me as a red rose type of woman. I eyed the colorful bouquet containing every shade imaginable. Blair helped me pick them out because I was typically a dumbass when it came to that stuff, and Becca mattered. A nervous sweat dripped down my back as I waited outside her front door.

Yes, we'd spent the last three nights together, but she insisted on getting ready at the house by herself.

I didn't argue. I was just damn happy we were together without doubt. It didn't matter it had been only a week of being with her, she'd changed me and wedged her way into my soul.

Footsteps. My heart sped up as the door creaked open. Becca stood there with a goofy smile as she twirled around. She wore a golden dress, the silky material clinging to her gorgeous body.

There's a slit.

Fuck.

"Goddamn, Becca." I couldn't stop staring at her. The tease of her smooth leg, the freckles lining her collarbone, the way her hair cascaded over her shoulder...she was beautiful.

"You look incredible." My voice cracked, and her grin grew.

"Thank you." She winked and struck a pose with one hand on her hip. "Are the flowers for me?"

I nodded and shoved them at her like a caveman.

Get a grip.

One day had me all twisted up in anxiety, even though we'd already slept together, survived a winter storm together, and knew each other's family bullshit. There was no reason I should be this nervous.

"These are gorgeous, Harrison!" She beamed at me before sniffing the flowers. "I love all the colors. My mom prefers red roses and says they're more romantic, but I disagree. Colorful ones are happier."

"They reminded me of you." There, that made me sound smooth.

"Aw." She kissed my cheek. "Let me put them in water. Thank you! I can't remember the last time someone brought me flowers. I absolutely love them!"

She hummed to herself as she opened a cabinet and pulled out a vase. Crouched on the ground, her spine curving in the position, her dress dipping low in the back and giving me a great view of her smooth skin. My fingers twitched. I wanted to trace them down her back and tease her skin until she went wild.

"You look so sexy in that dress, Becca."

"Yeah?" She spun around and bit her bottom lip. "You're giving me your bedroom eyes, and that ain't gonna happen, buddy. My parents would skewer me if I showed up late. Plus they still think I'm making you up."

"Might be worth it to be late." I picked her up around the waist and set her on the counter. She wrapped her legs around me, and I rubbed my palms down her legs. She giggled, licking the outside of her lip. My cock swelled. "I'm not sure I can wait another..." I checked my watch, "Five hours to have you to myself."

"You'll survive." She grinned and wrapped her arms around my neck. "You wear a suit very well, Harrison. They say seeing a man in a suit is the equivalent of a woman in lingerie. What do you think?" She ran her fingers through my hair, making me groan in pleasure. "Is it true?"

"With you, hell yes."

She laughed and traced my stubble with her fingers. "You might be the most handsome man, but I kinda fell for the stuff in there." She tapped her finger on my chest, just above my heart, before kissing me.

"You're not helping my situation down there," I said between kisses. I moved my hands from her legs to her waist and then up to her beaded nipples, teasing her through the thin fabric. "Mm, no bra?"

"Have you seen the back?"

"You should wear a jacket. Or a sweater."

"Can't. It'll ruin the look, but I do plan on driving you

crazy. Call it a hobby of mine." She grinned and wiggled her way out of my grasp. "Now, no more funny business until the drive home."

"Fine." I rolled my eyes, earning a laugh from her. With that sound, she was the one for me.

Sometimes you just know. It was that way for me. It took one horrible snowstorm for me to learn who I wanted to spend the rest of my life with. I had no plans to freak the hell out of Becca, but it provided a pleasant blanket of calm knowing what to work toward—getting her to agree with me.

I rubbed her arm as goose bumps spread across her skin. "You need a coat before we leave, Becs. It's still freezing."

"Obviously." She waltzed toward the hall closet and pulled out a bright red coat and yellow gloves. She looked like an ad, or a fan of McDonald's, and I couldn't stop smiling.

Catching my grin, she tilted her head and frowned. "Why the look? Judging my winter wear?"

"Not at all." I helped wrap a green scarf around her neck and lifted her hair from it. "I love your colors. I knew you'd be trouble when you picked up those balls of yarn with nothing that matched."

"I'll tell you another secret." She ran her tongue over her lip and looked pleased with herself. "None of my socks match. Not worth the time, and I love looking down and seeing explosions of neon colors."

"None of that surprises me." I held out my arm, and she looped hers through mine. "I don't want to one-up you, but my pillowcases aren't the same colors as my sheets. I'm wild like that."

She laughed super loud and leaned her head against my shoulder. "I noticed."

I couldn't remember the last time I was this excited for a night out. I tended to hate dinners and fancy events. Small talk was one of my biggest weaknesses, but knowing I'd be with Becca made all the difference. She made everything better.

I helped her into the truck and checked to make sure my gift for her was still wrapped behind my seat. Butterflies swarmed my gut just thinking about giving it to her. She didn't strike me as someone who wanted expensive gifts— not like Vivian. It had to mean something.

"Have you talked to Dexter today?" she asked once I pulled onto the road. "The girls officially heard about it and texted me. They're prepared to start a meal train for him and his family once they get back. Some of the girls are going to start a #DexterStrong campaign to talk about the dangers of drunk driving. I told them to reach out to you or the guys to see how they can get involved. I hope that's okay."

"It's more than okay." I slowed at a stop sign and gave her a reassuring look. "It's a phenomenal idea. And to answer your question, I stopped by for a bit during lunch and was able to see him. He's doing...okay. I worry more about how he'll be once things settle down and visitors stop. Football was his life, and it's gone now."

"He'll find a way back. There are other ways to keep it

in his life that don't require playing. And it sounds like the guys aren't going to let him disappear."

"True." I snuck a glance at her and smiled when I caught her staring at me. "I've already thought about having him keep stats or help with equipment."

"You're a good coach but an even better man." She patted my hand and, weaving our fingers together, brought it to her lips and kissed the back of it. The gesture charmed the hell out of me, and a confidence I had never experienced settled in me. Never in my life had I felt this secure in a relationship. And it had only been ten days.

Becca let out a long sigh as I turned onto the freeway, and I held on to her hand tighter. "That sounded sad."

"No, not sad. I realized we haven't talked about it yet, but once the girls come back, we'll have to figure out our sleeping arrangements. You're warm, and I've gotten used to the heat."

"That's what you're going with? That I'm warm?" I laughed. "It has nothing to do with how good the sex is between us?"

"I'm a cold lady." She grinned. "But the sex is a plus."

"Correction, the sex is fucking great." I, too, had been thinking about how I could keep her in my bed as often as possible. "You get a couple nights off a week, yeah?"

Please say yes.

"Two, but I'm already thinking you could sneak over a couple of nights. The girls rarely come to my room after ten unless there's an emergency. My bed is much smaller than yours, but we could make it work."

"Hell yeah, we can. If it means I get to sleep next to you, I'm in."

"And to think I once thought you were difficult to please," she joked. "As long as our sleeping together doesn't cause any issues in the house with the girls, we're doing it."

While I didn't love her answer, I respected it. "Fair enough. Now, give me the details on this party. I want to be prepared if I have to make small talk with strangers."

We arrived at the event right on time, and Becca immediately waved at a middle-aged couple. Her parents. She looked like them with their wide smiles, overexaggerated gestures, and same blond hair.

Her mom threw her arms around Becca, studying me over her shoulder. "Honey, who is this?"

"Harrison Cooper," she said with a hint of pride in her voice. That tiny amount of pride was like food for my soul, and I held out my hand.

"Pleased to meet you." Her mom and dad shook it, but their gazes remained tense. "Becca and I are neighbors and survived the blizzard together."

"Hmm, yes." Her mom pursed her lips and tilted her head to the side. "The football coach, yes? The one who never called for a second date after my daughter was smitten?"

"Mom. Gah!" Becca swatted her mom's arm and turned beet red. "He saved me, okay? Be nice."

"No, it's okay." My skin felt too tight. "You're right, Mrs.

Fairfield. I was a bit of an idiot two years ago. Things have changed."

"Let's get you a drink, Harrison." Her dad motioned with his chin toward a bar while Becca's mom hooked her arm around Becca. "We'll meet you beautiful ladies at the table."

"Don't do this Dad, please," Becca begged.

Her father ignored her. His face was set with determination, and I took a deep breath. He clearly cared for his daughter, and my gut said he was going to try and intimidate me or have some awkward talk.

"I'm going to ask Harrison about what the season will look like next year," her dad said. "You know I love college football."

"Right. I'd believe you sprouted wings before you had anything to do with sports. The man can barely catch. One time I tossed keys at him, and he missed, tripped over his own feet, and knocked over a vase." Becca shook her head. "Football, my butt."

"Come, Becca. Much to discuss." Her mom dragged her away while her father pulled me toward the bar.

"What'll you have? I do whiskey."

"Good taste, but I'll stick with a beer. I'm driving us back later."

He gave me an appreciative nod and handed over a Coors Light. "Becca is my pride and joy, and I don't think there's a person on this earth who deserves her."

"I don't disagree with you." I smiled at her as she watched us with a worry line between her eyebrows. "But I need to ask, why do you and your wife continue setting her up with men who don't deserve her?"

He closed his eyes and pinched his nose. "My wife tries, but I happen to agree with your opinion. Becca hates it, and the men are weasels."

"I'm not one of those guys." I met his steady gaze, my voice firm and confident. "I love your daughter. It's soon and she doesn't know, but I plan to ask her to marry me next year."

Her father paled and he downed his drink before ordering another. "Damn."

"She's different. She never matches her clothes, can't handle alcohol at all, loves everyone around her, and changes the lives of everyone she meets. She knows more random facts than should be legal, and rambles when she's nervous. It's rare for me to admire someone so strongly, but I admire her, Mr. Fairfield. She's bold and full of life. She's like sunshine."

He blinked fast and cracked his knuckles. "I've always called her My Sunshine."

"It's a true statement." I took a sip of beer and met her father's eyes. "You don't know me, but I can assure you I'll treat her right. I would never come between her family or her job at the sorority house, and I'll take whatever part of her life she gives me. I'm not going anywhere unless she tells me to."

"What if you get bored or annoyed with her?"

"It's hard to get bored when she's a never-ending source of laughter and finds joy in every scenario. Hell, she made a once-in-a-lifetime blizzard fun." I stared over at the table, and my chest tightened as I watched Becca flail her hands while talking with an older gentleman. He was as smitten as I was, and I patted her dad on the back. "I'm going to sit with my date before this guy charms her. It'll take time, but I'll prove it to you that I am enough for her."

"I look forward to it." He smiled and held up his drink as I gave him one last look. I hadn't planned on promising a proposal to her father when I'd agreed to be her date, but as soon as I said it, I knew it was the truth.

I'd give her one year to get used to the two of us, and then I'd do everything I could to ensure that she'd be with me forever. Keeping my gaze on Becca, I headed back toward the table where she waited with wide eyes.

"How did it go? Was he nice? Did he threaten you? He's a mild-mannered guy who wouldn't harm a fly. What did he say?"

I took her hand and kissed her palm before putting my arm around her. "He's a good father."

"Okay, that answers nothing." She ran a hand through her silky hair and pointed at her dad as he approached the table. "Behave, Father."

"I plan to." The man tipped his glass to me before joining his wife. Whatever storm was in his eyes before had lifted, and before I knew it, I found myself enjoying the evening.

We dined on steak and potatoes—my literal favorite substances on earth—and Becca lit up the table with her unique charm. She told stories about the girls in the house and rested her head on my shoulder.

At one point, she placed her small hand on my thigh and

squeezed. "I'm so glad you're here. This has been just the best...everything."

"Me too." I placed my hands on hers and did something I hadn't done in years. "Would you care to dance?"

"You don't strike me as a dancing type of guy."

"If I get to keep my hands on you, I'm in." I stood, offered her my hand, and steered us toward the dance floor. Appreciating the blush covering Becca's neck and cheeks, I pulled her against me. The band played an instrumental version of a slow pop song I couldn't name to save my life. My breath caught in my throat when she rested her forehead against my chin, and we swayed slowly like we had all the time in the world. She hummed to the music, totally off-key, and I simply enjoyed the moment and the new feelings going through me.

Content.

Peace.

Happy.

It didn't matter I had texts from my brother bragging about his win, or the guilt-inducing texts from my mother trying to make me feel bad.

I had Becca, and Blair, and now the team. The future wasn't as dark and negative as it had been two weeks ago.

I pressed a kiss to Becca's temple and almost confessed everything. "I gotta say, I've never been happier that your window broke and you ended up on my porch."

She giggled. "I busted my butt on your porch."

"You were cute."

"Awkward." She rolled her eyes and poked my side. "Then you saw me passed out in my bra."

"That's what did it. The bra and blood."

"You're so charming." She pretended to faint. I laughed, pulling her closer to me. "I'm so happy with you."

That did it. I cupped her chin with one hand and kissed her. "I love you, Becca. I know it's only been a couple weeks, but I know what love is and what it can do for two people. You've infiltrated every single thought I have, and I want to do life with you."

Her eyes turned the size of dinner plates, and her bottom lip trembled as the silence between us grew. She blinked, and her expression turned worried. I dropped another kiss on her. "There's no pressure to say it back. I wanted to tell you because it's the truth, and it's how I feel. I know you feel something for me, and when you're ready, you can tell me, too."

Her eyes glistened. "Awful confident I'll return the sentiment, aren't you?"

"Yes." I trailed my fingers down her arm and enjoyed the way goose bumps broke out on her skin. "I know you and your weaknesses. I'll tear down those walls."

"I like a man with a plan."

"I'll start with your hobbies and mismatched colors. Then I'll supply you with every brand of hot chocolate you can imagine. I'll bribe every one of the girls in your house to leave you crazy flowers, and most importantly, I will take you to Barcelona. I can't imagine anything better than experiencing something with you that you've dreamed about for years."

She sucked in a breath and pressed her lips together. "Harrison."

"Becca," I teased.

"I don't know what to say." Red splotches covered her cheeks and neck, and she opened and closed her mouth a handful of times. "You've wowed me. That doesn't happen. I always have something to say, and I'm empty. I don't have a comeback, or a joke, or anything. Literally, my mind is a blank white slate, and it's unnerving."

"Wait until you open your gift." I wiggled my eyebrows, and she squealed. "Want to open it?"

"Hell yes!" She dragged me off the dance floor and pushed me into a chair. "Where is it? You've piqued my interest, Harrison Cooper, and now I'm ready."

"I want you ready in other ways." I lowered my voice, my intent very clear. "But the gift is first."

"Give it to me." She held out her hand and I chuckled, jutting my chin toward the parking lot.

"We'll have to leave."

"Okay." She got up, put her jacket on, and hugged her parents all within a minute. "Let's go, handsome."

"Are you always so eager for presents, or are you wanting to get me naked?"

Her eyes flashed with heat, making my dick swell. She ran her hands down my chest, a wonderfully wicked glint in her eyes. "Yes."

"To which question?"

"Both." She laughed and walked quickly to my truck. I grabbed her hand and slowed her down, pushing her against the passenger side door and running my nose along her neck.

"You smell so good." I bit her earlobe and ran my hand up her thigh, teasing the outside of her panties. "If it wasn't so goddamn cold right now, I'd have some fun with you in the back of my truck."

"I'd let you." She ran her hand down the length of my dick and bit down on her lip.

Instead of responding, I picked her up and set her down inside the truck and then ran to the other side.

Give her the present first, then get her naked. I repeated the plan and took a second to catch my breath.

"Okay, to mirror your log gift, I got you something weird."

"I love weird." She grinned and searched the floor. "Where is it?"

I reached behind my seat and handed her the small box. She tore open the paper, and nerves racked my body. It wasn't the same as a playoff game that came down to a field goal, but it was similar. My heart beat way too fast, and I second-guessed my decision.

She looked up, and her face softened. "You look nervous. I'm going to love it no matter what it is. It's from you."

"Just get it over with." I tugged on the collar of my shirt and waited on edge when she pulled out the coffee mug with a large bull on it.

"It's a bull." She smiled as she studied it. "Whoa. A bull with very large balls hanging from it."

"I bought it from a shop in Barcelona. Apparently, all their bulls have balls there."

She met my eyes for a second before throwing her head back and laughing. "I adore this. I will use it every day."

"There's more." God, my throat was dry, and I kinda wanted to throw up. "Look inside."

She tipped the mug and pulled out the envelope I'd folded. It took her a couple of seconds to open it, and she gasped. "Oh my. Oh my!"

"You like it?"

The whites of her eyes grew huge. "Is this real?"

"Yup. You pick the dates, and we're there."

Her eyes filled, and she burst into tears before throwing herself across the cab and onto my lap. I rubbed my hand up and down her back before lifting her chin. "Hey, why are you crying? I thought you'd love it."

"I do. Oh goodness, I do." She kissed my face, my chin, my cheek, my temple, and then my eyebrow. "I can't believe you did this."

"I love your smile and your selflessness for the world. It's time you get to be a little selfish." I pressed my lips against hers before baring my soul. "I love you, Becca. I want to give you the universe, but we'll start with a ten-day trip to Spain. Spring break works for me and, if I recall my research, the girls leave the house then?"

"Yes. *Yes.*" She hugged me tight, her cheek squished against mine. "I love you, you big, wonderful man. I'm so happy you shared your heart with me," she whispered and then kissed the side of my neck. "I'll take care of it. I promise."

My breath caught in my throat at her confession. I held her tighter, so damn thankful we got our second chance. I got a taste of what life with her was like and I'd do everything to make her happy.

EPILOGUE

BECCA

One year later...

I ran my fingers over the banister near the fireplace, wincing at the dust I'd missed. It would be my last Christmas at the sorority house, and it hit me hard. I was thrilled to be going back to school, but that meant starting a new chapter and saying goodbye to the current one. The sorority house was my first love, and I had learned so much from it. Though my life needed to go in a different direction, it still hurt. So many memories. So many wonderful moments.

I wrapped my arms around myself and sniffed, just as Marissa joined me in the room. "I can't believe you're breaking up with all of us at the end of the year. I figured you'd always be in the house, even though I know it's selfish thinking."

"Stop it." I gave her hug and squeezed extra tight. "I'm not breaking up with you, and I definitely wouldn't live here forever." We embraced for several long moments before I pulled back. "I'm *growing up.*" I put the words in air quotes, and we both laughed.

"I guess I never thought about you having a family or getting a normal job." She eyed the family room and all the decorations before her gaze landed on me again. This time, her expression was filled with warmth and something I couldn't place. Glee? Excitement? "Promise me we'll stay in touch no matter what."

"Duh." I rolled my eyes and stared at the front door. Harrison was supposed to pick me up for dinner ten minutes ago but he'd texted that he was running a little late. "I dare you to try to get rid of me from your life."

"I don't know. You might become too busy with...your new life." She smirked and glanced over my shoulder. Turning, I found a handful of girls standing there with smiles on their faces. My skin tingled. Something was going on.

"Spill it. What did you all do?" I marched to the other room, expecting to see something that would explain the looks, but it was empty. "Did you sneak a boy in here or what?"

"Something like that." Marissa walked up to me and handed me a knitted square with a million colors. It was misshapen, poorly done, and looked like a child did it. "This is for you."

"Oh, thank you," I gushed because a handmade gift was better than any gift card. I knew a friendship was over the day I got a gift card in the mail. "Did you make this, Issa? I love it, but what is it exactly?"

She shrugged and walked out of the room. Quinn, a sophomore, approached me next and handed me a window ornament before walking away. It was a rectangular window—that was it—and also handmade. Next came a box of hot chocolate, a sweater that said *This is My Hallmark Movie Watching Shirt*, and a small box. "Okay, ladies, what the heck is going on?"

None of them answered, and my heart raced. Was this... could it be...

"Becca." Harrison appeared from the kitchen wearing a dark green sweater and jeans.

He was so handsome, and I melted when he gave me an appreciative glance from my head to my toes. His gaze landed on my mis-matched toe socks, one side of his mouth quirking up. The socks were the school's football team colors, and while they started out as a birthday gift, I wore them all the time. He'd bought me two more pairs.

Harrison gestured to the small box in my hand, and my throat closed up.

A box. A small box. Oh God. My hands shook as I blinked, trying to calm myself down. The gifts from the girls...he'd planned it. He'd been planting hints about proposing for the past six months, but I shrugged it off. It was football season, and my job required me to live at the house full-time.

But I move out in June to go back to school, and we haven't talked about where I'll live.

"Open it, Becca." He stepped toward me with a nervous smile.

I snuck a glance at the small crowd of girls watching, and Marissa gave me a thumbs-up.

I can do this. Deep breath.

The paper was dark red and poorly wrapped, making it all the more endearing that Harrison had done it himself. I set the paper on the table and popped open the box, expecting to see something resembling a ring.

Instead I found a small figurine of a man pulling down his pants. I cackled. "Oh my goodness."

"Do you remember?" He stood closer now, and his clean aftershave greeted my nose like an old friend. I loved how he smelled like home, and I fought the urge to jump into his arms. I hadn't seen him in two days, and I missed him. "We saw these in Barcelona."

"Yes! The Caganer." I held it up for the girls. "It literally means the crapper."

They frowned, clearly confused.

"It's used in Nativity scenes in various parts of Spain. Its meaning changes depending on who you ask, but my favorite one is that he's fertilizing the earth." I laughed at their bewildered expressions and closed the distance between me and Harrison. "I love it. It is the perfect Christmas gift."

"You are my favorite person." He picked me up and kissed me—not too passionately with the girls watching—and set me down. "Only you would love a figurine of a shitting man."

"If you wanted normal, pick someone out of a magazine," I teased.

His eyes warmed, and he gave me my favorite smile of his—the one showing off his dimple on one side. "I made that pot holder for you."

"The square thing? That's what it was? A pot holder?"

"Yes. I knitted it. It took me forever." He pressed his lips together in a frown as he eyed the pot holder. He was a perfectionist, so it meant a lot that he'd tried something he was horrible at.

"The fact you knitted is amazing. I'll use it every day, along with my bull with balls mug."

His eyes danced with humor, and he cleared his throat. "Okay. This is it."

"What are you talking about?"

He took a step back and retrieved something from his sweater pocket. Then, crouching down on one knee, he revealed another small box.

"Oh, damn."

"I'm going to pretend you didn't just cuss during my proposal." He wiped his forehead with the back of his hand before popping open the box. There wasn't just a single diamond on the ring. Instead, there was one centered in the middle, but it was surrounded by colorful gems. It looked like a flower, and all the moisture in my mouth went to my eyes. My vision blurred entirely when he spoke.

"Did you know I told your dad last year on New Year's Eve that I was going to marry you?" He paused and took a big breath before continuing. "I told him I'd prove I was worthy of you, and I asked his permission in May."

"May?" I croaked out.

"Yes. He and your mom were thrilled, and I'm shocked they kept it quiet." He smiled, clearing his throat and staring me in the eye. "I love how you sing all the time, even though you can't carry a tune. I love how you live life to the absolute fullest and get joy from the little things. I'm beyond proud of you for going back to school to become a guidance counselor, even though it'll be hard. I never imagined having a family of my own until I met you. So, Becca, will you marry me? I promise we'll travel anywhere you want and I'll buy weird figurines for you. There's a place in Belgium that's famous for a statue of a kid peeing—if you want to go there next, I'm in."

Time seemed to stop for me. The squeals of the girls and the sound of cars on the street disappeared. The familiar smell of the sorority house was overpowered by Harrison, and I took in the moment.

His declaration. His promises. His words. The fact he'd looked up the famous statue Manneken Pis.

It wasn't a choice, not really. I wanted to be his forever. "Yes, *duh*."

His grin had become my favorite thing in the entire world. He picked me up and swirled me around like in the rom-coms I loved watching. "We can have a long engagement. It's your choice. If you want to wait until you move out of here, or after you graduate in a couple years, it's all up to you."

"I'm thinking…a summer wedding would be nice. I think I know a couple people who would like to help plan it." I glanced over at the girls, and it turned into a mob of hugs and congratulations.

They hugged me, I hugged them. Even Harrison had his arms wide open as various girls embraced him. Our celebration lasted ten minutes before Marissa cleared her throat and motioned us into the great room.

"The final part of the night has arrived, so if you could please head in there, Future Mrs. Cooper, it would be appreciated." She grinned so wide and shared a scheming glance with Harrison. My heart almost burst. The fact he'd included the girls in his proposal told me all I needed to know.

He knew me. The good, bad, odd, and quirks.

He held out a hand. "Well, Becca, want to see what's next?"

I bit my lip to prevent my grin from hurting my face, and I practically floated toward him. "Hell yeah."

He led me into the great room where we were greeted by Blair and her family, along with my parents. Blair didn't wait a second before running up to me. "Let me see the ring!"

We laughed as I was passed around between Blair, my mom, and my dad. A hushed silence filled the room when someone I hadn't met cleared his throat. He was a younger, less handsome version of Harrison, and I went into protective mode. Since the blowup last Christmas, things were slowly getting better with Harrison's parents. They weren't amazing, but there was slow progress. But after Dexter's accident, things had changed with his brother. Harrison's perspective on football, competition, and teammates had changed. He had chosen to have a relationship with his brother. They were trying, and that meant I had to, too.

"Hank."

"Becca." He held out a hand with a hesitant smile. "It's really nice to meet you."

"I'm hoping I can say the same."

Hank's smile grew, and he clapped his brother on his shoulder. "You've got a keeper, man. She looks like she wants to beat my ass."

"I wouldn't stop her if she decided to." Harrison pulled me out of Hank's reach and into the crook of his arm. "And I know she's a keeper."

"So you got a sister, Becca?"

Hank's question broke the tension in the room, and everything was a dream after that. It wasn't until hours later, after champagne and cake, hugs and laughter, that Harrison waved goodbye to everyone and took my hand.

"I cleared it with the girls, you can stay at my place tonight."

"They'll know we're doing it!" I blurted, my face already turning hot. "You could've had me sneak out."

"Ah, sweet Becca. They know we're doing it." He kissed my temple and kept me nice and tight against him. "But it's cute you care."

"Shut up." I playfully punched him in the side, but it got him laughing more. "Be careful or I'll hit you with my left hand. I got a huge rock on it, so it'll hurt."

"Yeah?" He stopped us on the short walk to his house and held my hand in his. "It looks really good on you. I've been thinking about this since last winter."

My insides went all gooey, and I wanted to declare my

love for him in a million ways. "You're a little mushy, my Big Grump."

"Don't tell anyone. It'll ruin my reputation."

"I think the cat's out of the bag on that one." I stood on my tiptoes and planted a kiss on his perfect lips. "I love you. All of you. And I want to share a house with you, have kids with you, go on brunch dates with Blair, and pretend I like golf with you and my dad. I even kinda like football now."

"Don't push it. We all know you hate football." He picked me up, bridal style, as we walked toward his house. "But everything else you said, yes. I know we haven't talked about it, but are you moving in with me in June?"

"You bet your butt I am. I already moved some of your clothes in the closet to fit mine. I have a lot of them, in all different colors, too."

"Of course you do." He set me down on the porch, taking his time studying my face, and tracing my jaw with kisses. "Speaking of clothes . . . I need to take all of yours off. Immediately."

"Or what?" I teased, earning a growl from him.

He pressed me up against the front door, slowly moving his lips against mine. He gently tilted my mouth to deepen the kiss.

I couldn't believe I was going to spend my life with this man. "Let's do it in front of the fire, for old times' sake?"

"We can do it in any room you want. I just require that you wear the ring, and that's it."

"*That* we can agree on." I took the keys from his hands

and opened the door, dragging my man into the living room and shoving him onto the couch. "I can't wait to marry you."

His smile was the perfect response, and when the first snowflakes fell hours later, I sent a silent prayer of thanks for the blizzard a year earlier. Things happened for a reason, and it didn't matter how Harrison and I found each other.

We did, and life couldn't have been better.

ACKNOWLEDGMENTS

I wish I could go full *Mean Girls* at this part and just break this book into a hundred pieces so I can rave about how amazing my support system is.

This book wouldn't have happened without Noreen Mughees and Cathie Armstrong, and the summer of 2021 totally changed my life.

Noreen—that summer we Zoomed and chatted was the best. Your journey inspired me to query again after years of struggling. I was at my lowest point when your chat had me think, *Hmm, maybe I can try again.* It was fate. So thank you, dear friend. This book wouldn't be here if you weren't the inspiration for me to try again. If we ever meet in person, I will break my no-hugging rule.

That leads me to Cathie, my agent. Thank you so much for taking a chance on me! I know I'm your problem child. It's honestly just who I am. I ask too many questions all the time. (I was the child who had a question limit per day, so at least I've always been that way, lol.) You're so patient, and I am so grateful for you. I've learned so much working with you and can't wait to see what else we can do!

I owe a huge thank you to Alex Logan and the team at Forever! You helped bring these characters to life and took it to the next level. It's been amazing working with you, and I can't wait to see what other projects we get to partner on together.

Thank you so much to Katherine McIntyre, Kat Turner, Heather Van Fleet, Rachel Rumble, and Katie Erin. You've all been such amazing people to run an idea by, vent about how authoring is super difficult sometimes, and be a cheerleader. I love having you in my life!

A special, heartfelt shoutout to Katie Golding who coined the term Hot Henley Harrison. That obviously ended up in the story because, duh, its perfect. You've been an amazing writing buddy and I am SO thankful for you!

To Haley Walker, who lets me blend my author life with my day job AND who stepped up when I was like, hey, I need a sexy last name for Harrison. What do you think? And *bam*. We got Coach Cooper.

This story pushed me in a lot of ways, some harder than others. I couldn't have done it without the support of my husband. Thank you. I love you, our family, and our life. Being married to you the past ten years has been the most amazing thing, and I can't wait to see what other adventures we go on.

ABOUT THE AUTHOR

Jaqueline Snowe lives in Arizona where the "dry heat" really isn't that bad. She prefers drinking coffee all hours of the day and snacking on anything that has peanut butter or chocolate. She is the mother to two fur-babies who don't realize they aren't humans and a mom to the sweetest son and daughter. She is an avid reader and writer of romances and tends to write about athletes. Her husband works for an MLB team (not a player, lol) so she knows more about baseball than any human ever should.